Perm

Etched

In

My Heart

by

Angela Hairston

Highland Park Publishing

This book is a work of fiction. Name, characters, places and incidents are products of the author's imagination or are used fictitiously. Any resemblance to actual events or locales or persons, living or dead, is entirely coincidental.

Permanently Etched In My Heart
ISBN: 0-9834732-9-3

Published by:
Highland Park Publishing
P.O. Box 724651
Atlanta, GA 31139
hairston@highlandparkpublishing.com
www.HighlandParkPublishing.com

Book cover

Model/Actress
Asia Mills
hairston@highlandparkpublishing.com
Photographer/graphic design
Anthony Thomas
ecmanthony@gmail.com

Printed in the United States of America

A Special Dedication

I dedicate this book to my beloved sister Selena Hairston whom I lost June 11, 2009. I thank God for every moment I had with my only sister. Selena will always remain permanently etched in the hearts of her loved ones.

Thank You

I would like to thank all my family, friends, and especially my daughter for putting up with me while I pursued my dream of becoming a published author.

Permanently Etched In My Heart

Chapter 1

Everybody has a story and this is mine. My name is Selena Wright I am fourteen, and the oldest of three kids. I live in a very small city in the heart of Detroit, Michigan known as Highland Park the city of trees. It is the home of Ford Motor Company first automotive assembly line plant and the Davison Freeway: the world's first modern limited access urban freeway that runs through the center of the city. The city spans one square mile down Woodward Avenue.

Most of the homes are huge and several are considered to be mini mansions. When we first moved into Highland Park, the neighborhood was gorgeous. The streets were lined with beautiful tall evergreen trees until they became infected and the city had to cut most of them down. Every store up and down Woodward Avenue was bustling with businesses and neighbors took pride in their homes.

Chrysler Headquarters was three blocks from my house. The tan brick building took up seven square blocks off Oakland Avenue. It was the largest taxable asset in the city's budget, until Chrysler negotiated an early contract buyout and moved their headquarters to Auburn Hills. The city never did see any of the money, because the Mayor pocketed it all.

Declining economy was followed by poverty. Gangs increased criminal actives and flooded the neighborhood with drugs. Political corruption swindled away the city's funds. The three elements dramatically changed the city. Most of the police department was filled with relatives from Highland Park's most notorious residents. Eventually the bustling businesses closed or moved out leaving abandoned reminisce of their presence.

McGregor City Public Library is on the corner of my block. The entrance to this beautiful library is unusual since it is an ornamented between two impressive fluted Ionic columns. The inscription "Books Are Doors To Wide New Ways" etched in an arch above the highly ornate bronze doors. The exterior is designed in a dignified classical Roman style and the interior was inspired with Greco-Roman motifs.

I live in the middle of the block in a four-story brick house with lead plated windows and a two ½-car detached garage. The large front porch is built with limestone brick with three six feet long brick ledges. The inside of the house has solid oak wood detailing throughout. The brick fireplace in the living room is surrounded by built in oak cabinets and the mantel is covered with family pictures. Huge French double doors separate the downstairs' rooms.

My father had an entertainment room built to accommodate his 72' inch screen television with surround sound. The downstairs half bathroom is located under the front stairway. The front stairway leads to an oversized upstairs hallway. The back stairway in the kitchen leads up to the second floor hallway. One of the four bedrooms is transformed into a computer room. My bedroom is the second largest room on the second floor. My brothers have a sunroom off their bedroom that is filled with an electric train set. My father has a bathroom in the master bedroom, while I'm left to share the large upstairs bathroom with my brothers.

The huge basement has a half bathroom. When the weather is bad my little brothers are able to ride their bikes and skateboards in the basement. My father claimed himself a room that he turned into a carpentry workshop. They love the basement, while I find it creepy. The saw dusk from my father's workshop attracts centipedes, which creeps me out.

I grew up in a happy loving household until my fourth grade year. It was a month after summer vacation ended. My mother was stopped at a red light behind a semi-truck when a pickup truck driven by a drunk driver rammed into the back of her car at eighty miles an hour. The impact pinned the entire front half of my mother's car under the bed of the semi-truck. Her head exploded when the rear bumper of the semi-truck trailer came crashing through the car's front window. The police had to remove portions of my mother's flesh and hair from the bumper and under the bed of the trailer. The police determined that she died on impact and never saw it coming.

I still remember that day clearly. It was the first time I ever saw my father cry. I was sitting on the living room window seat reading Green Eggs and Ham to my brothers Milton and Dwayne when a police car pulled up in our driveway. We went running to the front door when we heard my father scream. He was kneeling down on his knees crying. My brothers and I instantly hugged him and began crying. His tears silently told the story. My mother has gone to heaven and is never coming home.

My mother was the glue that held our family together. She was the one that planned all holiday and birthday celebrations. The first year without her was emotionally hard. Each holiday and birthday reopens the wounds of her death. The next four years my father raised us by himself. I helped my father out with my little brothers as much as possible. The first two years I had to initiate putting up holiday decorations, planning birthday parties for my brothers, and back to school shopping. As time passed, it became a lot easier to handle.

My mother was a beautiful black woman. Her grandmother from her father's side was an Indian. With her straight black hair and dark chocolate skin tone, she looked more like a Cherokee Indian instead of a black woman. Her small body frame hid the fact that she was a mother of three. When she talked, it was if she was singing. Everyone that crossed her path have only good stories about her.

My father could pass for a white man. His father was white and his mother was a light skin black woman. He is an extremely light skinned, tall, and stocky with sandy curly hair. He has deep dimples in his cheeks and chin. His thin pink lips and slightly pointed nose resembles a white man. He once had a comical personality, but after our mother's death, he has become very withdrawn.

I inherited my good looks from the unique combination of genes. I am 5-feet 3-inches with a 136-pound athletic body perfectly packed in a size 2. My tan skin has a red under tone which gives me the appearance of always having a suntan. My perfectly arched eyebrows enhance my brown eyes. I have my mother's cute nose and full lips. My long black hair reaches down to my bra clasp. Both sides of my family come from a long line of women with beautiful legs. Thanks to my skin tone, I get away without wearing pantyhose on my sexy legs. My friendly personality allows me to fit any crowd.

My brother Milton is eight-years old and one of the tallest kids in his third grade. He is the indistinguishable image of our father. My seven-year old brother Dwayne is starting second grade. He took after my mother's side of the family.

Several years after my mother's death my father began dating. I truly disliked this woman the moment he introduced her to us. His girlfriend Rita Harvey is four feet tall and shaped like an orange. She wears her clothes were so tight that you can count the rolls of fat on her back. The three pounds of blonde weave piled on the top of her head blends in with her extremely thick foundation, three inches long eyelashes, five shades of blue eye shadow, and the brightest red lip stick I have ever seen.

Two weeks ago my father transferred to the afternoon shift. It left me home alone in the evenings with my brothers, so he moved his overly made-up girlfriend Rita and her three badass kids into our home. He thought it would be best for us to have an adult around the house in the evenings. Her two boys were the same ages as Milton and Dwayne so they moved into their room. Our computer room was converted into a bedroom for her ten-year-old daughter. From day one, I let it her known that I'm not conforming to her rules and regulations. That bitch moved into my mother's house!

Despite the changes in my home life, I am excited and ready to take on high school and all it has to offer. Highland Park Community High School is a fairly new but oddly constructed building that resides on an extremely small hill. From street level, it does not appear to be a school, but a white brick two story square shaped correctional facility without any windows. Once you enter the school, it feels as if you are completely cut-off from society. The smoke glass-ceiling window over the indoor garden and the glass framed main door entrance are the only connection to the outside. The first floor houses the main office, cafeteria, science labs, special elective classes, senior hallway, and the extension to the auditorium and athletic department. The second floor houses the vice principal's office, regular classes, and the library. The basement houses regular classes, special education, counselors, offices, and the school store.

I'm embarking on this new journey with my three closet friends. Leslie Roberts is my best friend and babysitting partner. We have been best friends since kindergarten. She is 5-feet 6-inches, with shoulder length hair, brown skin, big beautiful brown eyes, and the baby of seven siblings. Her witty personality makes her stand out in any crowd. We started our babysitting business a year ago with one customer and have grown to 9-regular customers.

Baron Smith is good-looking and very soft spoken. His rich black skin tone perfectly enhances his tall slim build. Because of his father and uncles influence, he thinks of himself to be a playboy. Our first grade teacher assigned us to become classroom partners. That was her way of forcing us to get along. I would never have kicked him if he had not pulled my braids.

Floyd Johnson is an average looking light skin brother with a stocky build and wears his hair in a long ponytail claiming that it enhances his athletic abilities. He attended one of the other middle schools in the city. We met at a track meet between the schools. Our friendship flourished the summer of my fourth grade year through the school district combined middle school summer track and field program.

I met Brandy Love in third grade when she transferred to my elementary school. She's an only child and her parents keep her extremely well groomed that deflects the fact that her left eye is lazy. She only befriended Leslie and me because she thought that was a way to get Baron to notice her. Once she realized his ego was bigger than hers the quest for his attention faded.

My first two months as a freshman at Highland Park High School drastically changed my whole outlook on life. It was only the third week of school and I'm standing at my locker on the third floor in freshman hall when I witnessed my first shooting.

My locker is at the end of a long narrow dead end hallway. While exchanging books and talking with several other classmates a loud deafening bang rang out. I turned around and there's a boy name Derrick laying on the floor with a single gunshot wound to his stomach. The loud bang from the gun left me unable to hear all the screaming and crying. I could not hear a thing, but the smell of gun smoke loomed in the air. The hallway immediately became filled with students pushing their way down the hallway to see what happened.

Derrick was a low-level weed dealer and bully that nobody liked. The word on the street was that he's looking for one of his foot runner's. He accused his runner of shorting him seven dime bags of weed. Derrick sneaked into school to confront the runner at his locker.

"Were the fuck is my weed!" Derrick asked.

"I told you I did not take any of your fucking weed!" he answered.

"Who do you think you are getting grim with? I should bust you in your motherfucking mouth!" Derrick replied.

"I did not take your shit!" he responded.

"Listen here you punk motherfucker you better come up with my weed or the money by tomorrow. If not it will be your ass!" Derrick demanded.

"What the hell do you mean by that?" he asked.

"Don't have my shit tomorrow and your scary bitch ass will find out!" Derrick threatened.

"Why wait for tomorrow I have something for you now!" he replied.

"That's more like it," Derrick responded.

The runner turned around and rambled in his locker. He unzipped his book bag and pulled out a .38-caliber handgun. He quickly turned around pointing the gun at Derrick's head.

"What the fuck!" Derrick yelled out.

"Who's the scary bitch now motherfucker?" he questioned.

Derrick tried his best not to show the fear he was feeling inside. He toughened up his voice and said, "If you shoot you better shoot to kill. Cause if I live your ass is dead!"

It looked as if the runner had a second thought. He was slowly lowering his arm then "Bang!" the gun went off. Derrick eyes widen and his mouth opened up as the look of disbelief came across his face. For a few seconds no sound came out of his mouth then he released a scream of pain. He grabbed his stomach as he fell to his knees. He clutched hold of a male student's pants as he started to lean over. The student panicked and started hitting Derrick's bloody hand until he let go. Derrick fell over on to his back. By then his scream turned into a loud distressful cry.

The runner started jumping around ranting. "Get the fuck up! Get the fuck up! I said get the fuck up! This is what your ass gets! I told you I didn't take any of your motherfucking weed! Motherfucker I guess you won't be coming after me now! Look at your bitch ass laying there on the floor! Who's the man now?

What the fuck did I do? How am I going to explain this to my mother? All you had to do was believe me. You brought this on yourself. I'm going to hell! Your fat ass bet not die on me! I want my mother!" he cried out.

I did not run or scream. Instead, my legs felt like two large blocks of cement. I could feel the crowd pushing up against me but they were unable to move me from my spot. I just stood there in amazement and watched as Derrick laid on the floor begging for help. His stomach swelled up until his t-shirt could not stretch any further. It was like a volcano. The blood squirted through the fabric of his t-shirt and ran down the sides of his t-shirt. His cries were reduced to a gurgling moan as he began to spit up blood.

Many of the kids were crying and screaming, while Derrick laid there choking on his own blood. I stared in his eyes and watched his soul fade away as he took his last breath. The runner began shaking and crying hectically. He dropped the gun and pushed his way through the crowd.

The hallway was jammed packed, which caused the

school security officers, police, and paramedics to reach Derrick after he took his last breath. Due to the chaos, the gunman was able to slip through the crowd and out of the building. Immediately after the police found out the identity of the shooter, they went over to his house to arrest him. His mother was home but had not seen him since he left for school that morning. They thoroughly searched the house but were unsuccessful with locating him. While searching the garage one of the officers noticed the family dog covered in blood. The officers followed the bloody paw prints straight to the dog's house. There they located the gunman's lifeless body inside. He slit his throat and bled to death.

Because the murder happened at an inner city school, there was no grievance counseling for students. The only thing we got was an early dismissal for that day. A week later, the school board implemented their crime prevention plan. Which, caused for all doors except, the main door, to be chained and bolted locked from the inside during school hours, metal detectors installed in the main entrance doorframe, and the security guards were given handheld metal detectors.

With all the preparations and anticipations for homecoming, the murder became old news. The Saturday morning of the homecoming game the day started off with a small parade. It began at one end of Highland Park marching up Woodward Avenue to the high school football field.

The football team led the parade in the school athletic bus. I waved at Floyd as the float carrying the football team rolled by. The high school cheerleaders and a band combined of students from all three middle schools marched behind them. They were trailed by floats from the freshman class, sophomore class, junior class, senior class, and all our school organizations and clubs. The last float carried the homecoming king, queen, and the royal court. Our high school pom-pom squad and marching band followed behind.

It was amazing how much hype was put into the day knowing the last time we won a homecoming game was 10 years ago!

This is my first homecoming game and I'm thrilled. I don't know a thing about football, but the enthusiasm from the crowd is amazing. It's exciting just to be part of it. The whole homecoming experience is totally different for Floyd. He is the first freshman to make our schools varsity football team.

The stadium was packed. I could feel the bleachers swaying whenever the crowd began stomping and cheering he football team off. It doesn't matter that we lost the game I'm still looking forward to the homecoming dance tonight.

Leslie and I got dressed for the homecoming dance over Brandy's house since her mother is driving. I wore a red knee length dress with a pair of red flats, my long hair was down with curls at the end, and clear lip-gloss as my only makeup. Leslie wore a black dress past her knees with a pair of black pumps, her hair straight back, and dark red lipstick. Brandy wore a tight black leather dress with a pair of snakeskin heels, a fresh short haircut, and enough make-up for all three of us. Brandy's father followed us out the houses taking pictures as we left for the dance.

The homecoming committee did a terrific job transforming the cafeteria into a ballroom with decorated balloons in our school colors. Tables draped with royal blue table clothes and white balloon center pieces surrounded an area cleared for the dance floor. Students from our school radio station D.J. the party.

I danced and talked with my peeps the whole night. We were having a good time until a big ass fight broke out. It never fails; a few punks always ruin it for everybody. The crowd turned into a stampede of wild horses as students flee from the cafeteria. I found myself ducking from flying chairs as we ran for the exit. We made it out of the building just as the police pulled up.

A week later, Leslie and I skipped school that Friday to attend a ditch party. Cathy who lives around the corner from Brandy was having the party over her boyfriend John's house. Cathy was doubled promoted twice and two years younger than any of us. She tried and did anything to fit in with a crowd. Her boyfriend John is seventeen, and a high school dropout. He stays across the train tracks with his mother in a big brick house in the middle of the block.

When we got to the house that morning four of John's boys and five of Cathy's girls were already there. They all lived in the neighborhood. John boys are members of Highland Park's gang that called themselves the Mob Squad. They prided themselves on terrorizing the neighborhood, robbing, and slanging drugs. Most of them either dropped out or were kicked out high school.

The first half of the morning was ok, but a little boring. All we did was talk and drink. John cut the music up loud and his boys fired up blunts. I hate the smell of marijuana so I grabbed a couple of beers and sat on the front porch. Leslie took a couple of hits from a blunt then followed me outside. We sat out on the porch, while they did whatever in the house. After a while we decided to walk up to the Coney Island restaurant on Hamilton Avenue to get something to eat. I see we are not the only ones skipping school. The place is packed with students. A few hours had passed by the time we made it back to John's house. It looks as if most of his boys left.

"So Leslie this is what goes on at a ditch party?" I asked.

"Pretty much. They drink, smoke, and some of them have sex," Leslie answered.

"Hell I could have stayed in school for this," I replied.

"Me too. This is my last ditch party," she responded.

“Girl, I have to piss like a race horse,” I replied.

“I have to go too. Let’s go back in,” she responded.

The smell of weed was lingering in the air and the music seems to be even louder than earlier. Beer bottles, liquor bottles, cigar tobacco, and clothing was scattered all over the living room floor. Cathy and John are back in his bedroom. Two of her girls passed out on the big lounge chair they are sharing. Another one of her girls lying on the floor behind the couch wrapped in a blanket with one of John’s boys. Another of Cathy girls on the couch sleep under a sheet partially covering her naked body and one in the downstairs bathroom passed out around the toilet.

“Should we go in there and wake her up?” I asked.

“Hell yea!” Leslie answered.

“Are you ok?” Leslie and I asked.

“Ney. I might be here for a while. There is another bathroom upstairs at the end of the hall,” she mentioned.

“Is there anything we can do for you?” Leslie asked.

“Nothing if you can’t stop the room from spinning,” she answered.

Leslie and I looked at each other before closing the bathroom door.

“You go first,” Leslie said.

“Thanks,” I replied.

“Damn, this is a big ass bathroom. I hate that there is not a lock on the door. Even though the toilet looks clean, I’m still padding the toilet seat before I squat over it,” I thought to myself.

Just as I was finishing the bathroom door swung open. I panicked when I looked up and it is one of John’s boys standing in the doorway. His pants were hanging and his dick sticking out.

"Get the fuck out of here!" I yelled.

"Bitch I don't know who you yelling at!" he yelled back.

"Get out before I start screaming!" I said raising my voice.

"Go ahead. Nobody will be able to hear you over the loud ass music!" he commented.

"Leslie. Leslie. Help!" I screamed.

I got up quickly and tried to pull my pants all the way up. Unfortunately, the bathroom was not that big. It happened so fast. He closed the door and rushed me. The next thing I knew I'm on the floor and he is lying on top of me.

"I told your dumb ass nobody can hear you!" he said.

"What the fuck do you want?" I asked.

"You know what I want!" he said.

I start screaming as loud as I could, but the music drowned my screams out.

"I know you don't think I'm not taking that pussy!" he demanded.

"No. Get the hell off me. This is not right!" I yelled as I tried fighting him off.

"Shut the fuck up, Bitch!" he ordered.

"Please don't!" I begged.

"Begging is not going to help your ass. One day bitch you will thank me for this!" he said.

"Go to hell you sick bastard. If you stop now I want report this!" I yelled.

"To who? The police! Bitch I am related to the sergeant!" he said in a laughing tone.

"You will get yours one day!" I angrily said.

"I'm not worried about that," he said.

I continued to scream, while hitting him with my fist and kicking at him. He grabbed me around the neck and choked me with one hand while using the other hand to push my pants and panties down my legs. He then used his foot to force my pants and panties down around my ankles as I continued hitting him with my fist.

He grabbed a hold of my arms and used one hand to pin my arms down above my head. During the struggle I crossed my legs trying to keep him from penetrating me, but he forced his legs in between mine and pried my legs apart. My screams turned into crying as my body started trembling as I felt the pain of him forcing his dick inside of me.

"Shit. You're a virgin!" he said.

"What the hell is going on?" Leslie yelled as she busted in.

"Who the fuck are you?" he asked.

"Get your motherfucking ass off her!" Leslie ordered as she jumped on his back.

"Bitch, get the fuck off my back!" he yelled.

The next thing I remember was sitting on the bathroom floor and Leslie holding me.

Leslie came upstairs to see what was taking me so long. When she opened the door and saw that punk on top of me. She jumped on his back and started hitting him in the head. He slung her off his back, pulled up his pants, ran down the stairs, and out the front door. Leslie and I stayed on the floor crying while she held me.

"You want me to call the police?" Leslie asked.

"No!" I replied tearfully.

"Why not?" Leslie questioned.

"How will I explain to my father that I was raped while skipping school?" I explained.

"Do you know who that was?" Leslie asked.

"No, but I have seen him around," I answered.

"Let's go?" Leslie instructed.

"I don't want to go home and I don't want anyone to find out," I answered.

"You can stay over my house this weekend. This will be our secret," Leslie suggested in a sympathetic voice.

"Thank you. Do you mind if we stop by my house to pick up a few things?" I asked.

"Not at all," Leslie answered. We left the party without alerting anybody. When we got to my house, I was glad to see that no one was there. I packed a bag and gave my father a call at work to let him know that I'm staying over Leslie's house for the weekend.

When we made it to Leslie's house, I jumped straight in the shower. I stood under the hot running water as I tried to scrub the dirty feeling off my skin. No matter how hard I scrubbed I could not get rid of the dirty feeling on the inside. All I want to do is cry.

The mental aspect of being violated overpowered my physical pains of the attack. It hurt having something so precious stripped away so violently. After I got out the shower, I put on my pajamas and placed all my clothing from that day in a plastic bag.

"Selena I warmed you up something to eat," Leslie said.

"Thank you. Leslie can you throw this bag in the trash?" I asked.

"Are you sure you want to throw away your clothes?" Leslie questioned.

"Yes, I am sure. I don't want any remembrance of the assault," I answered.

"I understand," Leslie replied.

When Leslie came back upstairs, she found me in the bed curled up in the fetal position. It's a damn shame the one time I decided to start the weekend early by skipping school was the worst mistake in my life.

Because Highland Park is so small it didn't take long before the rumor got around school and I found out that my rapist name is Charles Singleton. He was recently released from a juvenile boot camp where he spent two years for carjacking.

For the next couple of months I relived the attack every time I fell asleep. I would wake up in a cold sweat. I found myself filled with anger. The anger turned into hate towards the punk that did this to me. Feeling complete utter hatred towards that punk helped me to form a brick wall that I hid my emotions behind. The brick wall allowed me to emotionally shut down and not show any emotions. From the guilt and shame seeking counseling or reporting, the rape was not and never will be an option. I promised never to put myself in a compromising position like that again.

I needed to make my denial story so believable that I acted as if nothing had happened. I stayed friends with the same group of people, kept my grades up, continued to attend school activities, and group social events. Every time I ran into Charles and he said something rude to me, I would cuss him out claiming that his story was a lie. From the fear of running into him when I'm alone I dropped off the track team. Hopefully nobody notice.

Luckily, I only had to deal with that punk Charles only

for a couple of months. It was the Thursday before our school Christmas recess. Leslie came running up to my locker.

"Girl did you hear who was found dead this morning?" Leslie asked.

"No. Who was it?" I asked.

"It was that punk motherfucker Charles Singleton. They found him dead in an alley. Somebody shot him in the face," Leslie answered.

"That's what that punk deserved!" I replied.

At that moment, it felt like a ten thousand pound weight being lifted off my chest. It's the best Christmas present that anybody could ever give me. I would love to meet the person that sent that motherfucker to hell!

Chapter 2

I'm so glad to see the first day of summer vacation and the end of my freshman year. I'm going to enjoy my last quiet moment before my brothers and Rita's bad ass kids came home from school. Think I should catch a quick nap. This way I will be rested for the parties tonight.

I fell asleep on the backroom couch under the ceiling fan with headphones on. I was sleeping like a baby until Rita's stupid ass woke me up talking about the front door.

"Can I help you? " Rita asked after swing the front door open.

"Yes, is Selena at home?" the stranger at the door asked.

"She is. You can wait on the porch and I will get her," she answered smacking her lips.

Rita's rude ass slammed the door and left the person standing on the porch. She walked into the backroom and unplugged the headphones from my IPod. I jumped up shout, "Why did you do that!"

"There's some thug looking punk on the front porch for you. Your father will be home shortly and you know how he feels about having thug looking niggas at the house," she said.

"Did you ask his name?" I inquired.

"No," she said with a smirk on her face.

Upon opening the door I'm surprised to see this guy named Robert Harris on my front porch. He is the finest guy that I ever seen and one of the biggest drug dealers in

Highland Park.

Robert grew up in Highland Park. He is 17-years old; that's only 2 years older than me. His mother lives next door to my girl Brandy. He dropped out of the high school because slinging drugs interfered with his ability to attend school. He's following in his big brother Thomas Harris footsteps. Thomas was one of Detroit's biggest drug dealers until he got busted. He's currently serving a fifteen to thirty year sentence in Federal prison.

Robert's mother is Puerto Rican and his father is African American. They definitely had a handsome son. He is a little under 6 feet tall, bronze skin tone, short curly black hair, beautiful gray eyes, perfectly manicured mustache, deep sexy voice, well built body, and a charisma that turns heads when he enter a room. He's also known to have a mean streak. He either likes you or not. Because of his looks and money, he has many female admirers. Robert is always dressed from head-to-toe in the lasted designers. He has his own place, drive a black Mercedes Benz, and a BMW motorcycle.

"So why the hell is he on my front porch?" I thought to myself.

"Hi, my name is Robert," he announced.

"I know who you are, but I am puzzled as to why you're on my front porch," I replied.

"I want to talk to you," he responded.

I tried my best not to stare at him, but those gray eyes of his are so amazing and the way he keep softly licking his bottom lip makes it hard not to.

"Why would you want to talk to me?" I asked with an attitude.

"Why wouldn't I want to talk to you?" he responded.

"How did you know where I live?" I replied not answering his question.

"This is a small city and everybody knows everybody. Beside that I always find what I am looking for," he answered.

"I am not sure what kind of game you are trying to play, but you have to get the hell off my porch. If my daddy sees you, he will blow up," I replied.

"Why would he do that?" he questioned.

"Put it this way you really need to get off my porch and get that car out of my driveway," I demanded.

I went in the house and closed the door, but could not help myself from watching him through the front door window, as he walked to his car. That was strange, why would Robert be looking for me. I ran to the phone to call Leslie the moment he pulled out of the driveway.

"Damn, Rita is always on the phone and getting her off is nearly impossible," I mumbled under my breath.

"Rita, can you tell dad that I went over Leslie's house?" I asked.

"Yea," Rita replied.

"Shit, this seems like the longest four block walk to Leslie's house that I have ever taken," I thought to myself.

Knock! Knock!

"Come in," responded Leslie's mom.

"Hi, mama," I replied.

"Hi baby," she responded as I walk over to give her a hug and kiss as Leslie came downstairs.

"Leslie I will need you to pick up my prescription and come right back home with it. I mean right back," her mother ordered.

"Do you mind walking with me," Leslie asked.

"Not, at all. Walking to the pharmacy would give us plenty of time to talk about my shocking, but surprising visit," I mentioned.

"Come on I want to hear this," Leslie said excitingly.

"Girl, you will never guess who came over my house," I replied.

"Who?" she questioned.

"Robert Harris," I answered.

"For real! What the hell did he want?" she asked.

"I am not sure. But it shocked the shit out of me," I told her.

"How did he know where you lived?" she grilled.

"I asked him the same question. He said he finds what he is looking for," I said repeating his words.

"That's a spooky ass answer. It could mean a lot of things," she replied.

"I wondered if it has anything to do with that punk Charles," I commented.

"Why would you think that?" Leslie responded.

"Charles use to work for him. I know he don't think I'm going to fall for any shit," I told her.

"Do you think he's trying to add you to his list of freaks?" she commented.

"I don't know what to think. I hope he don't think I had anything to do with that batch's death," I suggested.

"If he does then he is the dumbest drug dealer in history," she cracked.

"I am going to try and avoid him like the plague," I

pledged.

"On the way back from the pharmacy do you mind if we stop by Brandy's house for a minute? I left a pair of shoes over there," she asked since it was on the way.

"I don't care only if Robert is not over his mother's house," I implied.

"We should be able to notice his car from the corner," she hinted.

On the way, back I looked down Brandy's block and was relieved not to see Robert's car. Brandy was sitting on the porch with Cathy and her girls.

"Hey! What's going on?" Brandy yelled out.

"We're just coming back from the pharmacy for my mother. Figured we stop by so I can get my shoes," Leslie replied.

"What going on?" I asked the group.

"Waiting to catch a glimpse at the cutie," Cathy revealed.

"Who are you talking about?" Leslie inquired.

"She's talking about Robert," one of them blurted out.

"I don't see his car," I commented.

"He parked further up the driveway," another one responded.

"He did that to hide from you hoes," Brandy snarled.

"I would love to fuck him," Cathy blabbered out.

"Is this the only reason why you hoes came to visit?" Brandy asked.

"Here he comes," Cathy said. I was flabbergasted to see Robert walking out of his mother's house.

"Hi Robert," they all called out.

Damn, he turned around before I could duck out of view. I'm hoping that he did not see me.

"So how are you ladies doing," Robert responded walking towards Brandy's house.

It was funny how they all started talking to him at once. Just as he proceeded to stroll up Brandy's walkway an incoming call on his cell phone distracted his attention. It saved me from another awkward moment.

"I have to go. However, ladies have a good day. Selena, hopefully we will get the chance to finish our earlier conversation," he requested looking at his phone.

Everybody turned around looking at me. I sat there with a blank look on my face and said nothing. The moment he drove off all the questions started.

"What conversation was he talking about?" Cathy asked with an amazed look on her face.

"I didn't know you knew him like that," Brandy commented.

"When did you meet him? Why didn't you tell us," Cathy asked.

"Hell, I didn't even know that he knew I existed until this afternoon when he showed up at my doorstep," I responded knowing that brought on more questions. I decided to tell them a little about the brief encounter on my front porch.

"He came over, introduced himself, and I put him off my porch," I claimed.

"Girl, why would you do some stupid shit like that?" one of them asked.

"I didn't want to talk with him," I replied.

"You are a fool!" another one commented.

"I would have pulled him in my house and fucked the shit out of him," Cathy replied.

"We have to cut this conversation short. Brandy can you get my shoes I need to get my mother's medicine home. Besides we will see you all at the party tonight," Leslie said jumping in to save me for their interrogation.

That entire summer, it was funny how Robert showed up every place I went. Damn is he stalking me. I'm not surprised but irritated to see him at the boat dock for Bob-Lo Island Amusement Park.

Bob-Lo Island is a Canadian island located on the mouth of the Detroit River that was transformed into an amusement park. For the last couple of years this is how we end our summer vacation. A slow four level steamboat docked downtown Detroit off Fort Street is one of shuttle location to getting the park. The boat ride is just as enjoyable as the park.

"What is it about Robert? He always seems to be everywhere I go lately. It's like he is following me or something," I whispered to Brandy.

"He is?" Brandy laughed.

"What you mean by that?" I asked with a puzzled look on my face.

"Remember his mother lives next door to me and every time he is over there he asks about you," she stated.

"I hope you didn't tell him anything about me?" I replied. "Sorry. My bad!" she laughed.

"Why didn't you tell me?" I questioned.

"He paid me not to. Besides, who do you think is paying for everybody's tickets?" she responded with a sarcastic smile on her face.

"Ain't this a bitch? You sold me out! I should take my ass home!" I fussed.

"You don't have to talk to him. He's not even going to Bob-Lo. Don't fuck it up for the rest of us," she pleaded.

Robert walked over with admission tickets in his hand. "Good morning ladies. Good morning Selena," he said with a smile on his face. They all said good morning to him like he was a celebrity. However, I refused to acknowledge his presence. He looked directly at me and smiled as he handed Brandy the tickets.

"I hope you ladies have a very good time today," he commented.

I tried my best not to stare at his beautiful eyes and smile. I knew he notice my half smile before he walked off.

"Hell. His fine ass could follow me anytime," Cathy said.

"He would not have to pay anybody to follow me around," Leslie remarked.

"Selena do you know how many girls would love the chance to get with him?" Brandy stated.

"We can move on to a new subject since, you bitches got your free tickets," I demanded.

"He's fine and got money. What more could you ask for?" Cathy added.

The comments and jokes lasted for the next fifteen minutes or so. I would never admit that I'm a little flattered by is gesture. Meanwhile, Robert drove back to Highland Park to take care of business and prepare for his next move.

After boarding the boat, we rushed to get a spot on the third deck around the concession stand. The morning ride on the Bob-Lo Boat is always cold and the heat coming from the concession stand feels good. I took in deep breaths of the fresh crisp morning air and watch the sea gulls hovering around the boat as I sat relaxing.

It turned out to be a good day. I had a great time at the park and no sightings of Robert. Of course, we decided to leave on the last boat back that night. We talked and laughed about the day while standing in line to board the boat. Everybody was ready to get on the boat to enjoy the party back home. Evening trips on the last boat back to Detroit was always a big party. All I wanted to do was enjoy the relaxing cruise home.

Teenagers and young adults always take over the third deck. Most of the third floor level chairs were cleared to create a dance floor. The boat's DJ plays the latest music. We found seats along the boat rails and near the dance floor. Since, I'm not much of a dancer I turned my chair around, propped my feet up on the boat rails, close my eyes, and enjoyed the cool breeze traveling across my face. I did not even notice that someone sat in the chair next to mine.

"Selena, can I talk to you for a moment," the deep male voice said startling me.

I'm shocked to open my eyes and see Robert sitting next to me. Robert has a cousin that works on the Bob-Lo Boat that arranged for him to ride on the last boat back to Detroit. He assumed it would give him more than enough time to force a conversation between us.

"Where the hell did you come from? What do we have to talk about?" I quizzed with a little bass in my voice.

"Why do you always have to be so defensive?" he asked.

"You guys are all the same. All you'll want to do is get into somebody pants one way or another," I responded.

"No, you are wrong about me I am not like the others. You can talk with me now or some other time, but I'm not going anywhere until you hear me out. I am not giving up," he informed in a serious tone.

"Who said I have to speak to you at all?" I asked being irritated at his persistence.

"We are stuck here on this boat together and I am determined to talk with you," he said.

"What do I have to do to get you to stop following me around?" I asked.

"Just give me a moment of your time. Is it possible that we can go someplace quieter and talk so I do not have to yell everything to you?" he proposed politely.

"Come on, we can talk if this will get you to stop following me around," I said with a sarcastic tone in my voice.

I got up and began walking out of the room and like a little puppy he followed. We went upstairs to the top deck, which is a popular spot for older people. My mother always said that the open air seemed to deafen the loud music from the dance floor.

We walked around to the front of the ship and found two seats next to the rails. I choose that spot because it was private but still open for everyone on to see us. That way it would lessen the chance of him trying anything stupid. And if he did, it's an ideal spot to push him overboard.

The view is breathtaking and the weather is perfect. The night breeze dropped the temperature down to a comfortable 74 degrees. The clear dark bluc sky allowed the moon and every star to shine bright. The water was calm enough to hear the humming of the steamboat engine and water splashing from the huge paddle wheel as it cruised back to Detroit.

"So what is so important that you need to talk to me about?" I asked.

“I have wanted to talk to you since the first moment I laid eyes on you,” he admitted.

“When was that?” I asked being taken aback.

“The night of your homecoming dance,” he answered.

“You were at the dance?” I responded trying to remember if I saw him there.

“No. I saw you from my mother’s living room window when you were taking pictures in front of Brandy’s house,” he replied.

“That doesn’t answer my question as to why you feel the need to talk with me,” I indicated.

“I would like to get to know you better. Is that a problem?” he asked with sincerity.

“The problem is that you were friends with that punk Charles and I don’t want anything to do with friends of his,” I stated.

“He was an acquaintance, but not a friend. Punks that like to exploit people even if they have to lie about it could never be a friend to me,” he explained.

“Then why did you hang around him?” I questioned.

“For business reasons, but that is enough about him. Let’s get back to my real concern, which is why you keep blowing me off,” he replied.

"Honestly, I do not trust any guys from Highland Park. Nor do I trust any guys affiliated with Highland Park," I said in all honesty.

"You should not put us all in one category. Their actions should not be a reflection on me," he argued.

"Why should I believe you? Usually birds of a feather flock together," I replied.

"That is not necessarily true. Hell, you are nothing like some of the girls you hang out with," he blurted out.

"Ok, you have a point. So say what you have to say," I said.

We spent the remainder of the boat ride home talking and surprisingly laughing. I actually enjoyed his company. That was the first time that I felt comfortable around a guy that had any ties to Charles.

This is the last Saturday before the start of school and Brandy is having an end of the summer vacation backyard party.

"Hey Selena, my mother has to work tonight and I need to spend the night over your house in order for me to go to Brandy's party tonight," Leslie belted out when I answered the telephone.

"Leslie I'm not sure if I want to go," I mentioned.

"Come on. She is counting on us to show up. It's going to be fun and my mother will not let me go if you're not going," she pleaded.

"Ok, but you need to come over early and help me clean my room up or my father won't let us go," I explained.

If it wasn't for Leslie calling this morning, I wouldn't be going. When we got over Brandy's house, I noticed Robert's car parked in his mother's driveway. This is the first time that

I did not have the urge to hide, but excited to catch a glimpse of his fine ass.

Three hours into the party everybody that is anybody from Highland Park High School was in attendance. The D.J. played all the jams. I was actually having a good time. Around 11 o'clock the whole mood of the party changed when members from the Mob Squad showed up. Everyone prepared for some shit to pop off. It always seemed like those punks deliberately act like fools, but the moment Robert came over the restless thugs calmed down. They walked over to him as if he was their king. I smiled as my heart began racing when he looked my way.

"I don't know who that hoe is smiling at. She thinks she's the shit," one of the punks as niggas commented.

"Not at your ass. She's too good for any of you. And by the way she's smiling at me," Robert responded in a mean voice shutting them up before walking off.

"Would you like to dance?" Robert asked.

"I don't dance to well," I responded.

"I don't care," he replied.

"Then I would like to dance," I accepted.

He took my hand and led me out to the dancing area. He grabbed me around my waist and I hugged him around his waist. We slowly moved side to side and stared in each other eyes as we talked. I could feel the butt of his gun pressing against my side as he bent over to whisper in my ear.

"I am glad to see that you stopped running away from me," he implied.

"You wore me down. I hope you stopped paying Brandy to find out information about me," I commented.

He laughed and kissed me on my forehead. I blushed and laid my head on his chest. We danced and talked until the police shut the party down.

"Robert, since you know where I live, would you drop me and my girl Leslie off at my house?" I asked.

"Anything for you," he said smiling.

As I got in his car, he handed me a piece of paper that had his home and both cell phone numbers on it.

"You can call me anytime," he said handing me the paper.

"I'll think about it," I smirked.

"All I want is the opportunity to show you that my intentions are nothing but good," he explained.

"Only time can tell," I replied.

I wrote my number on the back of an envelope that was sitting in his cup holder, and the biggest smile surfaced on his face. Later that night, Leslie and I were still up laughing and talking about the party when the phone rang.

"Hello?" I answered.

"Can I speak to Selena?" the voice on the other end of the telephone asked.

I started smiling and making hand motions to Leslie.

"This is she. And who's calling?" I asked.

"Is that him?" Leslie whispered in the background.

I nodded my head up and down, yes.

"Hi, this is Robert. I know it's late, but I just wanted to say goodnight and sweet dreams," he said softly and seductively.

"Well thank you. Goodnight and sweet dreams to you," I repeated.

Leslie and I began to scream after I hung up the phone.

"Stop all that damn screaming. I am trying to sleep," yelled the bitch on the other side of the wall.

The following afternoon, as I'm walking back from Leslie's house Robert, pulled up on his motorcycle.

"Hello there pretty lady!" he said.

"Hello to you," I replied with a smile.

"So when are you going to let me take you out?" he inquired.

"I will have to think about that," I said.

"Would you like to take a ride?" he asked.

"No, I think I'll pass on that," I replied.

"Why?" he asked being a little disappointed from the turndown.

"I have on shorts and don't want my legs to get messed up if we fall," I responded.

"Trust me I do not want to mess those legs up either. All you have to do is hold me tight around the waist," he ensured.

"I guess I can, but just for a little while," I said moving closer to him.

"Here you have to put this helmet on," he instructed handing it to me.

I put on his extra helmet and climbed on the back of his bike. It was scary when he first took off. Those first jerks made me lean in closer and hold him tight around the waist. Robert smiled as we rode down Woodward Avenue to Jefferson Avenue. We end up going to Belle Isle.

Belle Isle is the largest city island park in the United States. It is bigger than New York City's Central Park. It's located off Jefferson Avenue and completely surrounded by the Detroit River. One side faces the City of Detroit and the other side faces Windsor, Canada. Crossing the MacArthur Bridge is the only way other than by boat or helicopter to get on the island. It is enjoyed by people of all ages and walks of life for more than just picnics. There are nature trials, golf courses, a private yacht club, playgrounds, a beach, a greenhouse, athletic areas, outdoor theaters, zoo, and a police station. Deer would surface from the woods during the winter months and late nights.

We cruised around the island a couple of times before stopping at the James Scott Memorial Fountain, nicknamed the Magic Fountain. The 510 feet wide marble Magic Fountain sprays a water display 125 feet up in the air during the spring and summer months. The nightly exhibit is the reason behind the nickname. It lights up and turns colors, which gives the illusion that the water is actually turning colors while flowing.

"Hoping you give me the time to prove my intentions are good," Robert requested.

"I'm still cautious on your real motives," I admitted.

"What's so puzzling about me?" he asked.

"I have heard the rumors about you being a player," I commented.

"I will not deny that rumor. The problem is I never met anyone that I want to take the time to know until I saw you," he disclosed.

"What make me so different then the other girls?" I asked blushing.

"Have you ever seen somebody that you can't get them out of your mind?" he asked.

"No," I responded.

"You have a natural beauty that radiates from the inside out. The first time I saw you I have not been able to get you off my mind," he explained.

"I will admit you are very good looking. I see why all the girls scream after you. They act as if you are God's gift to women," I said.

"Thanks but I would not take claim to that. I do hope you will allow me the opportunity to prove that my intentions are all good," he requested.

"We will see. As much as I am enjoying this conversation I need to make it home before my father starts looking for me," I told him.

On the ride home, I felt a little more comfortable around Robert. The bike ride didn't seem to scare me as much.

"I hope you enjoyed the ride?" he asked.

"I did," I answered him with a smile.

"I would like for you to call me later," he requested.

"I will," I promised him.

I could feel him watching me as I walked into the house. That evening I was excited and nervous about calling him. Once I heard his voice, I seem to be unable to stop talking. We talked on the phone for hours. I could not wait until school the next morning to tell Leslie

Chapter 3

"What are you smiling about?" Leslie asked.

"I talked to Robert last night," I answered.

"Tell the truth, you like him," she said.

"Maybe. Just a little," I confessed.

"You like him. I can tell it in your smile," she responded.

"There is something sweet about him, but it also could be a game he is playing," I replied.

"Don't let your past rule your future," she suggested.

"It's still hard to trust any of the guys that knew Charles," I responded.

"Girl, Robert is just so fucking fine," she said.

"I have to admit he is," I agreed.

"So what are you going to do about him?" she questioned.

"I will give it some time to see if he is on the level. If not his ass is gone," I reveled.

"You know if he is on the level a lot of girls are going to be jealous of your ass," she warned.

"What lunch period do you have?" I asked.

"I got B lunch," she replied.

"Damn, I have C lunch. I will catch up with you after school," I responded.

After school, I was standing outside talking with the girls when Robert's car pulled up. The second he got out a group of chicken head girls ran up to talk to him.

"Selena, are you still running away from Robert?" Cathy sarcastically asked.

"I seen you all on him at Brandy's party," someone commented.

"I have no idea what brought him up here, and I was not all on him at the party," I responded.

"Looks like he is coming your way," Leslie said.

He walked right pass each one of those chicken heads. When he walked up and gave me a hug. The expression on their faces was priceless.

"I thought we could go and grab something to eat," he proposed.

"That would be nice," I answered.

"I guess you won't be hiding from him anymore! Remember I hooked you two up," Brandy jokingly yelled loud enough for everyone to hear.

"It's not like you did not profit from it. It's ok if you all drool," I laughed as I walked away. I did feel a little special since all eyes were on us. Especially when he opened the car door for me.

"How was your first day of school?" he asked.

"It was ok and how was your day?" I asked.

"It could be better if you decide to give me a chance," he encouraged.

"That's sweet, but you will have to see," I replied.

"I hope you don't mind going to Bahama Breeze Restaurant?" he recommended.

"Not at all, but where is it located?" I inquired.

"It's on Big Beaver off of I-75 Freeway in Troy. The food

is good," he claimed.

"I have never been there before," I mentioned.

"You will like it. Is there a certain time you have to be home?" he asked.

"I need to be home before seven o'clock," I said.

"That's not giving us a lot of time," he responded.

"If I'm gone to long my father will have a problem, since I did not come straight home," I mentioned.

"I want keep you too long," he promised.

The unofficial date went better than I thought. The restaurant turned out to be nice, the food was great, and the conversation was even better. We sat in a back booth. I am not sure what we were talking about, because when he leaned in for a kiss and I responded that is all I can remember. When I felt our tongues touch my hands became sweaty and my heart started to race. At that moment, it was the start of something unexpected.

From that day on we both adjusted our schedule to spend more time with each other. The next three weeks I saw him almost every day. The day he introduced me to his mother and sister everything about their reaction towards me seem exceptionally genuine.

Mrs. Harris is in her mid forties and a very good-looking woman. Robert had his mother's hair, eyes, and skin tone. Her curly black shoulder length hair complements her beautiful gray eyes, bronze skin tone, keen nose, and small lips. Robert is a momma's boy and her opinion means a lot to him, so he was truly thrilled to see that she approved of me. His lifestyle is the only thing they disagreed about. She was happy to see that he finally settling down with one person.

Robert and his big sister Sherries are extremely close. She is a mirror image of their mother. She is two years older and a second year student at Wayne State University.

I meet his father a week later. Mr. Harris is a very attractive man in his late sixties that still thinks he is a player. Robert has many of his father's features. They share the same build, facial features, and demeanor. His father has fourteen other kids by eleven different women. Most of Robert's siblings have a huge age gap over him and a few of his nieces and nephews are older than him. Robert and Sherries are Mr. Harris last set of kids.

Thomas is the only half sibling that Robert claims. I had the chance to meet him through a telephone conversation, since he's serving time in a federal prison. From the pictures that Robert showed me, Thomas also took after their father. He and Robert were the only two that picked up their father's hustler traits.

Introducing Robert to my father and his bitch was a different story. My father already had his mind made up that Robert was a no good, dope dealing, slick talking thug. Every time Robert comes to visit, my father tries his best to make him feel uncomfortable. It's funny that he wants me to accept his money hungry girlfriend and he won't accept my boyfriend. Even though my father did not care for Robert, that did not stop me from spending as much time as I possibly could with him.

At a blink of an eye, it was time for homecoming again. I'm meeting up with my girls for the parade and the game. After the game, I have to rush to the hairdresser to get my hair done then home to get dress for the homecoming dance. This was going to be the first big Highland Park event that Robert and I would be attending as an official couple.

Robert made it to my house around eight o'clock. When I walked down the stairs the look in his eyes and smile on his face expressed his amazement. I'm wearing a knee length, long sleeve, form fitting black dress. I finish the look with 3-inch black heels, and silver matching accessories. He is wearing the hell out of a black Giorgio Armani suit and a black pair of big block alligator shoes. If I didn't know any better I would have thought he walked off the cover of GQ magazine. I will admit we looked damn good together.

"Selena, I want you home right after the dance," my father demanded.

"I will bring her straight home," Robert said hoping to assure him.

"I'm talking to Selena, but I'm glad you're are listening Robert," my father corrected.

"Come on it's time for us to go," I insisted.

"Did you hear me?" my father asked.

"I heard you," I replied.

We left before my father could open his mouth again.

"I take it your father is starting to like me," Robert joked.

"What would make you think that?" I asked.

"He didn't call me a thug this time," Robert answered.

"You are silly," I said with a giggle.

"You are absolutely gorgeous," he complimented.

I began to blush. "Thank you," I said blushing.

"You're not going to give me a compliment?" he asked.

"Your head is big enough," I teased.

"Ok if that's how you want to be," he replied.

"You are truly handsome," I whispered.

"What is that I hear you saying under your breath?" he questioned.

"I didn't say anything," I answered.

"You don't have to tell me what I already know," he cracked.

"What is it that you think you know?" I asked.

"You will never find a brother better than me," he claimed.

"If that's what you think," I snapped.

"That's what I know," he snapped back.

Everything about the dance seemed magical. We danced all night long. He made me feel as if I'm the most gorgeous female in the room. All eyes were on Robert and me most of the night. I know everyone had to see the chemistry between us. I was the envy of all the females there.

As the night was coming to a close we were on the dance floor about to share a kiss when all hell broke out. Like last year, chairs began flying across the cafeteria, people running and screaming, and security shuffling in the direction of the commotion. From the cheering of the crowd, I could tell it was a fight.

"Babe, it's time to blow! Let's get the hell out of here," Robert said ushering me to an exit.

"I feel the same. It was fun while it lasted," I replied as we rushed off the floor.

"The dance is over. Everybody must leave the school immediately!" blurred a voice over the speakers.

Bam! Bam! Bam! Bam! Bam! We were heading for the car when gun fire erupted. The crowd scattered running in all directions. Robert grabbed my arm and rushed us to his car. He wanted to get off school grounds before the police showed up.

"Sorry, I grabbed your arm so tight," he apologized.

"It didn't hurt," I told him.

"I needed to make sure you were safe," he said being protective.

Ring! Ring! Ring!

"Hello," Robert said answering his phone.

It was not long before someone called and gave Robert details on the shooting.

"Damn, news travel fast. I just hit Woodward Avenue and the details are out," Robert commented.

"What happened?" I inquired.

"One of the twins that live down the block from you was killed. It sounds like a case of mistaken identity. The wrong one was killed," he explained.

"That's a damn shame. I feel sorry for his parents," I said sadly.

"On a lighter note you are gorgeous," Robert said changing the subject.

"Thank you. I had a wonderful night and you made me feel like Cinderella," I replied smiling at him.

"I am glad to have been your Prince Charming," he said reaching over to hold my hand.

When we reached my house, he opened my car door and walked me to the front door. We were about to share our last kiss for the night as the porch light came on and the front door swung open.

"I'm glad you got her home on time," Rita advised.

I rolled my eyes at her then turned and gave Robert a kiss.

"Don't you see me standing here?" she asked.

"Is that suppose to mean something to me?" I

questioned.

"You would not have done that shit in front of your father," she replied.

"Your right. Remember you are not my father or my mother," I snapped.

Rita stomped from the door.

"She likes you as much as your father likes me," Robert said jokingly.

"That's something we have in common," I laughed.

"One last kiss," he requested.

"You have to hold on to that thought until tomorrow. Knowing Rita she probably went crying to my father and he is on his way to the door," I responded.

Time is going by fast. It seemed like homecoming was only yesterday. Now it's the Friday before Sweetest Day and the Cheerleader Squad is holding their annual flower fundraiser sale. They pass out pre-ordered Carnations during the school day. I'm surprised but not shocked to receive an order from Robert during my first hour class but stunned when I received an order in all my classes.

When I got out of school, Robert was parked out front with a long white box sitting on the passenger seat. It was a dozen of red roses. I receive roses on top of the carnations.

"Thank you! I feel so special!" I said leaning in to give him a hug and kiss.

"You are special," he said smiling.

"I was not expecting all of this," I replied.

"The day is not over yet," he commented.

"What do you mean by that?" I asked.

"I figured that we would celebrate our Sweetest Day today, since you choose to babysit tomorrow," he answered.

"You know I rotate babysitting jobs with Leslie. So, what do you have planned?" I asked being curious. "Nothing big. Just dinner and a movie," he answered in a nonchalant manner.

"That's sounds good. Let me see your phone so I can call home," I requested.

Robert pulled a phone out of the driver's side door pocket.

"Whose phone is this?" I asked.

"It's yours," he answered.

"What are you talking about?" I asked being caught off-guard.

"I wanted to get you something that would make it easy for me to keep in touch with you," he said smoothly with a smile.

"Thank you, but you didn't have too," I said.

"Yes I did. I was getting tired of your father picking up the phone when I'm talking to you. My numbers are already programmed in it," he confessed.

We headed out to Benihana's Japanese Restaurant on Big Beaver Road in Troy. The place was packed and there is a two-hour wait for a table. Robert put his name on the waiting list and we drove down the street to the shopping mall.

Somerset Mall is not an ordinary mall. It was my first time going there because it consists of nothing but high-end stores. I followed Robert into the Gucci Store so he could buy a pair of shoes. While he was trying on a several pair of shoes, I browsed around the jewelry counter.

"Wow, I can't believe people spend this much money on

watches. They are sharp but way out of price," I thought to myself as Robert walked up behind me.

"Do you want anything?" he asked.

"No thanks. Just admiring the watches," I answered.

"You're sure?" he asked bending over and kissing me on the back of my neck.

"Yes, I'm sure," I answered.

When we got to Benihana's, the maitre d was able to place us at a table with the grill. A Japanese chief performed tricks with his cooking utensils as he cooked our food in front of us. We spent so much time eating and talking that we never made it to the movies.

It's Sweetest Day and I have an overnight babysitting job at one of Leslie and my best customer's house. Their three children are all under the age of five years old and a handful but a joy to be around. They live in a big six-bedroom home in one of Detroit's most prominent areas. Their big house is in the Palmer Woods subdivision located right out of Highland Park in the Seven Mile and Livernois area.

"Hey, there Sweetheart," I said answering my cell phone.

"Hello to you. Are you busy?" he asked.

"I'm getting the kids ready for bed. Can I call you after they kids are sleep?" I requested.

"Yes you can," he answered in a smooth and sexy voice.

"Talk to you later," I replied.

I gave the kids a bath and dressed them in their pajamas. We spent five minutes going through our ritual of hugs and kisses as they all climb in the guest bedroom king size bed to hear a bedtime story. It only made sense for them to fall asleep in that bed, since they all seem to end up in the bed with me by morning. I ended up reading Brown Bear twice before all three of them fell asleep. They looked like angels. I tuned on the night light and went downstairs to call Robert.

"Hello," Robert said answering his cell phone.

"Hey Baby," I replied.

"You got the kids to bed?" he asked.

"Yes. It took reading the same story twice to get them to fall asleep," I answered.

"So, what are you doing?" he asked.

"Thinking about you," I replied.

"Do you mind if I stop by?" he asked in a smooth and low voice.

"Not at all," I replied.

"I will be there in fifteen minutes," he responded. "What's the address?"

"Ok," I replied giving him the location.

I rushed around to put up the children's toys. I stood in the mirror making sure my hair was together when Robert arrived. He gave me a big hug when I opened the door.

"I hate that you had to work on Sweetest Day, but I am glad that I get the chance to see you," he whispered softly in my ear.

"I also was hoping to see you. So what did you do today?" I asked as he followed me to the living room couch.

"I spent time with the other woman in my life," he said teasing me.

"That's good. I know your mother was happy to see you," I said.

"She was and she asked about you. I told her that you stood me up for three other dates," he joked.

"Why would you say that?" I asked with a puzzled look.

"Well, you did," he replied.

"They were the perfect dates. They even got the chance to hug and kiss me," I said getting his point.

"I bet their kisses aren't better than mine," he teased.

"I don't know about that. Their kisses are kind of special," I teased back.

"I know their kisses aren't better than that," he bragged leaning in and giving me a small but tender kiss.

"You need to try a little harder," I suggested.

I locked eyes with Robert and I watch as he licks his lip while preparing to give me a kiss. Robert ran his fingers through my silky hair and pulled my face closer to his. He gave me three quick kisses followed by a deep, long, French tongue kiss. He place one arm around my back and gently lower me onto the couch. I wrap my arms around the lower part of Robert's muscular back. He licks my top lip as he pulled his tongue out of my mouth.

"I know their kisses could not top that one," he commented proudly.

"I'm still undecided," I replied teasing him and wanting more.

"I know the truth," he said with such confidence.

"If that's what you want to think," I replied with a sultry look.

"Then why is your heart racing?" he asked.

"Your right. There is no comparison," I admitted.

"You are so beautiful," he said wrapping his arms around me.

"You make me feel beautiful," I replied looking into his eyes.

Robert and I engaged in another deep tongue kiss. He sucked on my bottom lip then outlined my lips with his tongue. He stuck his tongue back in my mouth and we engaged in another deep wet kiss. His tongue passionately slide off my lips to my chin and then down my neck. I ran my hands up his back then back down until I reached the ass of his blue jeans.

My left hand stroked over Selena's shirt across her right breast as I nibbled my way back up her neck. I felt her body tense up when I reached her bra, so I only cupped the bra and began to kiss her until I felt her body relax.

His hands affectionately squeezed the cups of my bra. I touched his ass with my hands. My body trembled when his hands ran across my breast. My pussy began to tingle and moisten up when I felt the imprint of his dick as he stroked it against my pelvic area. I'm shocked at my body's reaction, but I became slightly scared when I felt his arms pushing my shirt up and his hands sliding under my shirt.

"I noticed that she's not stopping me. Could this be the night that we take our relationship to the next leave? I honestly picture our first time would be in my bed, but I want her so bad. I hope I don't scare her away. Damn I never felt this way about a female. Am I in love with her?" Robert had thoughts running through his mind as he was building up the courage to remove one hand from Selena's breast and reaching for the crouch of her pants.

So many thoughts ran through my head, "Should I stop him from exploring my body? Should I remove my hands from his ass? Is he still trying to run game on me? Could this be real that Robert Harris really wants me? Does he think that I'm a freak? Am I actually falling in love with this guy? Will I regret this later? Damn he is a good-looking! Does he really like me? If I stop him will he stop calling me? Could he ever love me?" The moment he tried to unbutton my pants, I panicked. I pushed him off and quickly sat up.

"Is everything ok?" he asked being surprised at my reaction.

"I'm not ready for that," I answered.

"I'm sorry. I didn't mean to do anything that would make you feel uncomfortable," he replied gently.

"I hope you understand?" I asked.

I softly placed my hands on Selena's face and looked her in the eyes. I needed to reassure her that my intentions are good.

"Baby, I understand. You can take all the time you need," he softly spoke.

"Thank you. I hope this won't change your mind about me," I said being timid.

"Believe me this will not change the way I feel about you. I'm not going anywhere and it will happen when the time is right," he said with sincerity. "I hope she don't think it's her fault. It will happen when the time is right. I hope I can find something on one of these channels to watch while my hard on goes down," he thought to himself.

He gave me the most enduring kisses on the lips and both my cheeks. He placed his head in my lap and began flicking through the cable channels. I know he has to be disappointed, but I'm glad he didn't get up and leave.

"Do you mind watching Menace to Society? That and Scarface are a few of my favorite movies," he asked being polite.

"Not at all," I answered.

"Can you do me a favor and lightly scratch my scalp," he requested.

"I would be happy too," I obliged and began scratching his scalp gently.

In a blink of an eye it's the night before Thanksgiving and Robert kept his word about staying around. He is picking me up around 4 p.m. this evening. The only thing I know is that he has a surprise planned for me.

"I know you're curious as to what I have planned for you tonight," he teased.

"Yes, but I am also intrigued," I admitted.

"Good," he replied with a devious smile.

"Can you give me a little hint?" I begged.

"Not at all," he answered.

"You know that I hate surprises," I pouted.

"That sounds like a personal problem to me," he sternly said.

"You are wrong," I fussed.

"No I'm not wrong. I like knowing that you don't have any idea what I have in-store for you," he taunted.

"Come on, just a teeny tiny hint," I pleaded.

He cut up the radio and started singing. That is his way of not answering any more questions about the surprise. I had no choice but to sat back and enjoy the ride. When he turned on to the bridge leading to Belle Isle the first thing that came to my mind is that we were only going to ride around the island before heading to my surprise. What else is there to do out here on a cold night?

"This is a beautiful fall evening. The trees have lost all their leaves and a thin layer of snow is covering the ground. She probably thinks this is a diversion to her surprise. There goes a park bench facing the Ambassador Bridge which connects Detroit to Canada. That looks like a perfect spot," Robert thought to himself as he pulled up.

"He must have lost his mind cutting his car off and getting out. So is my surprise hiding in the trunk! If so he didn't have to cut the heat off. I know he's not walking with a blanket to that park bench. This man is crazy," I thought to myself.

"Are you getting out of the car?" he yelled out.

"You're not serious?" I yelled back.

"Yes I am. Come on and get out the car," he said.

"You are crazy!" I stated savoring my warm spot.

"No, but you got to get out my car," he said walking away.

I got out the car and followed him to the park bench. He dusted off the thin layer of frosty snow and then sat the blanket on the bench before sitting on it. I sat on his lap and he wrapped us up in the blanket. He tried to kiss me but I turned away.

"So you're not going to kiss me now?" he asked.

"Not until you tell me what's going on," I answered with a shiver.

"You are so impatient. You need to work on that," he said holding me tighter.

"You got me out in the cold, so what is the big surprise?" I asked.

"I want to give you something that money can't buy," he stated.

"Now I am truly intrigued," I said warming up in his arms.

"I want to share a sunset with you. Look how beautiful and peaceful the sky is," he said pointing his finger towards the Ambassador Bridge.

"It is truly breath taking," I complimented looking up at the sky.

It's amazing to see nighttime overlapping daytime. Heaven is displaying a light show as a farewell to the day and a greeting to the night. The sky began coloring itself with several shades of pink and purple with splashes of yellow, red, and orange. The large pale splashes of bright colors slowly race across the sky darkening as they blend together. Once the colors completed blended together a brilliant dark blue sky with a faint outline from the white clouds and a glowing shadow casting around a bright full moon is all that's left.

"This perfectly explains how I feel when I am around you," he whispered softly in my ear.

I'm speechless as I smile from ear to ear. Embracing him in a deep long kiss is the only thing I want to do. We sat cuddling in each other's arms as we watched the sky cast a mirror image of God's perfect work over the Detroit River. I had forgotten how cold it was. All I could think about was how much I loved being with this man.

"This is the best present I could have ever received," I softly whispered to him.

"Talking about presents, what are some hints for your Christmas gift?" he asked me.

"I prefer not to exchange gifts," I answered.

"Why not?" he asked being puzzled.

"Spending more time is the only thing you can give me," I answered gently.

"It's only a Christmas gift," he replied.

"Can you please promise me that you will not get me nothing more than a card?" I asked.

He stared at me with a smirk on his face.

"I will obey your commend if you promise to bring in the New Year with me," he requested kissing my forehead.

"You have a deal," I responded and kissed his cheek.

We spent Thanksgiving at his mother's house and Christmas with my family at my aunt's house. I'm thrilled to see that Robert kept his promise and did not buy me a Christmas gift.

Chapter 4

It's New Years Eve and my father thinks Leslie and I are babysitting overnight for one of our customers. This is the only way I am able to ensure getting out of the house and spending the evening with Robert. My father dropped Leslie and I off at our customer's house. After the parents left for the night, I helped Leslie put the kids to bed before Robert came to pick me up.

"Leslie, Robert is out front. I'm going to put the downstairs alarm on and Happy New Years," I called to her upstairs.

"Happy New Years to you and Robert," Leslie yelled down the stairs.

When I got in the car, Robert gave me a hug and kiss before we pulled off.

"So what do you have planned for me?" I asked.

"I figured that you will help me finish cooking and then we can sit on the couch cuddling while the New Year comes in," he answered.

"Oh, that's sweet," I replied with a giggle.

Robert lives in the heart of Downtown Detroit at 1300 Lafayette on the 16th floor in a corner apartment. The apartment has two bedrooms with oversized closets, a full bathroom off the master bedroom, and a half bathroom in the hallway. The master bedroom is furnished with a dark cherry wood king size bedroom set. The spare bedroom has nothing but clothes and a wall full of alligator shoes and gym shoe boxes.

The outside walls have floor to ceiling windows that run the entire length of wall that gives a spectacular view of Downtown Detroit. The living/dining room is furnished with a black leather couch set, huge flat screen television entertainment center with surround sound, matching end tables, and a small glass top dining room table set for two located in a corner off the kitchen. Everything about his place signifies a single man, but exceptionally clean.

I could smell he already started cooking the moment we walked into his apartment. The dining room table is set for two with candles and fresh flowers. He cooked the steak and baked potatoes before picking me up. I helped with the salad, garlic toast, and steamed vegetables as we shared a bottle of white wine. The New Years Eve special on WJLB the local radio station is playing in the background.

"I know you told me not to buy you anything for Christmas," he said as we sipped wine.

"I'm glad you listened to me. You know one of the rumors around school is that I am with you because of your money. I want a relationship built on something solid and not something superficial," I said.

"Your beauty was not the only reason I became attracted to you. You are not like the other females out there. There is something definitely special about you," he said.

"I noticed you from a distance, but never imagined that you noticed me," I revealed.

"I also noticed you but was not sure on the correct way to approach you," he admitted.

"Almost every girl in school would love to get with you," I mentioned.

"They only want me for my money and my good looks. I feel that I deserved the best and nothing less. You are the best. That is why I fell in love with you," he confessed.

"I love you too," I said before I knew it.

This was the first time we said those three words to each other. I leaned over to kiss him, but he pulled away.

"Sorry baby but I need to seriously talk with you. I wanted to have this talk for a while, but was afraid that it would scare you away," he blurted.

"What is it?" I asked being mystified.

"Just like you I want a relationship that is built on a solid foundation. I need to be very honest with you. I am not sure as to what you may have heard about my life style. First, my profession is not considered legal and it is not something I plan to do forever. Second, I have been with many females, but none of them ever made me feel the way I feel when I am around you. You are my calm in this storm that I live in. And I truly do love you with all my heart," he said seriously and softly.

"With Highland Park being such a small city it would have been virtually impossible for me not to hear about your career choice or the females. The story about the other girls was not the only reason why I first avoided you. The main reason was the rumor about me," I confessed being ashamed.

He placed his fingers on my lips to stop me from talking.

"You do not have to discuss it," he said gently.

Tears started running down my face.

"Yes, I do. I love you with all my heart and I need to be totally honest with you, because it's indirectly affecting our relationship. I am not a virgin, but it was not by my choice. Charles raped me. I didn't report it because I was too ashamed of anybody finding out. He took something from me that was meant for that special someone. He made a moment in my life that was supposed to be so beautiful into something so ugly. You are the first person outside of Leslie that I have discussed this with. You will never know how many times before his death I wished him dead. I know it sounds bad but, it was like Christmas when I heard that he was murdered," I cried being relieved to get it out.

Robert wrapped his strong arms around me and cradled me the way my mother use to. I laid my head on his chest and cried. He rubbed my back and whispered.

"It's wasn't your fault. Charles was a monster and he got what he deserved," he said agreeing with me.

I looked up at him with tears still running from my eyes. He tenderly wiped them away and began to softly kiss my face. At that moment, his kind, compassionate, loving side had became my only perception of him. He pulled a wrapped gift box from under his couch.

"I want to give this to you because you came in my life at the right time," he said handing the box to me.

Like a girl, I broke out crying again before I opened the gift. This time they were tears of joy.

"Thank you, but you didn't have to get me anything. I feel bad that I don't have anything for you," I cried.

"You gave me your heart and that is something that money can't buy," he whispered.

I ripped open the box and to my surprise, it was an expensive diamond incrusted heart shaped pendant on a gold chain.

"It's beautiful!" I said through my tears.

"This was the only way I am able to give you my heart for the whole world to see," he explained.

"That is the sweetest thing I ever heard," I said looking at the pendant and then at him. "Wait until the chicken heads see this," I thought to myself.

"Turn around so I can put it on you," he said.

With my back to him I took one hand to sway my hair to one side like the women in the movies. After Robert closed the clasp to the necklace, he licked his lips and softly kissed the back of my neck. Without a second thought, any insecurity I had about sharing myself with him completely disappeared. He continued kissing on the back of my neck as he slowly unbuttoned my shirt. I unbutton the cuffs on my sleeves. With slow sucking kisses, his lips slowly moved down my back as he removed my shirt.

One at a time, I removed her sleeves from each arm. The second that my lips reached the bottom of her back and was making my way back up her back she let her hair loose and it brushed the top of my head as it swung downward. I stopped midway up her back. Wrapping my arms around her waist and with slow small circular movements my hands climbed up her stomach until they reached the wire in her bra. My hands cupped her breast and slowly rotated my fingers up and over her nipples. I repeated the motion four or five times before running my thumb over her nipples several times quickly.

I felt my pussy moisten my panties. He took hold of my bra straps and slid them half way down my arms. I cupped my breast to keep my bra from exposing my breast when he unclasped my bra.

"Turn around baby," he whispered.

I turned around still cupping my breasts and tenderly biting my bottom lip. Robert took my hands and removed them from my breasts. He smiled as he sat there and stared at my breast. I saw a sparkle in his beautiful gray eyes as he stared at me. I bit my lip slightly harder as I watched him remove his shirt. My heart skipped a beat as his muscles flexed when he raised his arms to take off his shirt.

I let my hands gently touched his perfectly sculpted biceps. Even with the hair on his chest and stomach, I'm still able to see his six-pack abs. I took my time and let my hands explore every detail of his hairy chest.

I grabbed her breast when we leaned in to meet each other for a kiss. While we were engrossed in a deep tongue kiss, I removed one hand off her breasts and placed it on her back. I lowered her on the couch as we continued kissing. I instantly stop kissing her and sat up.

I looked up at him as I lay on the couch. "Robert is everything alright?" I asked, being a little baffled.

"I don't want to rush you into doing anything you are not ready for. I will stop the moment you tell me too," he said assure me.

"I'm ok," I said softly.

"Are you sure?" Robert nervously asked.

She shook her head yes as I leaned back down and resumed kissing and touching her. I rubbed her breasts and she gently ran her hands along my biceps and back shoulder blades. I took one hand off her breast and placed it between her legs to rub her pussy through her blue jeans.

I'm somewhat embarrassed because my pussy had moistened up so much that the crouch of my blue jeans were soaking wet. He unbuttoned my pants.

"Do you mind if I touch it?" he asked for my permission.

"Sorry. It's wet down there," I said being embarrassed.

"There is nothing for you to be sorry about. I have never seen a pussy get this wet before," he said.

"Is that a good thing?" I asked.

"Hell yea. Every man loves a hot wet pussy. And yours is dripping wet. That's why I want to touch it," he confessed to me.

"Go ahead. You can touch it," I said being timidly.

He inserted one of his hands in my panties. Feeling his fingers exploring my pussy made it moisten up more. As one of my legs rested between his legs, I could feel his dick pulsating and swelling. That made my pussy throb in a way I never experienced before. I took one hand to rub his throbbing dick trough his blue jeans.

She used both hands to loosen my belt and unzipped my jeans. My dick popped out as far as the material of my boxers would allow. It started throbbing faster when her pussy secreted more hot juice on my hand.

"Are you sure about this?" he whispered in my ear.

"Yes, I am 100% sure," I whispered back.

I picked her up, carried her to my bedroom, and laid her across the bed. I took her shoes off one at a time. I grabbed her jeans and panties at the same time and pulled them down off her legs. I stepped out of my shoes and swiftly removed my jeans and boxers.

The song, Between the Sheets by the Isleys Brothers played in the background as he climbed on top of me. While he was taking turns to suck on my breast, I could feel his dick brushing my pussy. I twirled my fingers in his black curly hair.

When I was unable to hold myself back I slowly inserted my fully erect dick inside her pussy.

"Ohhhhhhhhhhhh. Oohhhhhhhhh. Ooooooohhhhhhhh. Oooooohhhhhhh shitttt," I moaned after loudly gasped for air.

"Do you want me to stop?" he asked.

"No. I want to feel you inside of me," I told him.

My body was exploding with pain and pleasure from his dick entering my pussy. I felt like a virgin again, but in a good way this time.

I will keep my strokes gentle and slow, since this is our first time. As her pussy became wetter, it excited me even more.

I tried to remember some of the movements I heard my girls talk about. However, my mind went totally blank.

"Baby, tell me what you want me to do," I whispered in his ear.

"Let your body move to the rhythm of my strokes," he whispered back.

I let my heart guide my body. Pleasing him was the only thing that came to mind. I rotated my pelvis area to the rhythm of his strokes. He intertwined my fingers with his and held my arms out to the side. We both moaned with pleasure as sweat dripped from every inch of our bodies.

"Baby, this is better than I ever imagined. Your pussy is tight, hot, and wet," he whispered.

"All I want to do is please you," I moaned.

"This was definitely worth the wait," he whispered softly.

"I love you," I whispered.

"I love you too," he moaned.

I rolled her on her back and instructed her to get on her hands and knees. I held on to her waist as my dick guided itself back into her pussy. She arched her back as I directed her body to go back and forth, as my dick plunged inside her pussy.

It felt like time is standing still just for us. The fireworks of excitement exploding inside my body blocked out the gunshots in celebration as a new year being born. His strokes became rapid as my body trembled with pleasure. Am I experiencing my first orgasm?

“Here I come. Here I come,” Robert cried out.

Robert pulled his dick out and ejaculated on the lower part of my back and ass. I intentionally watched his sperm erupt from the head of his dick.

“Thank you Selena,” he moaned.

“No. Thank you for being patient with me,” I said in a satisfied tone.

“Happy News Years, baby! That was the perfect way to bring in the New Year,” he said.

“Robert you are that someone special that I was saving myself for. And that was definitely beautiful. I love you,” I told him with a hug.

This completely took our relationship to a new level. I curled up in his arms and laid my sweaty head on his sweaty chest. Using the hand that was cupped under his shoulder I lightly held my heart pendent close to my chest. The fingers on the other hand twirled in his chest hair. He kissed me on the forehead as I dozed off with only one thought in my heart that I'm truly in love with this man.

That next morning Robert was up cooking breakfast, as I lay in the bed sore. He smiled as he watched me slowly walk to the kitchen. He knew that I'm sore from last night. We talked and laughed while eating a pancake breakfast.

Chapter 5

"I need to make a run before I drop you off. Do you mind?" Robert asked.

"Not at all," I answered.

We pulled up in front of a two family flat on Glenda Street off Hamilton Avenue. I started to get out of the car to go up to the house.

"I want you to wait in the car for me. It's only going to take me minute," he said.

I got back in the car and waited. He was only in there for fifteen minutes. Once he got back in the car, he handed me a brown bag.

"Can you put that in the glove box for me?" he asked.

As bad as I wanted to know what was in the bag, I did not ask.

"What do you have planned for your birthday this year?" he asked.

"To tell you the truth I have not even thought about it. Taking the road test for my driver's license is the only thing I have planned," I replied.

"This will be your sweet sixteenth birthday," he said with excitement.

"Honestly, I lost the thrill of my birthday the year that my mother died," I said sadly.

"I'm sorry," he said.

"You have nothing to be sorry for. My mother was

always the one that initiated all our parties. Once she passed I just stop having birthday parties for myself," I told him.

"I did not mean to make you sad," he apologized.

"You didn't," I guaranteed him.

"If you do not want to do anything I will understand," he said sympathetically.

"I will let you know. I still have time before my birthday," I replied considering the idea.

With the anticipation of my sweet sixteen party being ten days away, I didn't mind sharing our first Valentine's Day with Robert's mother. It means a lot to me that his mother likes me. Besides, I had my personal time with Robert. I skipped school and spent the entire morning with Robert all up in me and the afternoon shopping.

The big day was finally here. I went with Leslie's bowling party idea. Over sixty of my closest friends are meeting me up at the State Fair Bowling Lanes on Woodward Avenue just south of Eight Mile Road.

Ring! Ring! Ring! Ring! My cell phone rang.

"I know you're not here already!" I said somewhat surprised.

"No. Baby, I hate to do this to you, but is there a chance that you can ride up to the bowling alley with one of your girls?" Robert asked.

"Why. I know you're not standing me up on my birthday?" I asked being a little pissed.

"No. Something came up that I need to attend to," he evaded.

"Should I expect to see you later?" I asked.

"Yes. I will get there as soon as I can," he guaranteed.

When I called Brandy she had already left, but I was still able to catch Leslie at home.

"Hey girl, can you ask Brandy to pick me up when she leaves your house?" I asked.

"Is everything ok?" Leslie asked.

"Yea. Robert had business to attend to and he will be up there later," I said.

"I will call you when we are on our way," she said hanging up.

Chapter 6

Robert's boys Sean, Shannon, and Jason were walking down a dimly lighted alley behind the drug spot on Tyler.

"Motherfuckers, this is a stick up!" A punk said stepping out from a dark hiding spot holding a 35MM handgun and wearing all black including a black skullcap.

"What the fuck you mean this is a stick up!" Jason responded in a mean tone.

"You're that motherfucker they call Quick. You don't know who you are fucking with!" Shannon added.

They called him Quick because he slipped in and out of the dark of night in the blink of an eye. "Bitches what part of this is a stick up you didn't understand? Put all your money in this bag!" Quick demanded.

Shannon and Jason emptied the money from both of their pants pockets and dumped it in the bag. Sean pulled out a hand full of coins from his front pants pocket. Instead of dropping them in the bag, he tossed it in Quick's face to startle him. That split second allowed them to overpower him.

Sean knocked the gun out of Quick's hand and they all proceeded to beat his ass. They dragged him into the garage of an abandon house. Sean pulled an electrical cord off the wall, while Shannon called Robert. They tied his hands behind his back and stuffed his mouth with the skullcap he was wearing. They stripped Quick of all his valuables while waiting for backup.

Robert, Lamont, and Gator all pulled up at the same time. Robert and Lamont have been best friends since second grade. They consider themselves as brothers. Robert met Gator in the seventh grade when they both were sitting in the principal's office. It was Gator's first day of school and he was waiting for his class assignments. Robert was kicked out of class for fighting and waiting to see the principle.

"Great job men we can handle it from here," Robert ordered.

Shannon and Jason went back to the house on Tyler.

"This punk needs to be taught a lesson. I want to make sure the lesson sends out a message that actions like this will not be tolerated," Gator demanded.

"He fits the description of that nigga they call Quick," Sean brought to their attention.

"Isn't there a hit on his ass?" Robert questioned.

"Hell I believe there are several hits out on his ass!" Gator added

"Well the motherfucker ran into the wrong niggas this time!" Lamont said.

"I guess he wasn't quick this time," Robert suggested as they all laughed.

"Should we turn him over and get the reward?" Sean asked.

"No, were going to deal with this bastard ourselves," Lamont responded.

"I got something for your ass. Sean can you give me a hand?" Gator asked.

A few minutes later Gator and Sean walked in with two 5-gallon cans of gasoline and an ax from Gator's trunk.

"I know you're not riding around with that shit in your trunk," Robert commented.

"Actually, I do," Gator responded.

"Your one sick motherfucker," Robert said

"Never know when you might need to set a fire," Gator commented.

"Let's not set the whole garage on fire," Robert suggested

"Sean, run down the alley and get one of those industrial trash cans from behind the corner store," Lamont ordered.

"It looks like your bitch ass is about to become barbeque," Gator said.

Quick tried pleading for his life through his facial expressions. Robert yanked another electrical cord from the wall, tied Quick legs at the calf, and held his legs down as Gator chopped his feet off just above the ankles.

"Ain't this a bitch you got blood on my fucking coat!" Robert said.

"Robert, take off your coat so we can wrap his legs up in it," Gator ordered.

"Why my shit?" Robert asked.

"This way we can avoid getting blood on anybody else shit. Hell, you already have blood on it. Also, Let me get your motherfucking gloves," Gator requested.

"Now I have to go all the way back home to another other coat," Robert complained.

"I have a jacket in the back of my car that you can borrow," Gator offered.

"What don't you have in your car?" Lamont asked.

They threw Quick in the trashcan along with Robert's coat and the ax. Lamont doused everything inside of the trashcan with both cans of gasoline.

“What about his gym shoes?” Sean asked.

Gator put on Roberts gloves then picked up the gym shoes and walked out of the garage with them.

“Where are you going with his gym shoes?” Robert asked.

“He’s probably putting them in his trunk,” Lamont chuckled as they laughed at Gator.

“Fuck you’ll,” Gator said when he walked back into the garage.

“I hope you got gloves in your car,” Robert said.

“Fuck you twice over,” Gator replied as he tossed Robert’s gloves in the trashcan.

Sean threw the empty gas cans in and a lit match in the trashcan before closing the lid.

They all walked out of the garage like nothing happened.

“Sean you can ride with me up to the bowling alley,” Robert said.

“Watch out!” ordered Gator as they walked out of the garage.

“For what?” Lamont asked.

“Gator left the motherfucker's gym shoes in the middle of the alley,” Sean responded.

“I wanted everyone to know that Quick made his last run,” Gator joked.

“You are one sick bastard!” Robert laughed.

“Motherfuckers you’re going to get enough calling me sick,” Gator replied.

“Shut the fuck up and give me that jacket!” Robert demanded.

"Don't get any blood on my shit!" Gator fussed as he tossed Robert the jacket.

"Are you coming up to the bowling alley?" Robert asked.

"No, my sick ass promised my girl that I would pick her up from her sister's house," Gator replied.

"I will be up there after I check on Tyler," Lamont replied.

Quick screams of pain were muffled by the hat that was lodged in his mouth. Bumping sound of his body's rapidly squirming in the trashcan could lightly be heard over the roar of the flames from the fire. The sounds ceased once his body went into shock and passed out from the pain of being burned alive.

The fire in the trashcan blazed for over an hour before anyone noticed the clouds of smoke and flames rolling from the roof of the garage. All evidence was destroyed by the time the fire department was able to contain the fire. The fire in the trashcan rose to a temperature high enough for cremation. The heat was so intense that all his organs and soft tissue vaporized. The only thing left was the light gray dry bone skeleton of the deceased. Since the fire truck parked over his gym shoes, they were not discovered until the next day.

Chapter 7

Robert showed up at the bowling alley with Sean. It was so crowded that I had to share my seat with him. Actually, I just wanted to sit on his lap. He was there for about an hour before giving me my birthday present. He pulled a long jewelry box out of his jacket inside pocket.

“Happy birthday, baby,” Robert said sweetly with a smile.

“What do we have in this box?” I asked smiling at him.

“Just open it,” he said.

I’m shocked to see it’s the Gucci watch I admired at Somerset Mall on Sweetest Day.

“How did you know that I liked this watch?” I asked blushing from ear to ear.

“I will never forget the day that watch caught your eye. It was the first time that anybody turned down my offer to buy them something. That moment substantiated you were special,” he said.

“Thank you, sweetheart. I love you,” I said leaning in and gave him a big hug and kiss.

“Selena why the fuck would you want to kiss on that motherfucker?” Lamont joked as he walked in with Shannon and Jason.

We stopped kissing and started laughing from Lamont’s comment. I enjoyed the rest of the night.

We left the bowling alley around 1 a.m. in the morning. Robert had to drop off all three of his boys, since Lamont sneaked off with one of my girlfriends.

Pulling up to one of the few occupied houses on Elmhurst Street was eerie. With the absence of working streetlights the darkness of the night is concealing the scary appearance of the block. Robert and his boys got out of the car. As much as I hated to stay behind I wasn't sure if he wanted me to remain in the car. I'm relieved to see Robert walked back to the car.

"Aren't you coming?" he asked.

"I thought you wanted me to wait in the car for you," I replied.

"Not at this time of the night and especially not on this block," he said.

We walked up to the small wood frame one story house. A howling cold stiff winter wind softly ran across my face and made me gasp for breath as we walked up the stairs. The creaking wood from the front porch steps seem to echo through the blackness of the night. The front porch railing has missing poles. Security bars dressed the windows.

As Robert was unlock the security gate and front door I caught a reflection in the dark. The glow radiating from the full moon created a dim trace of light bounced from the fresh layer of white snow. I could not help from watching the rats running around an open bag of trash on the neighbor's porch.

I was surprised when we stepped in the house. It's a lot cleaner on the inside then it appeared to be from the outside. There was not much furniture in the house. The front room had an old black leather couch, card table, two folding chairs, and a weight bench. Several stacks of money with rubber bands around them and a handgun on the side of a money counter sat on the table.

I wasn't able to make out details of the rooms in the back of the house because they were totally dark. The side of the brown refrigerator was the only view of the kitchen that's visible from the front room. I could hear voices of other people in the kitchen besides Robert and his boys that rode with us.

Like a good girlfriend, I sat on the edge of the leather couch and waited for my man to finish his business. He walked out of the kitchen and placed the stacks of money from the card table in a brown paper bag. That explained what was in the paper bags that I place in the glove box.

"Come on baby lets go," he said heading back out into the night blackness.

"Robert I had a wonderful time. And I love my gift," I told him in a cheerful tone.

"I am glad you enjoyed yourself, but the watch was only part of your birthday surprise," he said with a smile.

"What's the other surprise?" I asked.

"Look in the cup holder. You already have the key to my heart now I would like you to have the key to my home. I want you to feel free to come and go as you please," he said.

"I would like to use my key tonight since, my father thinks I'm spending the night over Leslie's house," I replied with a smile on my face.

"I love you," he told me.

"I love you too," I told him.

This was the first time Robert exposed me to a part of his life that he kept shield from me. We talked and laughed the entire ride to his home. Never did he mention the other events that occurred earlier that night.

Later as I lay curled up in his arms I noticed that he

reaches out for me and kisses me on the forehead in his sleep. Those are the most enduring signs of affection to proof that his love for me is genuine. I have heard so many stories about him, but all I see is a beautiful man inside and out, not the ruthless drug dealer many people call him.

Chapter 8

The last year and a half flew by. I can't believe my eleventh grade year passed so fast.

"Wow. This really was our last day of school," Leslie said as we walked home.

"Next year we will be the big dogs in the hallways," I said.

"Senior year. Our last year up in that bitch," Brandy cheered.

"So what do you have planned for the rest of the day?" I asked.

"I'm babysitting tonight," Leslie replied.

"I'm going home to beg my parents not to send me to my Aunt's house in Louisiana for the summer," Brandy replied.

"How long are you going to be down there?" I asked.

"I'm stuck there until the end of August," Brandy complained.

"So Selena what do you have planned?" Leslie asked.

"You know me. It depends on whatever way the wind blows me and Robert," I replied.

"Sounds like a boring ass summer for me," Leslie responded.

"Why you say that?" I questioned.

"Brandy's going out of town for the summer and you

going to be under Robert," Leslie responded.

"Don't worry, I do plan on coming up for air," I replied.

"Tonight when Robert picks you up from my house do you think he can drop me over to the babysitting job your father thinks you doing?" Leslie asked, popping her lips.

"I don't see that being a problem," I responded.

"Your father still falling for that bull shit lie about you babysitting?" Brandy laughed.

"He thinks the extra babysitting and the nights that I claim to be staying over one of your houses keeps me from spending time with Robert," I disclosed.

"Only if he knew the truth," Leslie commented.

"You better hope he never check up on you," Brandy remarked.

"As long as that bitch Rita is not complaining he has no reason to check up on me," I said.

With the weather being so nice, Robert pulled out his motorcycle. He had to make an appearance in the neighborhood. We made several stops to talk with friends while cruising through the streets of Highland Park.

While cruising up Hamilton Avenue near Six Mile Road, we stopped at Sampson's Party Store. Robert went inside as I stood outside talking to Floyd when this loud mouth bitch Wanda and two of her hoe ass girls walked up. The bitch has a problem with me because she wishes to be me. It's not my fault that Robert treated her like the hoe she is. I don't have a problem fucking the bitch up!

The bitch graduated from Highland Park High School two years ago and lives next door to Floyd. She is one of the tricks that Robert messed around with long before we started dating. She's high yellow with a small face and big scary eyes. Hell she resembles a Chihuahua dog in the face. Her long bright red hairweave looks as if her head is on fire.

"I see that motherfucker left his bitch outside with his bike," Wanda said as she walked up.

I turned to look at Floyd and then back at that bitch Wanda.

"I know that cheap hoe ain't talking to me," I blurted out.

"I don't know who you think you calling a hoe!" Wanda snapped.

"If the name fits you need to accept it. Hoe" I said in a sharp tone.

"I hope Robert do your young stupid ass the same way that motherfucker did me! It is only a matter of time before he gets bored with a little girl and turn to a real woman," Wanda cracked.

"I know it won't be you're ugly ass," I responded.

"Ain't you kinda old to be acting like this? Didn't he kick your raggedy ass to the curve almost three years ago?" Floyd commented.

"What the fuck does that matter? You need to stay out of this!" Wanda growled.

"You need to grow your ass up! Face reality, Robert will never want your ugly ass!" Floyd blasted.

"Your psycho ass needs help. Get over him. Besides he's not going anywhere," I responded with confidence.

"Bitch you don't know who you fucking with," Wanda shouted.

Just then, Robert walked out of the store.

"What the fuck is going on out here?" Robert asked as he stepped to that hoe's face.

"That hoe was just expressing how much she wants to be me," I said.

Wanda rolled her eyes at me as she turned back to face Robert.

"Fuck you Selena. So Robert is this the reason why were not together?" Wanda inquired.

"We were never together. You were just one of my hot-and-ready hoes," Robert said.

"What the fuck you mean one of your hot-and-ready hoes?" Wanda asked.

"Think back, I never took you any place outside of your bedroom!" Robert said reminding her.

"You ain't shit!" Wanda barked.

"Get over it, you could never be on my level. You were nothing but a piece of cheap ass," I said while giving her the finger as I climbed on the back of his motorcycle.

We cruised down Hamilton Avenue to head back to his place for the night. Robert leaned forward and accelerated to a speed well pass the posted speed limit as we entered the Lodge Freeway. I leaned in close, held him tight, and closed my eyes. The excessive speed did not bother me, because I trusted him with my life. Riding on the back of his bike and hugging him tightly around the waist as we cut through the wind is one of the most exhilarating feelings.

Robert slowed down to a slower cruise when we got downtown. Jefferson Avenue was jammed with the traffic trying to get on Belle Isle. We turned on to Chene Street, right on Lafayette, and then cruised home.

"Were you scared of that bitch and her girls?" Robert jokingly asked on the elevator ride to his floor.

I pushed him slightly and replied, "Hell no! That bitch is

all talk when her girls are around, but won't say shit when she's by herself. Beside that she doesn't want to get her ass kicked."

"I forgot I was hanging out with big bad Selena," he teased

"Fuck you," I said.

"No problem I'm planning on you doing that tonight," Robert said as he grabbed my ass while stealing a kiss.

Being out in the air all day made us smell like two little kids that played outside all day. When we got to the apartment, I headed straight for the shower knowing Robert would follow me.

My eyes scanned up and down his body as he climbed in behind me. I loved staring at his naked body. He is a good-looking man in and out his clothes. I understand why Wanda is so jealous.

I stood behind Robert and lathered up the washcloth. In a soft slow circular motion, I started washing him across his shoulders. From his shoulders, I slowly washed down each of his muscular arms to his hands. I took my time to enjoy the well-developed definition of his back and ass. As I wrapped my arms around him to wash his sculptured chest, I leaned in close enough for my nipples to rub against his back.

I turned around and kissed her on the forehead then proceeded to lather up my washcloth. She turned around and I lovingly kissed her neck while washing her arms, then gently washing her back, and ass. I bent over close enough for her to feel my dick rubbing up against her back, as I slowly used a circular motion to wash her breast. She leisurely turned to face me. I lathered the washcloth and rung bubbles out over her breasts. I watched the bubbles run down her chest. Cupping my hands to fill with water I enjoyed the sight of the water rinsing the bubbles over her nipples. I see the love in her eyes.

He stood like a perfect gentleman as I lathered up my washcloth and began to massage his dick and balls. I proceeded to lightly wash him as I softly said.

"Robert I love you," I whispered.

"I know you do. I love you too," he replied.

"These are the moments I treasure," I shared.

"Me too. They make me feel as if we are the only two people left in this world," he said.

"I'm glad to be yours," I admitted

"I'm glad you are mines. Before I met you I never imagined that one woman would make me this happy," he said.

"You make my heart dance. I never want this feeling to end," I gushed.

"I will try my best to ensure that it will last," he promised.

We began kissing as the water ran down our faces. He sucked on my bottom lip. I tilted my head back as he nibbled on my chin and kissed down my neck. The palm of my hands cupped under his chest. I gently ran my thumbs back and forth across his nipples.

I dropped my washcloth and used my middle finger to flick and tickle her clit. The nipples on her breasts became hard. I ran my fingers along the inside of her virginal lips. Her pussy moistens in my hands. It was the perfcct invitation for me to insert two of my fingers into her hot wet pussy. She moaned with excitement as I enjoyed the moist warmth of her pussy on my fingers.

I gently held his testicles in one hand as my thumb caressed the base of his dick. With my other hand I used my thumb and index finger to make ring shape. I gradually slid the ring up and down his dick. I stroked his into a state of throbbing arousal. It excited me so much that my pussy got even wetter as I felt his dick became fully erect.

I lifted her up so she could wrap her legs and arms around me. Her head fell back as she gasps for air from the excitement of me inserting my dick inside her pussy. I wrapped my arms around her for support as she moved her body up and down on my dick as the hot water ran down between us.

"Mmmmmmmm," Robert moaned.

"Uhhhhhhhhhh," I moaned.

We fucked until the water started to cool down. Robert pressed my back against the shower wall, placed his hands on the wall, and enjoyed stroking my pussy with his dick. I nibbled on his ears and lightly sucked his ear lobes. It felt so good that I started talking nasty to him.

"I love to feel your beautiful dick inside of my pussy," I cooed in his ear.

"Whose pussy is this?" he asked.

"It's all yours. Your name is all over this pussy," I assured.

"Yeah, this dick has your name on every inch of it," he said stroking deeply.

"Give me more," I begged.

We fucked in the shower until the water became ice cold. I stepped out the shower with her still attached. I lowered her on the counter.

I grabbed the sides of the counter to balance myself as he continued stroking his dick in and out my pussy. I contracted my vaginal muscles around his dick on his down swings in my pussy.

I enjoyed the sucking feeling of her vaginal muscles contracting on my dick. The sensation is highly stimulating.

“That’s it baby, fuck this pussy. It’s all yours,” I ordered.

“Damn your pussy is dripping wet,” he said being pleased.

She hugged me around the neck as I lowered us to the floor. We continued to fuck missionary style sharing open mouth kisses. She thrust her hips to meet my every stroke on my upswing. Her pussy quivers while devouring my throbbing dick.

Feeling his dick growing thicker and stiffer excites me so much that my pussy muscles began to twitch and contract uncontrollable. Our bodies shivered as we both reached a full orgasm. We lay on the floor for a couple of minutes with him on top of me as we shared more kisses.

“What did I do to deserve that?” Robert asked.

“It’s for the little things you do that shows how much you love me,” I answered while gazing in his eyes.

“Thanks for loving me,” he said gazing back in my eyes.

“Thanks for loving me,” I said smiling.

We were worn out but eventually made it to the bed. I love falling to sleep in my favorite spot. Wrapped in Robert’s arms listening to his heartbeat.

Around 2 a.m. in the morning, Robert’s house phone rang.

“H.e..l.l..o,” I answered the phone in a slow sleepy voice.

“Sorry to wake you up, but I need to talk to Robert,” Dean said on the other end.

“No problem, hold on a minute,” I said with a yawn rolling over to wake Robert.

"Baby wake up, Dean is on the phone," I said gently shaking him.

"Hey, what's going on?" Robert asked being alert.

"I am calling an emergency meeting at my house. I need you to be here within the next hour. Don't call anyone. I will alert all that needs to be here," Dean instructed.

"I'm on my way," Robert said hanging up. As much as I hate getting out of bed, but when business call I must go. I rolled over, kissed Selena on the back of her neck, and got up to get dressed.

"I have to go. I will be back in a couple of hours," he said.

"Ok baby. Be safe," I said giving him a hug and kiss.

Chapter 9

Dean is my brother's best friend and my boy Shannon's uncle. Dean is brown skinned and slightly shorter then my brother. As the females claimed, he has that Denzel Washington look. He carries himself like a regular nine to five man. He's like a big brother to me and I have mad respected for him.

Him and Thomas started as number runners under our father's supervision and graduated to selling marijuana for Dean's uncle right out of middle school. It wasn't long before they were introduced to the money that could be made from selling of crack. By their eleventh grade, they formed a family and had more than half of the local drugs dealers working for them. Within two years, they had the entire city on lock down.

When I pulled up to Dean's house I noticed an out of state car in the driveway. I assumed it was our boy Corey since the license plate is from Ohio. It has to be serious to make Corey drive in from Ohio unannounced.

Corey is our main drug connection in Ohio. He's average height with a stocky built of a man fresh out of prison, jet-black complexion, and very soft-spoken. He always wears a patch over his left eye to hide his glass eye and is over dressed for every occasion.

I scanned the basement and observed that it was only Dean, Gator, Corey, and myself in attendance when Dean called the meeting to order. Lamont was the only top ranking family member not in the meeting. At that moment, I knew whatever was going on Lamont had to be part of the problem.

"I'm sorry I had called at such an early hour, but this meeting is of an urgent matter. First, I would like to thank Corey for making the trip up here to inform us of the problem. I regret to say that Lamont's has jeopardized the reputation and safety of our organization. At this time I am going to let Corey explain the situation," Dean introduced and sat down.

"Gentlemen over the past weekend Lamont came down to Lucas to make a drug buy. He was looking to make a twenty thousand dollar deal. Within ten minutes two of my partners were dead, twelve thousand in cash, and twenty-five thousand in drugs went missing. Lamont unknowingly left a witness behind.

The witness was in one of the back bedrooms. The person stepped out in the hallway and saw Lamont pulling out his gun. They were able to slide back into the bedroom without being noticing. Before my partners died, they positively identified Lamont.

My men first reaction was retaliation, but I assured them that Lamont had to be acting on his own. I guaranteed them that my Highland Park connection goes through me and only me when setting up any dealings happening in Ohio. I promised them that this matter will be dealt with swiftly," Dean explained.

"Is there any particular way that your family would like retribution?" Gator asked.

"Yes, they would like for you to deliver Lamont to them in Ohio within the next two weeks. We will handle everything from there," replied Corey.

"Corey, I can guarantee that we will deliver Lamont within that time frame. I'll contact you with the date so you can make arrangements on your end for the pickup. Thank you for taking the time to come up here and informing us on the situation," added Dean as Corey was preparing to leave.

I sat speechless while Dean escorted Corey out to his car. "I don't believe what I just heard. Not my boy Lamont. What the fuck is he thinking?" Robert thought to himself.

"When the time is right I will inform you on how we are going to handle this situation. For the time being please, watch Lamont very closely. Obviously, he has another agenda and it's clearly not good for the family. I still expect to see the both of you at tonight's meeting," Dean said as we departed.

Chapter 10

When I woke up Robert was sitting on the end of the bed.

"What time is it?" I asked.

"Going on eight o'clock," he answered.

"Is everything ok?" I asked being concerned.

"Yes. I'm just tired as hell," he responded.

"Is there anything I can do to help?" I inquired.

"There is something you can do," he said.

"Name it," I replied.

"I might need help at a one or two of the spots," he mentioned.

"Is that it?" I questioned.

"You can drive," he suggested.

"Give me an hour to get ready?" I requested.

"Go ahead. I need to make a few phone calls," he said.

We made cash pickups and drug drop offs all morning long. By late afternoon, we made stops at five of his seven houses. I waited in the car while he went inside and conducted business. When he got back in the car, he would put stacks of money in a black bag that he kept behind his seat.

"Selena I need you to make Glendale Street our last stop," he ordered.

"Ok," I replied pulling away from the curb.

“Take me over to Dean’s house,” he said as I drove off.

“Thought I was going to do more then drive you around,” I commented.

“You are, when we get to Glendale. If I knew that you were this willing to help I would have put you to work a long time ago,” he said being surprised.

Dean lived in a big beautiful brick home on the west side of Detroit in the Rosedale Park area. Dean’s black BMW was parked in the back of the driveway. I pulled behind Dean’s car. Robert went in the house through the backdoor. He surfaced fifteen minutes later carrying a black gym bag that he placed in the trunk of the car.

I cut up the radio to hear an old school jam by Tupac as I jumped on the Southfield Freeway, to the Jefferies Freeway, and then to the Davison Freeway going back to Highland Park. We made a few more stops before heading to Glendale.

We finally made it to his last stop. A small one-story two-bedroom aluminum sided home on Glendale. Weeds and patches of dirt covered the lawn and the aluminum siding is in desperate need of repair. The front porch is nothing more than a slab of cement with two unleveled steps. The windows and doors are dressed with steel security bars and steel gate doors. It blends in with the other homes on that block.

Not one room in the house is the same color. The bedrooms would be completely empty if it wasn’t for the large piles of dust balls. The living room has a cheap wooden table with two matching chairs. The only things on the table are rubber bands and several stacks of money. Robert went in the kitchen with Shannon and Jason while I sat at the dining room table to count and rubber band the money.

“Selena, can you come here when you’re finished?”

Robert called out.

"I should be finished in a few minutes," I answered.

I walked into the tiny kitchen after I verified the last stack of money. The kitchen cabinets are missing their door fronts. A grocery bag of items rest on the counter next to the sink. An old stove with two pots sits in the back of the kitchen. Small glass jars, silver spoons, a pair of tongs, and boxes of baking soda are on the counter next to the stove.

Robert, Shannon, and Jason are seated at an old round glass top table. A scale, razor blades, zip lock baggies, brown paper bags, box of rubber gloves, several pistols, and pile of little white rocks of crack that look like broken pieces of soap were on the table.

"I hate to ask this of you but, I am shorthanded today. Lamont did not show up this morning," Robert said.

"What do you need me to do?" I asked.

"First put on a pair of gloves. You need to put one rock in a tiny zip lock bag. Place ten and only ten in the larger zip lock bags. Two large zip lock bags per brown bag," Robert explained.

"That's it?" I responded.

"Yes," he answered.

Robert continued his conversation with Shannon and Jason as if I'm not in the room. As I worked, I observed how they were able to use razors blades and shave off almost perfectly even amounts from the larger rocks. I sat quietly and did my task as they continue to hold a conversation amongst themselves.

Occasionally a crack head would come to the side door to make a buy. Between Shannon and Jason they would crack the door open wide enough for the crack head to slide their money through a bar on the security gate. They would close the door and return giving the crack heads their purchase.

We were there for hours. Robert collected our gloves and the money off the front table as we left the house. He later disposed of the gloves in the grates of a sewer drain in Detroit.

“Thanks for your help today,” he said.

“I did not mind helping out,” I replied.

“Good. Since you were so willing to help I need you to strap some more money when we get home,” he commented.

“Only if you don’t mind me driving your new car tonight,” I suggested.

“The Beamer?” he questioned.

“Yes, your BMW,” I replied.

“That’s fine. What you got planned for tonight?” he asked.

“I wanted to get my nails done before I go shopping. Then I’m meeting a couple of friends for Go-Cart Racing at the Butterfly in Warren,” I responded.

“Remember I’m having a meeting this evening at the house,” he said reminding me.

“I didn’t forget. Why don’t you meet me at the Go-Cart place later,” I suggested.

“That sounds fun I just might. I will call you after the meeting breaks up. Later this week I’m taking you to the firing range,” he commented.

“That’s a strange place for a date,” I responded.

“I will feel a lot safer knowing that you know how to use a gun if needed,” he replied.

"It doesn't seem to be that hard," I said.

"Trust me it is not as easy as it looks," he replied.

"I guess it's a date," I responded.

Once we got home, he sat the bag of money from the day on the table, alongside the gym bag from Dean's house. He picked the gym bag up and put it in one of the bedroom safes. After we counted, verified, and rubber banded all the money from the pickups he grabbed everything up and put it in the other bedroom safe.

I went to get ready for the evening. When I got out of the shower, I heard Gator's voice coming from the living room. I noticed that Robert left the car keys and a nice stack of money next to my purse.

"Hi, Gator," I said emerging from the bedroom.

"Hi, Selena how have you been?" Gator asked.

"Life couldn't be better and yourself?" I asked.

"Can't complain," he responded.

"Thanks for the gift on the dresser," I said to Robert as I walked over to give Robert a hug and kiss before leaving.

"I will see you later and again thanks for your help today," he replied slapping me on my ass as I walked away.

"Robert, man every time I see you two together it's like the Twilight Zone," Gator said jokingly.

"What makes you say that?" he asked.

"Before you meet Selena you claimed that you would never be a one woman man. What happened?" Gator asked.

"It's something about her that's hard to explain," he answered.

"You're a different person," Gator commented.

“I’m still the same person,” he said.

“You gave her a key to your castle, let her drive your new car, and the biggest shock was when you introduced her to the family. Looks like somebody is pussy whipped,” Gator teased.

“Fuck that shit,” he responded.

“Hell, everyone can tell that you are in love,” Gator replied.

“Is something wrong with that?” he questioned.

“No, she is fine. It’s just you, the last motherfucker I thought would ever fall in love,” Gator answered.

“To tell you the truth, Selena caught my attention almost a year before I approached her. Hell it took months before she stopped running from me,” he disclosed.

“What? The Mack did the chasing. Now that is some blackmail shit,” Gator laughed.

“If you tell anybody I would fucking deny it. Who would they believe you or the Mack,” he said jokingly.

“Don’t worry I wouldn’t tell that story, because I’m embarrassed for you. When was the last time you hung out with us?” Gator asked.

“Last week. Didn’t we all meet up for dinner,” he answered.

“I’m talking about with just the fellas,” Gator replied.

“I’m not sure but it hasn’t been that long,” he responded.

“It's been months, since you hung out with us,” Gator informed.

“I see your asses every fucking day,” he blasted.

“It’s still funny I’m talking to the same man that claimed he’s the Mack,” Gator teased.

“That was back then. It’s good having someone that loves me for me and not for what I can buy her,” Robert responded.

“Man I am happy for you,” Gator replied. Thanks, man. Enough with that mushy shit,” Robert demanded.

Chapter 11

"Hey girl, see I missed your call," I said when Leslie answered her phone.

"Hopefully I was able to catch you before you left the nail salon," Leslie responded.

"I am waiting for my nails to dry. What's up?" I asked.

"Do you mind picking me up before you leave Highland Park?" Leslie asked.

"I'm going to the mall," I mentioned.

"Good I can pick up an outfit or two," she replied.

"That's cool. What's happening? I thought you were riding with Brandy tonight?" I questioned.

"I decided that was a bad idea after I found out she has to stop by Cathy's," she explained.

"I should be there in fifteen minutes. Be ready the mall closes in a couple of hours," I reminded her.

Beep, beep! I tooted my car horn and Leslie came right out.

"Thanks girl for picking me up," Leslie said when she got in the car.

"My pleasure," I replied.

"I'm not mad that you have a man, but it would be nice to see more of you," Leslie commented.

"Don't worry, I will make time for you," I responded.

"Good to hear that. What mall are we going to?" she asked.

"I was running out to Oakland Mall. I need to pick up a few things for Robert's place. I want to soften up the look," I answered.

"How did you get Robert to let you change his bachelor pad?" she questioned.

"I didn't ask him, so technically he didn't say I couldn't," I replied laughing.

"Do you think Robert is going to mind?" she asked.

"If he does then that's his problem," I responded.

"Girl you are crazy," she giggled.

Ring! Ring! Ring! My phone began to ring the moment we pulled up to the Butterfly.

"Hey baby, I guess your meeting is over," I said answering my cell phone.

"It just broke up. Have you left the mall yet?" Robert asked.

"Yes, I am walking into the Butterfly as we speak. Will you be meeting me up her?" I inquired.

"That is the reason why I called. I want to let you know that I am hanging out with the boys tonight," he mentioned.

"Have a good time. Love you sweetheart," I replied.

"Love you too. See you when I get home," he responded.

We hung out in the arcade area while waiting for Brandy and a few others to show up. I was able to get in a few games of pool before Brandy showed up with Cathy and her girls. Of course, they were drunk and high as usual.

"Hey there Leslie and Selena!" one of them yelled.

"See you made it up here," I replied being polite.

"Hope we didn't miss the go-carting," Cathy yelled.

"We were just about to buy tickets," someone in the crowd shouted back.

After purchasing the tickets, we went outside to stand in line for the go-carts. Everyone was talking and laughing while waiting for the group on the track to finish up. Just before our turn, shit broke out. There were three white people ahead of us. One of their friends hopped the gate and got in line to join them. It didn't seem to bother anybody, but one of Cathy's girls had a problem with that.

"What the fuck is this shit! You think your white ass can take cuts!" she hollered to the white boy.

"No. They held my spot and besides that it's none of your fucking business anyway!" he replied.

"Ain't that a Bitch? I know you're motherfucking ass not talking shit!" she blasted.

"Fuck you!" he mumbled and turned his back.

The next turn of events was a predictable reaction for Cathy's group. One of Cathy's girl charged passed the crowd and punched the white guy in the back of his head. The white guy stumbled forward bumping his head on the fence. His girlfriend swung her purse in defense hitting Cathy on the shoulder. Cathy retaliated by punching the girl in her face until her boyfriend jumped in between them. One of the other girls grabbed a helmet from the rack and wacked the white guy in the face. His friends made an attempt to break the fight up. It was like a scene out of a cheap street gang movie. All of Cathy girls came out fighting.

One girl pulled a pipe out of her purse and started

swinging. The first blow to the white boy's head was my cue to call it a night and head home. Leslie and I pushed our way out of the line. We were not the only people that wanted to get the hell out of there.

"Somebody call the police!" one of the employees yelled out as we hit the door.

The word police was the only thing needed to clear the building. I had just turned on to the main street seconds before five police cars came racing towards the Butterfly. Two of the police cars blocked the entrance and exit of the parking lot.

"Damn Selena we made it out of there in the nick of time," Leslie said.

"I don't have time for bullshit like that. Everybody knows those motherfucking cracker ass police in Warren are notorious for racial intimidation," I mentioned.

"You're lucky you're always with Robert, because you miss a lot of bullshit," she said.

"Cathy and her girls were fucked up!" I stated.

"Every time they go any fucking place they are drunk, high, or both. They are true ghetto trash!" she replied.

"Why would Brandy bring them in that condition?" I asked.

"She is too scared to tell them bitches NO," she answered.

"She needs to man the fuck up! One day they're going to get her caught up in some deep ass shit," I replied.

"What's sad is that they fuck it up for everybody else," she responded.

"That is why I try to avoid them as much as possible," I revealed.

"I don't blame you. I try my best to avoid them but Brandy's scary ass want cut them loose," she mentioned.

"She needs to get a motherfucking backbone before she end up just like them," I reiterated.

"Hopefully she will find a back bone in Louisiana this summer," she responded.

I'm glad to see that Robert was not home when I arrived. This will give me time to replace his ugly items with the new things that I brought for his apartment. I was in the shower singing my head off when he came in.

"You scared the shit out of me!" I scream from Robert sneaking up and pulling back the shower curtain.

"Baby your singing scared the shit out of me!" he laughed at me. "I see you made changes around here," he commented.

"I needed to soften up the place. Do you mind?" I questioned.

"It's a little too late to ask that. Should I expect to see any other changes?" he quizzed.

"There might be a couple of small ones," I answered.

"How was your evening?" he asked.

"Either come in or close the shower curtain," I said.

"You giving orders and changing shit around, pretty soon you will try to wear my pants," he teased as he closed the shower curtain. He continued to talk shit on his way out of the bathroom.

When I came out the bathroom, Robert was not in the bedroom.

"Baby can you come here?" he called out.

"Give me a minute to dry off," I answered.

"Don't dry yourself off. I would like to see you wet," he replied.

"You must be in a freaky mood?" I stated.

"I am always in a freaky mood when it comes to you," he responded.

I stepped out of the bedroom and Robert was standing in front of the living room couch butt naked.

"Baby, slowly take your towel off as you walk towards me," he instructed.

"So you want me to give you a peep show?" I responded.

"Hell yea!" he answered.

"What does my dirty minded man have planned for me tonight?" I asked.

"Don't worry about what I have planned, but I can guarantee it is a treat that will satisfy us both," he promised.

"I can't wait to for my treat," I replied.

I walked in a very slow sexy strut towards Robert before stopping and striking a pose. Bending my right leg and fiercely tilting my head, I slowly spin half way around.

"All shit, my baby acting like this the tryouts for "America's Next Top Model," he joked.

With my back facing him, I held my arms out wide and let Robert watch me lower the towel down my back to expose my ass. I continued holding my arms wide out as I completed my spin.

I only permitted him a brief enjoyment of the magnificent view. I quickly closed the towel and continued my slow sexy strut toward him. With each step I alternated lowering the towel to expose one breast at a time.

"You like to see me naked," I said with a devilish smile as I watched him softly lick his top lip.

"You got that right!" he responded.

I stopped a few steps from Robert. I slightly held my arms out then lowered them letting the towel slide down my back. Then I let the left end of the towel fall to the floor. I finished my slow sexy strut with the towel dragging behind me. When I reached my destination, I released the other end of the towel dropping it to the floor.

While Selena stood in front of me I sat on the couch and ran my hands slowly up her thighs and around to her ass. I continued rubbing her ass as I licked and sucked on her belly button. She took my hands and placed them on her breasts. I massaged her breasts while clamping her nipples between my fingers.

I ran my hands through Robert's black curly hair as I climbed on the couch with my legs straddled over his lap. I caressed my man's strong shoulder blades, while he softly licked and sucked my nipples.

With a strong grasp around Selena's waist I lowered her onto the couch. I spread her legs open and rubbed the hair on her pussy as if I'm patting a cat. She rotated her pelvis while I took my time to slowly thrust two fingers in and out of her wet pussy. I took my fingers out and licked off the hot juices from her pussy. I want her so bad.

Robert kneeled down between my legs, lifted my legs over his shoulders, grabbed my ass, and went to work. My pussy moistened up more as his tongue ran up and down the sides of my pussy. I bite my bottom lip, rubbed my breasts, and moaned as my body exploded from the sexual pleasure. His tongue gliding in and out of my pussy as he tried to lick and suck it dry is so arousing. Before I could exchange the same pleasure Robert guided his hard stiff dick into my dripping wet pussy.

The anticipation of my dick penetrating Selena's pussy made her gasp for air. She kept one leg draped on my back and arched the other over the couch. Thrusting her pelvis upward ensured my dick deep penetration in her pussy on my down strokes. My dick enjoyed each one of my strokes inside of her pussy as if it was the first one. We both moaned with pleasure on my down strokes.

The sweat rolling down Robert's forehead and chest dripped on my body and made my pussy throb. My nipples rubbed against his chest as I held on for the ride. The friction between our bodies pleasured my nipples and made me want him even more. My moaning became louder as he began talking aloud.

"Damn baby this is some good ass pussy. It's hot and wet," he commented.

"Your dick is making my pussy wet," I replied.

"How much do you love this dick in your pussy?" he asked.

"I love every inch of your dick," I answered.

"You want more?" he asked.

"Give me all you got. Fuck this pussy like it owes you money," I replied.

"I know how to work this dick," he said with such confidence.

"Yes you doing an excellent job on this pussy," I complimented.

Robert's dick felt so good inside of my pussy. I could not stop the small explosions inside of me. I loved feeling this man's dick all up in my pussy.

"That's it! That's it baby!" I yelled out.

When I felt Selena's body trembling from the explosions it only made me want her even more. I pulled my dick out and signaled for her to get on her knees.

I did as Robert instructed. I got on my knees and laid my face down on the couch with my ass lifted in the air. His dick slowly entered my pussy from the back. We were like two dogs in heat. Sweat was dripping from every pore on our bodies. I could feel my wet hair lying against the sides of my face and on my back.

"That's it. Please don't stop, fucking me! I love to feel your dick in my pussy!" I yelled out.

"Whose pussy is this?" he asked.

"It's yours and only yours," I screamed out.

"This is the only pussy my dick craves for," he admitted.

"Your dick is the only one that my pussy craves for. Just thinking about your dick in my pussy makes it wet," I moaned.

"I love being all up in your wet pussy. My dick could live up in here," he said thrusting in and out.

"This pussy is never going anywhere," I promised.

"Good I never plan on letting it out my sight," he moaned out.

"Roll over on your back. I want to ride your dick," I instructed.

"I don't have a problem with that," he replied as he lay across the couch.

With one knee on the couch and the other leg on the floor I descended my wet pussy onto Robert's hard dick. I leaned forward and laid my hands on the side of his head. I watched as his dick disappeared inside of my pussy and then reappeared. I rode the shit out of his dick.

She slowed her strokes trying to delay a full orgasm as long as possible. It worked for several strokes until she couldn't stop her body from trembling. With her last deep stroke she kept my dick inside her pussy as our bodies trembled with excitement.

"Robert, that was good," I praised being breathless.

"That was some good shit," he agreed.

"I am glad you enjoyed it. Now you can carry me to the bed," I said laughing.

"Ooh, did I wear my baby out?" he teased.

The next morning while we were eating breakfast he noticed the other changes scattered around the apartment.

"Did you pick up anything for me?" he asked.

"Yes, all the pretty household items," I answered.

"Are you saying you didn't like the way I decorated my place?" he questioned.

"It's was ok for a bachelor pad," I responded.

"Gator is going to really talk about me now," he replied.

"Why would he do that?" I grilled.

"When you left last night he told me that I was pussy whipped," he answered.

"You are. What did you say to him?" I laughed.

"You know me. I took it like a man and told him the truth. You're whipped over my dick," he responded.

"Yeah, right. You whipped for my pussy," I joked.

"Face the truth. It's you that's whipped for my mighty python," he teased.

"You can think that if it makes you happy," I responded.

"You know the truth. How was go-carting last night?" he asked.

"It was a waste of money," I responded.

"What happened?" he asked.

"Cathy and her girls showed up and they were high as kites," I answered.

"They are always high," he replied.

"After we bought our tickets they started a big ass fight with some white kids," I stated.

"You didn't get involved?" he questioned.

"No. I got the hell out of there. I try to avoid them as much as possible," I responded.

"I am glad to hear that. Enough about those crack heads. We are riding this evening. No matter what you do today, be back at the house around four o'clock," he requested.

"I will be here," I assured.

I decided to stay close. I went to the Eastern Market to purchase fresh fruit, flowers, and meat. I made it back to his place early enough to get in a good nap. Robert came home shortly before four o'clock rushing.

"I am going to start getting ready so we can make it into Highland Park by five o'clock. We're meeting up at Palmer Park," he explained.

"Is there anything I can do to help?" I asked.

"Can you put me an outfit on the bed," he responded.

"Any particular outfit?" I questioned.

"No. Whatever you think I would look good in," he answered.

"If it was up to me you would go naked," I teased.

"I have no problem with dat. Don't get mad when other women check me out," he sarcastically said.

"Don't anybody want you but me," I teased.

"Yeah right," he replied.

Not only did I decide that we should dress alike we wore colors to match his new motorcycle. The bike is jet black so I picked out our matching black short set.

"Ain't that cute the love birds are dressing a like!" Gator shouted out when we pulled in the parking lot at Palmer Park.

"They both match Robert's bike," somebody else yelled out.

That was the first time Robert notice what I did. He turned to face me.

"Did you do this on purpose?" he questioned.

All I could do was laugh. "It'll be Ok, because you can take it like a man," I teased.

"Pay back is a bitch!" Robert replied with a laugh.

"Listen up! We are show-boating tonight, since everyone seems to have gotten new bikes this year. We're going to cruise down Woodward Avenue too Hart Plaza, then park on Jefferson along the Lodge Freeway. We'll hang at the festival before hitting Belle Isle. Let's roll out!" Dean yelled out.

When we rolled up to Hart Plaza, the group got a lot of attention. All the bikers without women hung near the bikes to hit on females walking by. Robert and I left to explore the entertainment and food of the Caribbean Festival.

The Caribbean Festival is held downtown Detroit at Hart Plaza. Each corridor is lined with vendor booths selling everything from food, clothes, artwork, accessories, and furniture. Most of the items represent the Caribbean but there are a few vendors selling local items and CDs. There are multiple entertainment stages which gives a variety of exposure to the diverse Caribbean culture.

After purchasing samples of several different Caribbean foods we found the perfect spot right off the Detroit River to sit and eat. We shared food and swapped kisses.

"This is really enjoyable," I said smiling at him.

"Don't try to butter me up hoping that I will forget that you made a joke out of me," he teased.

"Did it really bother you to have Gator tease you about our outfits?" I asked.

"No. Just don't make it a habit," he requested.

"I'll think about it," I replied while nibbling my Jerk Chicken.

We made it back to the bikes ten minutes before the group was ready to leave. Once we made it to Belle Isle the group slowly cruised around the island a couple of times to showboat. We eventually parked at the end of the hangout strip. All of us that were girlfriends or considered main women talked amongst ourselves. The non-mattering chicks stayed to themselves.

"Selena, what have you done to that man? How did you get him to agree to y'all wearing matching outfits?" Dean's girlfriend Fran asked.

"He asked me to pick out something for him to wear, and I thought it would be cute if we matched his bike," I answered.

"He didn't say anything?" someone asked.

"He had no idea until Gator said something," I commented.

"It's been two years, and I still don't believe that Robert is in a committed relationship," one of the other girls remarked.

"I tried my best not to talk to him when we first met," I responded.

"That first time he brought you around I knew you were different," Fran mentioned.

"How were you able to tell that?" I asked.

"He actually introduced you to us," someone interrupted.

"Why was that so strange?" I questioned.

"He never introduced any females to us. He treated them like it was a privilege for them to be in his presence," another person answered.

"He would always say that there weren't any females out there good enough to be his woman," someone added.

"He never mentioned that to me," I responded.

"Girl, that man is in love and he has it bad!" Fran replied jokingly.

"He is my heart. My father hates the ground he walks on," I replied.

"My mother thinks Gator is the devil," Gator girlfriend said.

"It's good to know that I'm not the only one whose parent hates their man," I replied.

"Hope you never have to sit in court with him. That last case Gator beat the prosecutor almost got her ass kicked after court. She painted a picture that made him sound like a monster," his girlfriend said.

"Get use to it. People only see one side to them. What I learned to do is ignore the comments. They are no different from any business man running a large corporation," Fran explained.

"The only time I have ever seen Gator's other side was when that bastard tried to rob us. It excited me to know that my man could protect me in any situation," his girlfriend said.

"Robert is my gentle giant. The little things he does are so touching. He has a heart of gold," I said.

"Robert has a heart!" one of the girls joked.

They all busted out laughing.

"Just kidding," she said.

It felt like we were on the island for hours. Robert and the other bikers spent all their time bragging about their bikes or checking out other bikes. By the end of the night, Robert was leaning against his bike as I stood between his legs with his arms around me.

"Hey let's roll down to Cedar Point this Saturday," Gator suggested.

"That's a good idea. We should stay the weekend," Dean replied.

"We can ride out Friday evening and come back sometime on Sunday," Robert suggested.

"I'm gamed," Lamont said hoping that no one noticed his uneasiness to the idea.

Loud cussing followed by an eruption of gunfire ringed out. Robert pushed me behind him and grabbed for his gun. The peaceful night was interrupted with screaming, crying, yelling, cussing, and car tires screeching off. People were running to their cars. We hopped on the bikes and rode off.

Thank God! Robert and his boys are skillful bike riders. They weaved in, out, and between cars. We were able to cut through traffic and exit the island before the police locked it down We called it a night.

After being out in all that fresh night air the only thing I could think about was taking a shower and fucking the shit out of my man.

Chapter 12

Ring! Ring! Ring! Ring!

"Hello," Leslie said as I answered my phone.

"Hey girl," I replied.

"I was hoping to catch you before you left the neighborhood," she responded.

"I have to babysit tonight and I need a ride. Do you think Robert would drop me off?" she asked.

"He would not mind dropping you off. Hell the way that you cover my ass with my fake babysitting jobs. That is the least he can do," I replied.

"I was going to ask Brandy until she talked about going by Fat Cat's with Cathy and one of her crack head girls. I'm not sure which is worst, the thought of going over Fat Cat's house or hanging with Cathy and her crack head girls," she commented.

Fat Cat is the only name I know his slimy ass by, and that is too much information for me. He sales weed out of a rundown single family home on the corner of Pilgrim and Third. His house is a second home for Cathy and her girls.

The first and only time I went over to his house, it totally and utterly grossed me out. The outside of his house blends in with the other homes on the street. The four homes directly across the street are abandon and open. Two other homes further down the street are burnt down skeletons of forgotten homes.

His front yard is completely bald. Pieces of the dirty white aluminum siding is missing off the front and sides of the house. A dead tree branch that fell on the roof several years earlier is still hanging from the edge of the roof. The front porch steps are missing which means going through the side door is the only option to gain entrance into the house. The driveway leading to the side door is lined with several partially stripped cars.

The inside of the house is worst then the outside. A foul smell from the dark basement greeted us when we enter through the side doorway. The light blue paint on the stairway walls has the appearance of a slimy coating of dirt covering it. The basement door to the kitchen freely swings open since the doorknobs were missing.

The kitchen has thick streaks of grease drippings running across the ceiling and down the walls. The cabinet doors are hanging off their hinges. The dirt clinging on the window drapes give them a greasy black furry look. Flies hovering over the sink full of dirty dishes and the old food containers on the counters. The floor is so filthy that the bottom of my shoes kept sticking to it. Thank God my gym shoes were tightly tied or I might have walked out of them.

The living room and dining room is one open room. The windows are covered with the ugliest black curtains I ever seen. The curtains blocked the sun which left the room in a state of darkness. The mixture of rotten food, old musk, and funky feet lingers in the air. Large layers of brown paint strips dangle from the walls and ceiling. The television's glaring dim light makes it possible to see roaches moving in the corners. I could only imagine that the upstairs rooms look the same if not worst.

Fat Cat is in his late thirties but looks sixty years old. He barely stands five feet and weighs a good four hundred and seventy-five pounds. He is extremely light skin with red freckles covering his face. He wears his hair in one long nappy braid down his back. The skin around his breast has discolored round circles from old ringworm scars. The red rash around his armpits looks alive when he moves his arms. He has moist clumps of baby power seeping from the creases of fat on his stomach. The dry patches of skin on his legs didn't bother me as much as the thick layer of dirt on his feet. When he leans back, in the recliner and lifts his feet off the floor the bottom of his feet looks as if he has black rubber soles on. His toenails are long, brown, chipped, and extremely thick.

The recliner that Fat Cat sits in should be condemned. The worn off material on the armrest is coated with old dirty grey duct tape. Dried up streaks of food run down the side of the recliner and three of the four legs are broken. The end table on the right side of his recliner has a pile of dirty dishes and carry-out food containers stacked on and around it. He sits in the recliner with nothing on but an old nasty pair of boxer underwear. Just the sight of his underwear mentally gave out the scent of old hot yellow acid smelling urine. He probably has dried streaks of shit in them.

He rubs and scratches his dick like he can really find it under the layers of fat from his hanging belly. He hits on anything with a pussy that walks through his door. He actually thinks talking nasty and the sight of him rubbing in the area were his dick is hiding excites someone. Since he knew I was Robert's girlfriend is the only reason why he didn't hit on me.

Fat Cat is only one of many reasons why I avoid hanging out with Cathy and her crew. Getting high is part of their daily routine and they blend in with the surroundings at Fat Cat's house perfectly. Between the four of them, they tried almost every drug known to man. They started with marijuana and graduated to harder drugs trying to find higher highs. This summer I'm going to completely disassociate myself from them crack heads, especially Cathy.

Cathy's habit is so bad that the other three junkies rarely hang out with her. It is funny that drug users are particular about who they get high with. Cathy's boyfriend John has her so strung out that she have no idea what goes on when she's passed out. He sales her to anybody that is willing to pay. Some of the stories of what he has allowed other men to do to her are horrible. The worst story is the one of her and a dog.

Like always John had a house full of niggas over. Cathy was over in the corner nodding off when one of John's boys came over with his dog. The dog started sniffing around her pussy area.

"John your bitch must be in heat," the dog's owner said.

"With enough drugs in her system my bitch is always in heat!" John said jokingly.

"Is the hoe on her period?" one of John's boys asked.

"She must be. Look at the way my dog is sniffing around her pussy," the dog's owner commented.

"Would a dog fuck a hoe?" one of John's boys asked.

"I don't think so," the dog's owner responded.

"I believe a dog would fuck anything in heat," John said.

"I heard of crack heads doing that before," someone responded.

"There are known as Dog Lady's," John responded.

"Man, get the fuck out of here with that nasty shit!" someone said.

"Donald Goines wrote about it in his Dopefiend book," John responded.

"What the fuck would he know about some sick shit like that?" someone asked.

"He was a motherfucking junkie himself," John

answered.

"That's some shit that I would need to see in order to believe," someone said.

"Bet your dog would fuck the shit out of my bitch," John suggested.

"I think my dog has more sense than that," the dog's owner opposed.

"Put some money on the dog fucking the freak," someone yelled out.

"I got fifty that my dog has standards and won't fuck the stink ass bitch," the dog's owner offered.

"I got fifty that the dog would fuck her ass!" someone else added.

"I also got fifty that the dog will fuck the shit out of her," John said betting.

"That's some retarded shit, but I got fifty on the dog," another one of John's boys commented.

"Cathy, Cathy, CAAAATHY!" John yelled.

"What, what, what? Why you yelling at me?" Cathy asked as she woke up from her nod.

"Bring your ass here!" John demanded.

"Heeere I comeee," she mumbled stumbling to her feet.

"Daddy got something for you," John said knowing his words seem to put a pep in her step.

"I hope it's good," she said wishing it is a hit of dope.

"It is," John said in a sinister voice.

Cathy tied a belt around her arm and tapped to find a vein as she stumbled over to John. He injected her with a small hit from a needle filled with Crystal Meth. Cathy's head fell as her body became limp. He laid her across a footrest on her stomach. His boy held his dog back while John stripped Cathy from the waist down and spread her legs apart.

“Let your dog loose,” John ordered.

“Look at that motherfucking dog. He is licking the shit out of her bloody pussy,” someone said as the room filled with laughter.

“The damn dog doesn’t know the difference,” someone said.

“Cathy is one nasty bitch,” the dog’s owner stated.

“She is just like a dog. She will fuck anything with a dick,” John commented.

“Oh shit your dog is getting a hard on,” someone noticed.

“There he goes,” John coached.

“It looks like your dog has no standards,” someone else mentioned.

“That’s my boy. He mounted her like a pro,” the dog’s owner cheered.

“He’s all up in that bitch's pussy,” John laughed.

“He is fucking the shit out of her,” someone blurted out.

“Pay up. Give me my motherfucking money,” John ordered.

They laughed and chanted the dog on as they watched. Cathy let out a deafening scream from the pain when the dog’s dick swelled up inside her pussy.

“Man can you shut that bitch up!” one of John’s boys yelled out.

“Shut that bitch up,” several other of the guys yelled out.

“Hand me that belt and the needle,” John said.

John tied it around her arm and hit on her arm until a vein appeared and injected her with the remaining Crystal Meth in the needle.

"That's how you stop the bitch from screaming," John loudly said as Cathy passed out.

After the side show Cathy needed medical attention. John dropped her off at Detroit Receiving Hospital. He pulled up to the emergency entrance, put her in a wheel chair, and pushed her into the waiting room. Security thought he was going to park his car. Instead he pulled out of the parking lot as fast he could. I wasn't surprised when the stupid bitch went right back to John after she was released from the hospital.

That next day was Brandy's last day before she leaves to Louisiana for the summer. Since it turned out to be such a beautiful afternoon Leslie, Brandy, and I decided to hang out at Belle Isle beach. We lay out on the beach with takeout meals from Fuddruckers Restaurant and a cooler full of ice cold beer.

"Leslie what happened with you last night? I thought you needed a ride?" Brandy asked.

"I wasn't in the mood to hang around those crack heads," Leslie replied.

"You're talking about Cathy and her crew?" Brandy questioned.

"Yes," Leslie responded.

"I was only going to drop them off," Brandy mentioned.

"It always starts out that way," I stated.

"I try to avoid them," Brandy softly said.

"It doesn't show. You need to get a backbone and start telling them no," I commented.

"That's easy for you to say. For one they don't live around the corner from you and two you have Robert for back up," Brandy stated.

"Hell they know not to ask me for anything. I nip that shit in the bud a long time ago," Leslie mentioned.

"You both right. My parents hate me hanging around them too," Brandy confessed.

"Why haven't you told them crack heads to fuck off?" I questioned.

"I don't want to hurt their feelings," Brandy admitted.

"They don't give a fuck about your feelings," I replied.

"If they did they wouldn't drag you into all their crack head shit," Leslie added.

"Going away for the summer will give me time to work on an approach," Brandy suggested.

"Girl we are going to miss your ass," I shared.

"Don't go buck wild while you are down there," Leslie joked.

"Not with my stiff ass aunt. She probably will hire a babysitter to watch me when she's gone," Brandy mentioned.

"Luckily you want be left here with a friend notoriously known for popping up missing," Leslie replied.

"So Leslie, you're going to avoid me this summer?" I asked.

"You're ass is going to be so far under Robert's ass that I will barely see you," she said.

"That's not true," I answered.

"You need to face reality. You and Robert are like shadows," Brandy commented.

"What the hell does that mean?" I asked.

"Where there is one the other is not far behind," they both said laughing.

"Can you imagine yourself being with Robert forever?" Leslie asked.

"It's funny how at one time I didn't want anything to do with him, but now I can't picture my life without him," I replied.

"You and Robert would have beautiful children," Brandy commented.

"I'm not ready to be somebody's mother," I stated.

"What would you do if you found out he cheated on you?" Brandy asked.

"If he cheated on me, he kept that hidden very well. He has never done anything to make me suspicious. Besides he definitely takes damn good care of home," I responded.

"Girl he got your nose wide open," Leslie noted.

"He does. There is a whole other side to him that would surprise people. At first I thought all he wanted to do was add me to his list of hoes, until he introduced me to his mother as his girlfriend. It was even more surprising when she said that she heard so many nice things about me," I divulged.

"Out of all the years that I lived next door to his mother you are the only female I ever noticed him bring over there. I was shocked when he asked me about hooking him up with you," Brandy commented.

"I found it funny that he actually paid you," I laughed.

“The money was good while it lasted,” Brandy responded with a laugh.

“Talking about money, I might need to look for another business partner if I plan to enjoy our senior year,” Leslie proposed.

“So you are kicking me to the curve?” I questioned.

“Kick you to the curve. Your ass did the kicking. Don’t get me wrong, the extra money is great, but I would be nice to enjoy some of the senior events,” Leslie pleaded.

“I’m not mad at you. What about Brandy?” I suggested.

“I can always use the extra money this year,” Brandy stated.

“I’m fine with that as long as it doesn’t cause problems between us,” Leslie brought up.

“I’m ok with it. As long as my father continues to think that I’m baby sitting with you?” I recommended.

“Not at all. It might cost you a small fee,” Leslie hinted.

“First you dump me as a business partner then you want to charge me a fee!” I yelped.

“Yea. It would help to be able to still depend on you for a ride,” Leslie replied.

“I don’t have a problem with that,” I said.

Chapter 13

The morning before our Cedar Point trip Robert got an early start. When I woke up he was gone. He met up with Gator and Dean to discuss this weekend's upcoming event.

"I have done some investigative research on Lamont. He set up a drug house in Pontiac with his crack head white girl Cindy. I can only guess where he came up with the money and drugs for that venture," Robert said.

"I talked with Corey last night. This weekend trip will be the last one for Lamont," Dean informed.

"Is there anything we need to do?" Gator asked.

"The only thing that we have to do is get Lamont across state lines and Corey's people will handle the rest," Dean replied.

"Did Corey give you any details on how Lamont is going to be dealt with?" Gator inquired.

"No, but he ensured me that no one else will get hurt as long as they don't interfere," Dean stated.

"Robert, are you Ok with this? I know Lamont is your boy and all?" Dean asked.

"It's part of the game," Robert responded.

"I know it's hard to turn your back on your boy," Dean commented.

"It's him or the family. Lamont turned his back on me and the family for that I have to protect my best interest and the best interest of the family," Robert demanded.

"Some of the fellas are talking about meeting at the strip club and we would like you to ask Selena if it's Ok for you to come out tonight," Gator said jokingly as they both started to laugh at Robert.

"I don't have to ask permission to go out. I am the man in my house and I call all the shots," Robert claimed.

"Ok, if that's what you want to believe," Dean advised.

They laughed even harder.

"Fuck you both," Robert said as he left them.

Chapter 14

"It's nice to take my favorite girls out to dinner. Did you call Sherries and tell her to meet us at mom's house?" Robert asked.

"She had to cancel," I answered.

"What did she have to do that is more important than hanging out with me?" he questioned.

"She has a class tonight," I informed.

"I guess we can go some place a little nicer," he implied.

"So if Sherries was coming you were planning to take us to a dump?" I asked.

"Something like that. She eats like a horse and I want to save money," he answered with a laugh.

"Little did you know you were taking us some place nice any way," I chuckled.

"Now you're trying to call the shots?" he questioned.

"I know you are only trying to butter me," I hinted.

"Why would I want to do that?" he asked.

"I know you plan to ditch me at home and hang out with your boys tonight," I stated.

"No it's not like that," he suggested.

When we pulled up at his mother's house the street was packed with police cars, ambulances, news reporters, spectators, and the Wayne County Medical Coroner's van. All the action is coming from a house on the end of the street.

"Mama, what's going on down the street?" Robert asked running in the house.

"Baby, they said something bad happen to Sonya," Mrs. Harris replied.

Chapter 15

Tyrone, Tony, Manny, and David are all going to the eight grade this fall. Tyrone is the younger brother of the bastard Charles Singleton and his only goal is to become part of the Mob Squad when he gets out of middle school. Tony, Manny, and David are three lost souls that need to be part of something. Therefore, when Tyrone wanted to form a gang named of the Junior Mob Squad they agreed. Tyrone automatically appointed himself the leader. An empty garage belonging to a vacant house on Webb Street became their clubhouse.

“This is the day that the Junior Mob Squad becomes a household name in Highland Park. We are the founders and our names will go down in HP history. We will make my brother and the Mob Squad proud of us. Everybody else will fear us or want to join us. We will smash anybody that gets in our way! In memory of my brother we take our first victim on the Junior Mob Squad train ride tonight,” Tyrone said opening their first official meeting with a speech.

“So, which, one of the freaks will get to ride the train first?” asked Manny.

“Everybody will put the name of one freak in the bag and I will pull the name of the lucky trick that gets the first ride on our train,” Tyrone said.

They all wrote a name on a piece of paper and placed it in the bag. Tyrone shook the bag and then pulled a name.

“Men the lucky freak is Sonya Butts,” he announced.

"You know that ugly bitch is a virgin. I figured breaking in a virgin would make the train ride more fun," David proudly said while receiving hi-fives.

"Hell yea. That bitch will be losing her cherry the right way," Tony commented.

Unknowingly Sonya was sitting on the porch reading a book when David came walking up her walkway. She was so extremely excited to see him coming to visit her that she never notice the others gathering on the side of her house.

"Hi, David, I'm surprise to see you," Sonya said.

"I don't know why you would be surprise since you are the one that have a crush on me," David responded.

"No I don't.," Sonya said blushing.

"You don't mind if I hang around for a little while? I think it's time for me to get to know you better," David requested.

"I would like that. We can sit on the porch and talk," Sonya sweetly replied.

"That's cool. Do you have anything to drink?" David asked.

"Yes. Wait here I will be right back," Sonya instructed. Sonya walked in the house leaving the front door open. David jumped up and signaled for the others. Sonya was coming from the kitchen with a glass of water when she saw David and his boys rushing through the front door. The fear of danger immediately struck Sonya when she noticed the last one closing the front door behind him.

"David, what's going on?" Sonya screamed.

"Bitch I said I wanted to get to know you better," David replied.

"What the hell are the others doing in my house?" Sonya asked.

"We are all going to get to know you better!" they all said.

Sonya dropped the glass of ice water then turned and started running back towards the kitchen screaming. The glass shattered as it hit the floor splattering water and ice everywhere. They all chased after her. Tyrone grabbed the collar of her shirt and punched her in the back of her head. She felled face forward slamming her shoulder on the corner of the stove before hitting the kitchen floor hard tile.

Tyrone flipped her over. David and Tyrone grabbed her legs and began to drag her back into the living room. As they dragged her through the spilled water, she cried out in pain as pieces of broken glass tore through her shirt and became embedded in her back. Sonya arms waved frantically as she tried gabbing for anything she could use as a weapon. She got a very tight grip on a leg of the dining room table. Manny lifted his fat foot up and stomped on her wrist until she let go.

The kicking of her legs, swinging of her arms, and cries for help became more hysterical as David and Tyrone dropped her legs. They all started to attack her. They began kicking her in the side and punching her in the face.

"Bitch stop all that yelling!" Tyrone yelled before he busted her in the mouth.

Sonya would not stop yelling so Tyrone continued punching her in the face. Sonya began spitting out blood as she continued screaming out for help. Tony picked up a napkin off the dining room table and stuffed it in her mouth.

"When we finish you will always remember what it felt like to have us pop your motherfucking cherry!" Tyrone commented.

"You know you wanted us to fuck the shit out of you!" David said.

"Let's get this bitch's clothes off!" Tyrone ordered.

Sonya was on the floor crying and still swinging as they ripped her clothes off and tied her shirt around her head covering her mouth. Sheer panic set in from the disturbing feeling of forty fingers invading her body. Her skin crawled as they fondled and took turns sucking on her breasts. The pain and discomfort from them shoving their fingers in and out of her pussy was stomach turning.

"Please stop! Please stop! Please stop!" Sonya tried to muffle out through her covered mouth.

"Men it is time for us to break this bitch in and David should be the first to tear that pussy up. No one can come out of that pussy until they bust a nut in that bitch," Tyrone instructed.

"No, no, no, no, no," Sonya muffled as Tony, Manny, and Tyrone held her arms and legs down as she watched in horror as David unzipped his pants, pulled his hard dick out, and kneeled down in between her legs.

Sonya's muffled begging and pleading turned in to a stifled cry as the stream of tears running down her face became heavier from the pain. David forced his dick inside of her tight dry pussy. Every inch of her body shivered from fear and pain with each stroke of David's dick inside of her. She tried to block out the cheering and laughter of the other boys, but it seem to get louder as David continued to strip her innocence away.

"Is her pussy supposed to be this dry?" David asked.

"Manny run in the kitchen and get some cooking oil," Tyrone ordered.

"Here you go," Manny said as he ran back with a bottle of cooking oil.

"David pull out and grease your dick with this," Tyrone said as he poured a hand full of oil into David's hand.

"Look at the blood coming out of her pussy," Tony noticed.

"That's means David popped that bitch's cherry," Tyrone responded.

"That's better," David said as he reinserted his dick back into Sonya's dry pussy.

When David finished he stood up to fasten his pants while Tony unfasten his pants and rubbed his dick with cooking oil in preparation for his turn. The other boys left her arms and legs unattended. With the little energy Sonya had, she tried to get up and escape, but Tyrone was too quick. He pushed her down before she could stand to her feet.

They held her legs and arms down so Tony could take his turn. She silently cried as Tony's thin but very long hard dick penetrated her sore pussy. He lay on top of her pumping his dick back and forth inside of her pussy with fast deep strokes. The pain of his long dick was unbearable. Her body became numb of the pain and her eyes were completely dry of tears. By the time, that Tony finished up and Manny was preparing for his turn Sonya lost the urge to fight off her attackers.

Sonya felt like a prisoner in her own skin. As she prayed for the horror to end, her mind had escaped from reality. She closed her burning eyes and quietly lay on the floor gasping for air as Manny's fat ass laid on her chest to take his turn raping her. He inserted his short thick greased hard dick inside her sore pussy. This was the first time Manny actually penetrated a pussy.

She had not even notice that Manny was finished and that Tyrone was taking his turn. Tyrone was so irritated that Sonya laid numb while he was raping her that he decides to leave a mark. He bit her right nipple so hard that he drew blood. He uncovered Sonya's mouth and withdrew his dick out of her pussy when he felt himself about to bust a nut. He kneeled down on the side of Sonya's face, held her mouth open, and jacked off in Sonya's face.

Her body and soul was too tired to move. She laid there and stared in space as they talked shit while Tyrone fastens his pants.

"I thought you had to stay inside of her pussy until you busted a nut?" Tony questioned.

"Last minute change of plans. The bitch got the chance to taste my sperm," Tyrone laughed.

"Do you think she is going to tell anybody?" Manny asked.

"The bitch better not if she knows what's good for her," David answered.

"Hoe if any of our names come out your mouth I will be back and the next time will be worst. Hell we will fuck the shit out of you and your motherfucking mother," Tyrone said in a mean threatening tone.

"Yea, if we have to come back we will break both you bitches in!" David added.

"The hoe enjoyed it. We did her dumbass a favor," Tyrone claimed.

Just as Tyrone completed his comment the front door swung open and in walked Sonya's mother followed her big brother that was home from the army. The only thing he noticed was his baby sister's bloody naked body laying on the floor and four punks heading for the back door. Her mother's scream was bone chilling. Her brother's blood boiled into a hot rage. He pulled out his government issued gun and ran after them.

Manny and Tony never made it out the kitchen. Both

were struck in their backs from the spray of bullets. He had to kick Tony out of the way, as he headed out the back doorway. Manny and Tony lay on the kitchen floor crying like two little bitches.

David made it half way through the back yard as Sonya's brother emerged out the kitchen door. Her brother let one shot out. The bullet tore through the back of David's leg blowing his knee out. David crumbled over in pain and hit the ground face forward. A partial metal pole from an old broken fence sticking out of the ground plunged into his left eye and burst out the back of his head.

Sonya's mother covered her daughter's battered body with a blanket after calling the police.

"Why God, why did this have to happen to my baby?" her mother cried out.

Sonya's brother chased Tyrone down the alley. He let loose several rounds of gunfire. Bullets ripped through Tyrone shoulders and thighs. Tyrone dropped to his knees. Then in slow motion, his body leaned to one side then toppled on top of an open bag of trash.

Tyrone screamed out in pain when Sonya's brother grabbed his bullet rattled shoulder and rolled his ass over. There was nothing but fury in Sonya's brother eyes.

"I know your ass! You're that puck bitch Charles Singleton's little brother!" Sonya's brother yelled out.

"You're lucky he is dead or he would fuck you up for this!" Tyrone cried out.

"Fuck that sorry motherfucker! His bitch ass got what the fuck he deserved! I'm sorry I wasn't the one that blasted his ass!" he shouted.

"How's your hoe ass sister?" Tyrone asked in a sarcastic tone.

"She is the last person you're sick ass will ever hurt!" he informed.

"Fuck you," Tyrone replied.

"I feel sorry for your mother. She gave birth to two fucking perverted bitches!" he replied.

"That bitch will never forget how we split her shit wide open," Tyrone painfully replied.

Tyrone's last words enraged Sonya's brother. He opens fire on Tyrone striking him in his dick.

"Go to hell you sick bastard. I am going to make sure your punk ass pay for this every day of you're sorry as life!" he yelled out as he repeatedly kicked Tyrone's in his open wounds.

Tyrone yelled out in pain as Sonya's brother took hold of his arms and dragged him down the alley. The police arrived, as he was dragging Tyrone's bloody ass down the alley.

"Police. Drop the gun and put your hands in the air!" the police yelled out to Sonya's brother.

"You're fucked now," Tyrone said.

"No, you're the one that's fucked!" he said as he put his hands in the air.

Chapter 16

The incidents shook up his mother up so bad that she is unable to go out for dinner.

"Do you mind staying over until all the commotion dies down?" Mrs. Harris requested.

"Do you mind Selena?" Robert asked.

"Not at all," I answered.

"I have some leftovers I can warm up or I can fix you something," Mrs. Harris offered.

"The leftovers would be fine," I replied.

"I might want you to fix me something," Robert said.

"You don't have to cater to Robert. He will be fine with leftovers," I stated.

"Now you are speaking for me?" Robert commented.

"No, you acting like a spoiled child. Besides that I have never seen you pass on leftovers," I said.

"I have some meatloaf and mashed potatoes. Let me steam some vegetables to go with that," Mrs. Harris mentioned.

"That sounds great Mama," Robert replied.

We headed home once the block quieted down and his mother's nerves settled.

"That's what those bastards deserve. The only good thing to the tragedy is that they did not get away," Robert commented on our way to the car.

The ride back home was silent. Just the mention of Charles's name and rape in the same sentence brought back haunting images of what he did to me.

"You're ok?" Robert asked understanding my silence.

"Yes." I answered.

"I can cancel my night out with the boys," he suggested.

"No. Go out and have a good time, I will be fine. I am going to get something to drink then go to bed when we get back to the apartment," I said.

"You're sure about that?" he asked.

"Yes, I am sure about it," I claimed.

I grabbed a Smirnoff Ice and lay across the bed, while Robert got ready to go out. I could not stop thinking about the brutality of Sonya's rape. He kissed me on my forehead and I instantly broke out crying. Robert took off his shoes, got in the bed, and held me. I curled up in his arms and cried like a baby. I could hear the phone ringing while dozing off.

"Hello?" Robert said as he answered the phone in a low voice.

"Hey, man this is me Gator. I should be there in about ten minutes to pick you up," Gator informed.

"I have to cancel," Robert replied.

"Why are you whispering?" Gator asked.

"I don't want to disturb Selena. A family emergency came up and I need to stay home tonight. I will see you tomorrow," Robert answered.

"The fellas will be disappointed," Gator responded.

"Have a good time for me," Robert said as he hung up.

Chapter 17

Lamont kept looking at his watch. "I hate to leave the party early, but I have to attend to my hoes since they have to do without me for the weekend," Lamont said as he arose to leave.

"Remember we're taking off from Robert's at seven o'clock tomorrow," Dean said reminding everyone.

Lamont rush home to pick up a package of dope before heading up to Pontiac. He has to make sure that his business affairs are covered for the weekend. The ride up there gave Lamont time to go over his plan in his head.

"Thanks to them dead motherfuckers, I am going to make a killing in Pontiac. Their money and product is just what I needed to jump-start my business. With the help of those stupid ass niggas from Ohio, I should be in the position to move my operations to Highland Park in six months. Those HP punks will never know what hit them. If anyone survives the fall out maybe, I will consider giving them a job. As much as I hate going back to Ohio, I have to keep up my fake loyalty to the family. I'm surprise that those dumb bastards haven't retaliated by now. They might need some help. This trip could turn out to be an opportunity to add more fuel to the fire," Lamont thought out loud to himself.

Lamont set up his operation in Pontiac out of a crack head's home. It was easy for him to get Cindy to let him use her house for his drug venture. She did anything for him to ensure that he would fuck her from time to time.

Cindy is a thirty-year-old white woman that once was a very attractive woman. The years of drug abuse took a terrible toll on her appearance. Her face and arms are blotched from her picking at her skin while being high and thinking her skin was crawling. The gums around her rotten teeth expose black cavity holes in the roots of her brown teeth. Her hair has that dirty greasy look and is thinning out around the hairline. Her skin smells like embalming fluid.

"Cindy. Big Daddy is home!" Lamont yelled out as he entered the house.

"Hey there Big Daddy, I was hoping to see you," Cindy answered coming from a back bedroom with nothing on but her panties.

"I had to see my number one girl before I left for the weekend," he said.

"Where you're going?" she asked.

"I have to leave town for a couple of days for business," he answered.

"Can I go?" she whined.

"I said it's a trip for business. Besides, I need you to watch the store. You are the only person I trust to take care of my business," he lied trying to make her feel important.

"You know I would do anything for you. Baby, can you fuck me, because I missed your dick?" she said walking closer to him.

"No problem," he answered pulling out a condom.

Cindy followed Lamont in the bedroom. He pushed her on the bed and ripped off her panties. He did his job and fucked the shit out of her. He put his pants on and headed straight to the kitchen to prepare his packages for the weekend. Cindy came stumbling in moments later with nothing on.

"I'm leaving you with enough products that will hold you over until I return Sunday night. You better not smoke my shit up. I do not want to come home and have to beat your ass," he harshly threatened.

"You don't have to worry about me. I got you covered," she squeamishly answered.

"Like I said, this product is for selling. I know exactly how much is here and my money better add up or an ass whipping is in order," Lamont explained in a firm tone.

Lamont handed Cindy a nice size package of blow for personal use to guarantee that she did not smoke up his shit. To show Lamont her gratitude for the extra blow she got on her knees, unzipped his pants, and pulled his dick out. For the next five minutes, she sucked his dick and balls clean.

Cindy got off her knees and lay across the kitchen table on her stomach. To ensure her loyalty to Lamont she held her butt cheeks open to allow him to fuck her in the ass. She was completely unaware that he lied about loving her while he fucked her in the ass.

Chapter 18

"Good morning Sleeping Beauty. How do you feel?" Robert asked.

"Good morning. I feel great after a good night sleep. How long have you been up?" I replied.

"I've been up for a couple of hours. I want to take care of all my business early so I can relax before the ride," he answered.

"Is there anything I can do to help?" I asked.

"Your job is to pack our stuff," he answered.

"Do you have a small suitcase around here?" I asked.

"You don't need a suitcase. All you need is this backpack," he responded while handing it to me.

"You expect me to pack everything we need in that. My shoes will take up half the room," I replied.

"All you need to pack is two outfits each. One for the park and one for the ride home. Pack our swimsuits there's a Jacuzzi at the hotel. Don't make the backpack too heavy," he requested.

"Now you're trying to regulate what I can pack?" I responded.

"No. You can stuff as much shit in it as you like, but you have to wear the backpack," he answered.

"Don't complain when you are wearing the same outfit and underwear all weekend," I replied.

"Ok, be funny. Remember you have to ride behind me. By the way we are pulling out at 7 o'clock," he sarcastically responded.

"Whose place are we meeting at?" I questioned.

"I forgot to tell you that everyone is meeting over here. It would be nice if you could have some light finger food ready," he suggested.

"How many people do you expect will be riding?" I asked.

"Last count was seventeen people," he answered.

"I will see what I can do," I replied.

The weather turned out beautiful for a ride. We hit the freeway eleven bikes strong for the ride. The air flowing down my back as we cut through the wind is refreshing from the beaming evening sun on the open road. We rolled up in record time to the Radisson Harbour Inn at Cedar Point in Sandusky, Ohio.

After checking in we all met up for dinner at the hotel's restaurant. Following dinner everyone went bar hoping except Robert, myself, Dean, Gator, and both their women. I went back to the room to change into my swimming suit to enjoy the Jacuzzi with their women. Robert stayed behind at the table with Dean and Gator to settle the bill and discuss unsettled business.

There are several small bars near the hotel. The first couple of bars the gang stopped were dead for a Friday night. The last one they tried seem to be jumping. Since, no women seem to attract Lamont's attention he was ready to go until three young women walked in. They sat at a table facing the bar. This gave Lamont perfect view of the women.

The first woman is the true definition of a ghetto fabulous sack chaser. Her long wavy black weave with blonde highlights, long multi-color air brushed acrylic fingernails, and blue contact lens is not a flattering combination. All her clothing revealed the designers name for all to see and her jewelry had to add ten pounds to her weight.

The second woman was wearing a long black straight weave, three-inch fake nails, eye lashes the length of spider legs, and enough make-up for two women. The low-cut mini dress she wore showed off her extremely shapely body and double D breasts.

The third woman was short, caramel skin tone, with a plump round body shape. Her hair is pulled back into a ponytail and no makeup on. She's almost invisible next to the other two.

"Ok, ladies we are here to do a job. Do you recognize the man?" the first woman asked.

"Yes, the one sitting at the end of the bar, wearing the blue jogging suit. He was the one I saw that night. I will never forget that face," the third woman replied.

"That's your target," the first woman said instructing the second woman.

"This will be a piece of cake. No man has ever been able to resist my double D breasts," the second woman replied pushing her breast up.

"All you have to do is deliver him to the location and they will handle the rest," the first woman said.

"That bastard has no idea what's in store for him," the second woman stated as she walked to the bar to order a drink. She made sure that her breast rubbed against Lamont's shoulder as she leaned in to place her order.

"Sorry, they seem to get in the way sometimes," she laughed.

"No problem, I didn't mind one bit. Let me pay for your drink," he replied.

"Hi, my name is Veronica," she said introducing herself.

"My name is Lamont. Are you from around here?" he asked while staring at her chest.

"Yeah, somewhat, I live about fifteen minutes away," she answered.

"I see that you're here with your girls," he implied.

"They're trying to cheer me up from the separation of a long time lover," she insisted.

"What man would let a woman like you go?" he questioned.

"It wasn't by his choice," she answered as they chatted for a while longer.

"Is there anything I can do for you?" he asked after their third drink.

"I'm not sure," she answered.

"When was the last time a real man stepped to you?" he inquired.

"It has been a little while," she responded.

"Would you like to come back to the hotel with me?" he asked.

"I have a better idea. Why don't you come back to my place? This way I can pull out some of my toys," she suggested.

"That's fine," he answered gulping his drink down.

"Let me tell my girls that I'm leaving," she informed.

Lamont turned to Sean and said, "Double D invited me over her house for a night cap. If I'm not back in the morning don't wait for me."

"Man, are you sure about this?" Sean asked.

"I never give up the opportunity to please a damsel in need," Lamont answered grabbing his crotch.

Veronica went back to give an update.

"Damn, that did not take long," the first woman commented.

"Told, you it was easy" Veronica said.

"You don't think he recognized me?" the third woman asked.

"Girl, all he noticed was my breasts," Veronica responded.

I'll call and let them know that you should be there with the target," the first woman said.

The moment Veronica and Lamont walked out of the bar the first woman called with the news.

Chapter 19

"Have you heard anything on the Lamont issue?" Gator asked Dean.

"I got a call from Corey this afternoon and what he told me was alarming," Dean answered.

Robert and Gator carefully listened as Dean spoke. "This is definitely going to be Lamont's last ride with us. It was shocking to hear the information that Corey held back when he was in Detroit. The witness heard Lamont bragging on how they would blame everything on the family and declare war on us. He figured it would be a matter of time before we are all dead or in jail. With the family out of the way was going to allow him to take over our territory."

"Why didn't he tell us that at the meeting?" Gator angrily questioned.

"He had to make sure that we would deliver him," Dean responded.

Robert sat there speechless for a few seconds before he responded. "That bitch wanted to take down the family. We've been boys since, we were seven years old. I thought of him as a brother."

"Remember we have to act normal no matter how you feel about this," Dean enforced as they left the restaurant to join their women in the Jacuzzi.

Time went by fast as we sat in the Jacuzzi. We sat talking and laughing for nearly two hours. On our way back to the room, Robert and I ran into Sean.

"You're back early," Robert said.

“It was dead. The only single women were acting funky,” Sean replied.

“You mean they turned you down” Robert jokingly commented.

“Yeah, it seemed like after Lamont left with this big breast chick the other ones did not want to be bothered,” Sean responded.

“Did Lamont know this chick?” Robert asked.

“No. She walked up to him and struck up a conversation. They talked for a little while and then he took her home,” Sean explained.

“He’s going to get enough of those one night stands,” Robert replied.

“I’m calling it a night. I’ll see you both in the morning,” Sean responded.

We both said, “Good night Sean.”

When we got back to the room, we both jumped in the shower. I could tell that something was bothering him, because we silently washed each other up. Robert sat on the end of the bed wrapped in a towel flicking the television channels.

“Is everything ok?” I asked standing in front of him.

“Nothing I can’t handle,” Robert mumbled.

“Is there anything I can do to help?” I asked.

“No. It’s business,” Robert answered.

“I wish there was something I could do,” I replied.

“Just having you in my life helps more then you know,” Robert expressed.

I ran my hands through his hair and engaged him in a deep passionate kiss. I want him to know that I’m always here for him. I hate it but I do understood there will always be a grey area in his life that he won't share with me. He unwrap my towel and it fell to the floor. His hands softly ran up my back then around to my breasts. He slowly began caressing my breasts flicking his thumbs across my nipples. We continued to kiss. My teeth lightly held on to his tongue as I sucked on the tip of it. He returned the favor and sucked on my tongue.

I cupped her breasts and massage while I squeezed them. With slow nibbling kisses I worked my lips from her chin down her neck. She ran her hands up and down my shoulders as I circled each nipple of her breast with my tongue. I cradled one breast in the palm of my hand while sucking on the other. I took my time to give each breast equal time in my mouth. She twirled her fingers in my curls and softly kissed my forehead as she enjoyed the attention I gave her breasts.

He ran his hands up and down my back before rubbing on my ass. Just the mere touch of his hands on my body moistened my pussy. His hands glided softly around to my pussy. He sucked on his bottom lip as his fingers rubbed back and forth against my pussy hair. He inserted his fingers in and out of my wet pussy as he watched me slowly run the palms of my hands down my breasts then back up in a circular motion. I continued the circular motion around my breasts while he enjoyed the wet juices of my pussy running down his hands as his fingers moved in and out.

My towel opened up as my dick rose to a full erection. I scooted up on the bed to lie on my back. She climbed in the bed right behind me. She straddled on top of me and lean down to kiss me as she rotated her pelvis back and forth. Her wet pussy rubbed the tip of my dick on each stroke. Her pussy became dripping wet as she felt my dick pulsating for permission to enter.

I got in the squatting position, arch my back, and placed my hands on his thighs for balance. He held my waist as I lowered myself on his dick. I leaned my head back and moaned with pleasure as my pussy descended onto his dick. I slowly moved myself up and down as he held onto my waist. He bit his bottom lip and moaned with pleasure on my downswings. He raised his pelvis to meet my down strokes. It felt like time had slowed down. I could not help from saying what my heart was feeling.

"I love you more then you will ever know," I said.

"I never thought that I would fall in love," he whispered.

"You are my first thought in the morning and my last thought at night," I replied.

"You are the first woman I have ever loved," he revealed.

"I dream about you even when I am lying next to you," I whispered.

"I never thought I could find a woman that would complete me," he whispered back.

"You are my life and I plan to love you forever," I confessed.

"You are etched in my heart and I plan to love you forever," he softly said.

"You are also etched in my heart and I will always love you," I moaned.

"My love for you is what gets me through the day," he admitted.

I lowered my back on the bed. Robert kneeled on the bed with one of his legs straddled over one of my legs. He lifted the other leg up pressing it against his chest forcing me to lie on my side. I bit my bottom lip and moaned as he stroked his dick in and out of my hot wet pussy. The sweat from his chest rolled down my leg. Each slow deep stroke of his dick excited my pussy. I used my hands to massage my breasts with the sweat from my body as he watched.

With my dick still inside her pussy I lowered her leg to the bed, closing them, then placing them it between my legs. I lowered my chest on top of hers. My sweaty chest slide up and down her sweaty breasts as my dick continued with the strong deep strokes inside her wet pussy.

My body is on fire with passion for Robert. I rotated my pelvis to the rhythm of his strokes. Every inch of our bodies are dripping wet. I held him tightly as our bodies climaxed together.

I gracefully wiped the sweat off her face. Then I softly kissed her forehead, her right eyelid, her left eyelid, her right cheek, her left cheek, and then her lips.

"Thank you. You don't know how much this means to me to have you here with me at this moment. You are my happiness in my mad life," he whispered out of breath.

"Robert I can tell how you feel about me from your actions. You show it in your kisses, the way you touch me, and the look in your eyes. Being with you is magical and I love you with every fiber in my body," I replied.

We engaged in a long kiss before he rolled over on his side and retreated back into his thoughts. I lay alongside him and softly kissed him on his back. He grabbed my hand and held it tightly pressed to his chest. I could feel his heartbeat slow to a relaxing rhythm as he fell asleep.

Chapter 20

Veronica had Lamont park his bike in the backyard.

"Are you sneaking me in the house?" Lamont questioned.

"No. I lost the key to the bolt lock on my front door," Veronica quickly answered.

"For a moment it felt like a set-up," Lamont replied with a chuckle.

"That's funny. What reason would I have to setup you up? I just need a man to make me feel like a woman tonight," Veronica responded.

"I will make sure that you feel like a woman when I'm finished," Lamont replied as he squeezed Veronica's ass while following her through the back door.

"You don't mind if I check the house out?" Lamont asked.

"Go right ahead. I have nothing to hide," Veronica replied.

Lamont pulled out his gun and carefully searched each room. He put his gun up when he felt confident that they were alone and the feeling of being set-up faded.

"Sorry about that, but coming from Detroit you learn to stay on your toes," he told her.

"I understand. We have neighborhoods that make you watch your back too," she responded.

"Lately some scandalous punks out of Highland Park have been trying to expand their market area," Lamont commented.

"Enough of the gangsters talk. Make yourself at home, while I go and slip into something more comfortable. I don't have much food in the kitchen but there is plenty to drink. Can you grab two tall glasses and the bottle of Absolute?" Veronica yelled as she walked into the backroom bedroom.

While Veronica was changing her clothes she had to talk herself out of killing Lamont herself. "I can't believe that motherfucker is trying to shift the blame. He really thinks he has gotten away with killing my man. That bastard just doesn't know how bad I want to be the one to blow him away.

Girl get yourself together you have a job to do and besides that you don't want to disappoint your man's peeps. I have to do my part and they will handle it from there. Baby this is for you," she whispered kissing two fingers and holding them up to heaven.

Lamont was walking towards the back when Veronica resurfaced from the bedroom. She was wearing a very short white nightgown that enhanced her large breasts and a pair of six-inch white thigh high boots.

"Daaaamn, I'm going to enjoy this!" Lamont said as his eyes scanned up and down Veronica's voluptuous body.

"Follow me to the living room. I have a surprise for you," she instructed.

"I have a big long stiff hard surprise for you in my pants!" he informed.

"Sit on the couch so I can give you a show that you will never forget," she demanded.

Veronica dimmed the lights, cut on some booty popping music, and poured Lamont a drink.

She performed one of her routines from the strip club as Lamont sat back and enjoyed. After gulping down his drink he began drinking from the bottle. He was so engrossed with watching Veronica making her butt cheeks clap that he didn't notice she hadn't touched her drink. Nearing the end of her routine, she realized that the tranquilizer in his alcohol was kicking in slowly. She sat on his lap and poured him another glass of Absolute. She placed the glass between her breasts. Lamont cupped the sides of her breasts while drinking from the glass.

"G...i...r…l yo..u got my h..e..a..d sp..in..ning," Lamont slurred out.

Veronica put the glass up to Lamont's mouth and forced him to finish the drink.

"S…t..o…p the r…o….o….m fro…m s…pin…in….g," Lamont begged.

"The room is not spinning. Open your eyes," Veronica replied slapping him across the face.

"Biiiitch I ca…..n't th…..ey….re he….a…v…y," Lamont mumbled as he passed out cold.

"I told you that I have a big surprise but it's not for your ass. This is for my baby, may he rest in peace," Veronica responded after slapping him across the face again.

Veronica got off his lap, cut off the kitchen light, and opened the backdoor. The garage door opened, a van pulled out, and eight men rushed out. One man looked out, while they placed Lamont's bike in the back of the van and rushed in the house.

The men ducted taped Lamont's mouth and eyes shut. They pulled him off the couch on to a painter's tarp. His hands and ankles are handcuffed together before they rolled him up in the painter's tarp and carried him out to the van. They drove off with Lamont while Veronica stayed back to clean up all the evidence and fingerprints of Lamont's presence in the house.

Someone viciously ripped the duct tape off Lamont's eyes. He woke up from the pain of his eyelashes and eyebrows being ripped right out from his flesh. The duct tape over his mouth made it impossible for him to yell. The pain was so intense that he was unable to immediately open his eyes. It took a couple of seconds for his eyes to adjust from the pain. Once his vision cleared up he realized that he was not in the house Veronica took him too. He became very uneasy when he could not recognize the surroundings.

Corey's right hand man Giant walked through the door talking shit. "That fucking plan you came up with would have been a good one if you weren't such a dumb ass motherfucker! My first instinct was to go after the niggas from Highland Park, but your bitch ass had no idea that you left a witness behind and she identified your ass tonight at the bar," he said.

Lamont's heart began beating fast and his eyes started moving rapidly as he continued to listen. "Yea, you were set-up by your boys. They beat your good-for-nothing bitch ass to the punch," he stated.

Lamont is amazed his plan unraveled so fast and that the family knew. He knew there was no way they are going to let him live. His mind started racing from the sheer panic of fear that no one was coming to rescue him. His chest began hurting from the pounding of his heart. He knew this was the end for him.

"One of my boys that you killed was Veronica's old man. She asked me to make sure that you received your surprise," he said kicking Lamont in the face. "Men I'm going to leave him to you. I do not care how he dies. Make sure that his hands, feet, and head will never be found. This way his mother will never know what happen to his bitch ass," he ordered kicking Lamont in his stomach before walking out the house.

Giant's boys had fun for the next couple of hours taking turns beating on him. Lamont laid there with tears running from his eyes and hoping that they would end the pain. He just wanted them to kill him.

It's nearing four o'clock in the morning. They needed to clear out of the house before daybreak. One of the boys grabbed Lamont's head and snapped his neck. They rolled his body up in the tarp and carried his lifeless body out to the truck.

They drove out to a large deserted heavily wooded field to discard Lamont's body. They unrolled the blue tarp near a river edge. With a hacksaw they cut off Lamont's arms, feet, and head. All fingerprints on the handcuffs and hacksaw are wiped off before being toss them in the river. The rest of his body was rolled back up in the blue tarp with two large boulders tied to the end and pushed into the river. Each body part was placed in separate plastic trash bags and given to a friend of Corey's that raised dogs for illegal dog fighting so he could grind the remains up and feed it to his dogs.

Chapter 21

The next morning we made it to the park by 11 o'clock. We broke off into groups and planned to meet near the exit at closing. We walked from one end of the park to the other end to ensure that we did not miss any roller coasters. The last couple of hours Robert and I broke away from the group and spent it in the midway area eating and playing games. He wasn't able to win me a teddy, so he offered to buy me a big expensive teddy bear from the souvenir shop.

"That is really sweet of you but it is not necessary," I said.

"Don't you want something to remember the trip by?" he offered.

"The pictures from the roller coaster rides are enough for me," I answered.

"They are funny!" he added.

"Especially the ones of you screaming like a little girl!" I teased.

"You better not show anybody," he fussed.

"And if I do?" I asked.

"Remember I am your ride back home," he proudly announced.

"Like you would ever be able to leave all this," I cracked.

"There you go using my lines," he responded.

"Don't get mad at the truth," I claimed.

"You not really going to show anybody those pictures?" he questioned.

"It depends," I retorted.

"Depends on what?" he snapped.

"Act up and you will find out," I taunted.

"That's how it is?" he mocked.

"Never know when I need to remind you that you have a feminine side," I jokingly reminded.

"Payback can be a bitch!" he fussed.

"You always say that same old lame line," I teased.

"Bet you want be talking shit when we get back to the hotel," he laughed.

Later that night when we made it back to the hotel, everyone noticed that Lamont's bike is not in the parking lot.

"Did anybody talk to Lamont today?" Dean asked.

"No," they all answered.

"I called him this morning and he hasn't called back," Robert said knowing he didn't place any phone calls to Lamont.

"His phone is going straight to voicemail," Gator mentioned as he hung up his cell phone.

"Maybe his phone battery is dead," Sean said.

"It's been a long day. He knows we're checking out tomorrow. This is not the first time that he has pulled a disappearing act like this. He'll probable shows up in the morning," Dean suggested.

"Dean's right. Well I don't know about the rest of you but I'm calling it a night," Sean said.

That Sunday morning as we checked out the hotel's front desk clerk informed us that Lamont checked out some time Saturday afternoon.

"Did anyone get the name of the woman he left with?" Robert asked.

"No," answered those that went to the bar.

"Did anybody ask?" Robert questioned

"He called her Double D because of her bra size," Sean blurted out.

"Did anyone catch the names of the other women with Double D?" Gator requested.

"None of those other hoes would talk to anybody," one of the other guys replied.

"Lamont said if all goes his way with Double D he would catch up with us in HP," Sean revealed.

"He's a grown ass man that knows his way home. I guess we will see him at home," Dean commented.

Chapter 22

We made it home around 2 o'clock that afternoon. I truly enjoyed the trip, but glad to be home. All I wanted to do was catch up with my girl Leslie.

"Babe, I have to meet up with the fellas tonight, so I'm going to jump in the shower than take a nap," Robert said.

"I'll join you in a minute," I replied.

"I would prefer if you could make me something to eat while I'm in the shower," he suggested.

"Any preference?" I asked.

"Anything that is hot and quick," he answered.

Robert stood in the shower with the hot water running down his head as he thought, "I need a moment to myself. The weekend events surrounding Lamont is consuming my thoughts. I can't let that happen. I know Lamont is dead and there is not a motherfucking thing that can change that. This is not the first time and it definitely is not the last time a friend of mine is murdered. This is the first time I lost someone this close. As much as I want to hate Lamont for what he had planned for the family, it's hard to forget all the history behind our friendship. SHIT, we been boys since the second grade. I considered him family. Hell, our mother's knew each other.

I can't stop revisiting the day that my big brother introduced us to the game. We had big ass plans to take on the drug world together. He swore that he would never let anything come between us. I trusted Lamont with my life. At first I hated turning Lamont over but that was before I found out he put my life in harm's way.

Why the fuck am I wasting any good thoughts on that motherfucker! His bitch ass wanted me dead! Hell he planned to take the entire family down! The family was good to his foul ass! That motherfucker was making crazy money with us! Fuck that hoe ass bitch! He let the love of money and power turn him against his fucking family! I'm glad Corey did not say anything about Lamont's plan to eliminate the family. He would have never made it to Ohio. Not alive. Whatever they did with his ass, he deserved it. I hope his bitch ass suffered." Robert's thoughts flooded his mind then faded away.

I jumped in the shower while Robert ate. When I got out the shower, he was already laying down. I put on one of his big t-shirt and climbed into bed next to him. I wrapped my arms around him and softly kissed the back of his neck. I want to comfort him the same way he comforted me last week.

"Baby, I can tell that something is bothering you. I realize that your line of business can be stressful and I understand that there are things you cannot share with me. Always remember there is nothing about the way you play the game that will change how I feel about you. I love you," I whispered.

"Thanks Sweetheart that means more than you will ever know. I love you too," he replied.

I lightly scratched his scalp as he dozed off to sleep. When I woke up from my nap the apartment was dark and Robert was gone. I curled up on the couch and gave Leslie a call.

"Hey, girl I'm back," I said.

"How was the trip?" Leslie asked.

"We had a wonderful time. We spent the first evening in the hot tub," I answered.

"Did you give him a piece of ass in the hot tub?" Leslie questioned.

"No. There were two other couples," I mentioned.

"Were did the other's go?" Leslie asked.

"They went to some hole in the wall bars not far from the hotel. Lamont ran off with a chick from the bar," I stated.

"He is truly a hoe," Leslie replied.

"Hell, we left him down there," I responded.

"What happened?" Leslie asked.

"He checked out of his hotel room while we were at the park. He told a few of the guys that he would catch up with us in the city," I answered.

"One day he is going to run into the wrong hoe," Leslie replied.

"What went on in HP this weekend?" I asked.

"The Troy police arrested three of the crack heads for shoplifting at Oakland Mall," she blurted out.

"Damn. In a minute they will be banned from every mall in the surrounding areas," I replied.

We talked on the phone for hours covering every aspect of her weekend, my trip, and the stupid shit that Cathy and the crack heads did.

On the other side of city, Robert is meeting wlth Dean and Gator. They are discussing Lamont's disappearance and the impact it will have on daily operations. They also had to talk about who was going to fulfill Lamont's spot.

"Robert, I know that Lamont was like your brother," Dean inquired.

"You don't have to go there. My brother would never have set me up to take a fall. Yeah, I feel bad about what happen to him, but he put his self in that position," Robert admitted.

"I'm glad to see that you are handling it well," Gator added.

"Shit stinks, but life goes on," Robert commented.

"Corey is satisfied on the Lamont dilemma and that topic never needs to surface again. Remember to act truly concerned about his disappearance by asking around and checking on his mother," Dean recommended.

"Enough with the small talk we have business to take care of. Who and when are we going to fill Lamont's position?" Gator brought up.

"I would like to recommend Shannon as Lamont's replacement," Robert suggested.

"I don't have a problem with that and I'm not just saying that because he's my nephew," Dean added.

"He definitely has your work ethics, but I think Jason works just as hard," Gator mentioned.

"You right," Robert agreed.

"We should let the next few weeks tell who deserves the promotion," Gator proposed.

"Good idea Gator. Not putting someone in place immediately will seem like we are hopeful that Lamont is still alive. Robert I hate to do this to you, but I'm going to need you to pick up Lamont's slack for a while," Dean instructed.

"No problem, I could use the extra money," Robert responded.

"What the fuck do you need extra money for?" Gator questioned.

"I have a new outlook out on life. I am getting my GED so I can take business classes at Wayne County Community College. I want a legitimate business one day," Robert unveiled.

"Ah shit! A man falls in love and now he wants to change his life," Gator laughed.

"Fuck you man!" Robert replied.

"Your brother will be proud to hear that you are making plans for the future," Dean complimented.

"Maybe you could help us all get legit," Gator said.

For the last month, Robert worked his ass off to cover Lamont's absence. Robert's new hours meant he spent long hours handling business and less time with me. Thanks to his hours I spent more time with my peeps.

Getting a quickie in is the only time I have him to myself, but it always seems that he puts me to work after. Stopping by one of their dope house to help counting down money and bundling up the product is the only time we are able to have a long conversation.

Over the past weeks I have gotten good. I'm able to count money extremely fast with either hand. I accepted the fact that I never get paid as a contribution to my lavish life style. If it wasn't for Robert I won't be wearing expensive clothing, unique pieces of jewelry, expensive perfume, and carrying the latest purses. Hell, he always keeps cash in my pocket and let me drive his cars.

"I know you are tired of my long hours, but tonight is the last of it," Robert said as he strapped the last stack of cash.

"Are you going back to your old schedule?" I asked.

"Somewhat," he replied.

"Will you be home early tonight?" I asked contemplating if I should go to his place or go home.

"I am not sure what time I will make it in tonight, but be prepared. I plan to tear that ass up when I come in," he warned.

"You better hope that I am up for it," I replied realizing his comment settled my decision.

"I'm not worried about that. Those quickies held me over, but I am ready for a real workout," he proposition.

"Hopefully you won't fall asleep on me," I joked.

"You will see. So what are you doing tonight?" he asked.

"We're going to a birthday party at the Dairy Workers Hall," I mentioned.

"Be careful. Call me if anything pop off," he replied.

"That's cute you going to put on your superman cape and come save me," I teased.

"Ok smart-ass. Have a good time and I will see you later," he said.

My phone started ringing the moment I got in the car. "Hello?" I answered.

"Hey girl, are you still going to the party?" Leslie asked.

"Yes, I am. How did your shopping trip go?" I replied.

"Girl I'm so mad. I ran into one of Cathy's girls. That bitch was shoplifting!" She followed me from store to store. It almost look like we were together," she angrily stated.

"What mall were you at?" I asked.

"Fairlane. She knows that those white folks don't want our black asses out there anyway!" she blurted.

"She could have gotten you in trouble," I said.

"I know. I cussed the bitch out when she followed me out of the mall," she fussed.

"Are you still riding with me?" I questioned.

"Yea, what time you picking me up?" she inquired.

"I should be at your house around 8 o'clock. Be ready," I noted.

While going through my closet, I choose to wear one of my designer outfits that still have sale tags on it. This is perfect. My two-piece red linen short set. I can set it off with my red sandals, a matching purse, and a couple of expensive accessories. "Damn I look good." That is the only thing that comes to mind as I checked myself out in the mirror. It's hard not to out dress the birthday girl.

Ring! Ring! Ring! I called to Leslie. "Hey girl I'm walking out the door. I'll toot when I'm out front," I said when she answered.

"I will be ready when you get here," she responded.

"Ok," I replied.

Leslie came right out when I tooted for her.

"So we are hanging out in the Benz tonight," Leslie mentioned.

"I forgot to tell Robert that I wanted to drive the BMW," I responded.

"Shit, we still riding in style," Leslie replied.

"Your outfit is sharp," I complimented.

"Hell, it has nothing on your outfit," she critiqued.

"Robert picked this out for me," I mentioned.

"Are we getting out of the car at Floyd's house?" she asked.

"Only if the big mouth bitch that live next-door is sitting on her porch. I can't pass up the opportunity to piss her ass off," I admitted.

When I pulled, up to Floyd's house Baron and Floyd's new girlfriend were sitting on the porch. I'm glad to see Wanda sitting on her porch. Every since that bitch walked up on me in from of Sampson Party Store I enjoy getting under her skin.

"Look at the outfit Robert bought Selena!" Leslie shouted out.

"Damn that outfit is bad!" Floyd's girlfriend shouted back.

"That man must love the hell out of her! She is wearing designer from head to toe," Leslie added.

I slowly twirled around and then struck a pose. Wanda got up and ran in the house. We busted out laughing before she slammed the door.

"You hoes did that shit on purpose," Baron said.

"She makes it so easy," I laughed.

"I will never understand women. You are all crazy. Every last one of you," Baron commented.

"That haven't stopped you from using your lame ass pick up lines," Leslie cracked.

"Men are the reason why we are crazy. Most of them never grow up," Floyd's girlfriend said.

"Floyd, come on they are getting out of hand!" Baron called out.

Robert had two good reasons to be happy about today. This is his last day he had to fill in for Lamont's absence and he is the one that will deliver the good news. Both Shannon and Jason stepped up to the plate and pulled more than their weight. They never complained, never late, and their money was always correct. When Robert walked in the house, Shannon and Jason were in the kitchen preparing product.

"Hello gentlemen," Robert said.

"Hey Robert," they both replied.

"How are things going?" Robert asked.

"Business is booming," Shannon answered.

"It almost feels like the first of the month when all the crack heads get their government money," Jason commented.

"That's a good thing. It means more money for the family," Robert responded.

They continued talking with Robert while packaging up product and attending to customers. Around one in the morning he decided to call it a night.

"We are going to wrap it up. I'm going to run and pick up something to eat and you all can start shutting down. I will be back shortly," Robert instructed.

"Ok," they both said.

"I wonder what's going on!" Jason commented.

"Why you say that?" Shannon asked.

"Robert is shutting us down early," Jason answered.

"I hope it has something to do with the open spot," Shannon replied.

"You will have my full support if they promote you to Lamont's position," Jason replied.

"Man I believe you deserve that promotion," Shannon responded.

"No matter who gets the promotion lets promise that it will not change our friendship," Jason suggested.

"It want. I think of you as my brother," Shannon replied.

"I feel the same. I'll be glad when this waiting period is over," Jason shared.

"Me too," Shannon agreed.

"Hey, I'm back with the food. Take a break and come eat," Robert yelled.

They both came and sat at the front table. Robert felt that it is the perfect time for breaking the news. "I know that you both have been waiting to find out who was going to fill the open position. This move will affect the family as a whole. It was definitely a very hard decision. Both of you have proven to be ready and capable to handle more responsibilities.

Unfortunately, you still be working side by side. We are pulling four guys off our corner and opening two new houses. That means the open position comes with more responsibilities. That is why we have come up with our decision," Robert stated.

Robert stopped talking to eat all his food slowly. He wanted them to sweat. He enjoyed keeping them in suspense. They both sat there with nothing to say. The looks on their faces were priceless. They had no idea what was about to happen to them.

"Because of the work ethics and dedication you both showed to the family we decided the split the position and promote both of you," Robert said.

Their excitement from the news is over whelming. They both started to thank Robert and the family for their promotions. "Ok hurry up and eat so we can wrap it up. Your big day starts tomorrow. You will need to give Gator a call in the morning and he will give you further directions," Robert instructed.

Selena was sleep when I made it home. I pulled the blanket back and smiled to see that she was wearing her birthday suit. She woke up to me sucking on her breasts and my hand messaging the lips of her pussy. I climbed on top of her and continued to suck on her breasts. She opened her legs so my hard dick could enter her hot moist pussy.

I loved waking up to Robert sucking on my breast. My hips moved upward to greet his dick. I held on to his back as our bodies moved to the same rhythm. My pussy welcomed each slow and deep stroke of his dick as if it was the first time they met. We fucked like animals in heat with our bodies dripping wet.

"Thanks for putting up with my schedule," Robert whispered.

"You are welcome," I whispered back.

"I love you," he whispered.

"I love you too," I softly said.

He rolled over and I remained wrapped in his arms. We started kissing and the next thing I knew he is ready for round two, three, and four.

The next morning every muscle in my body was sore from the work out last night. I have not felt this sore since our first time.

"Are you getting up this morning sleepy head?" Robert asked.

"No. I'm not ready to get out of bed," I answered.

"What's the matter are you a little sore and stiff?" he laughed.

"Yes, and it is your fault," I snapped.

"I told you, I was going to tear that ass up," he teased.

Chapter 23

"I have to meet with Corey down in Ohio next week," Robert mentioned.

"Will you be back for the Fourth of July?" I asked.

"No. I figured we leave after the big fireworks show downtown and spend the Fourth in Ohio," he answered.

"When were you going to tell me?" I questioned.

"I just did," he replied.

"Thanks, know I have to scramble for a lie to tell my father," I said.

The morning of the fireworks, I drove Robert to Detroit Metro Airport to rent a low-key economy car. I went back to his place and packed our suitcases. Robert made quick stops at the spots before heading by Dean's house to pick up the items that was needed for the trip. We pulled out shortly after one o'clock that next morning to avoid traffic. As much as I would love for this to be a vacation, I'm fully aware that it was a business trip.

"So what excuse did you tell your father?" Robert asked.

"He thinks I'm with Leslie in Louisiana visiting Brandy," I answered.

"That's cool how your girl covers for you," Robert commented.

"We got each other's back. Her mother thinks she went with me to visit Brandy.

"She's hanging with her man?" Robert asked.

"Yes, his parents are out of town for the holiday. Do you have a lot of friends in Ohio?" I asked.

"They are actually friends of my brother and Dean. This is my first time meeting with them by myself," he answered.

"Is it going to cause any problems with you bringing me?" I asked.

"No. Corey knows that you are driving up with me," he stated.

"What will I do while you're meeting with Corey?" I questioned.

"I thought you would like to hit the mall," he stated.

"Why would I want to spend my time in a mall?" I asked cracking a smile.

"I thought shopping was every woman's favorite past time," he commented.

"It is but, shopping by myself ain't much fun," I replied.

"You are not going to be alone. Corey has two sisters that doesn't mind taking you shopping," he responded.

"What do you have planned for us on the Fourth?" I asked changing the subject.

"Corey invited us to his annual barbecue," he said.

"Good, I was scared that you were going to feed me barbecue from a cheap fast food restaurant," I teased.

Ring! Ring! Ring! Just then, his phone rang and I found myself listening to music as he talked on the phone for the rest of the ride. After checking into the hotel, we ordered room service and called it a night.

The next morning we meet Corey and his sisters for breakfast. I noticed that Robert was much younger than him. Corey had at least a good ten to fifteen years over him. After breakfast, Robert left with Corey and I left to go shopping with his sisters.

We ventured to two malls and made a few stops. I had a good time shopping and site seeing. They took me out for dinner before dropping me back at the hotel. I'm surprised to see Robert was already in the room when I arrived.

"Did you enjoy your shopping trip?" he asked.

"Yes I did. Corey's sisters are cool. We hit two malls and they showed me around," I answered.

"I can tell you had a good time from all the bags. Did you buy out the mall?" he questioned.

"I found clothes I haven't seen in Detroit. I also bought some candles I hope we get the chance to use," I answered.

"I am glad you enjoyed yourself," he replied.

"Did your meeting go well?" I asked.

"It did, but Corey would like to introduce me to a couple of his fellas tonight," he answered dryly.

"So, that means I'm not invited?" I commented.

"Yes. It's only going to be guys tonight. Is that a problem?" he questioned.

"No. I wanted to hang out with his sisters," I answered.

"Oh, you were trying to dump me anyway," he replied.

"No, I made back up plans," I responded.

"Do you need me to drop you off?" he politely asked.

"No. They are picking me up in an hour," I answered.

When I got back to the hotel, it was after one o'clock in the morning and Robert was still out in the street. I took a hot shower and went to bed. The next morning I woke up and found him lying next to me. I could smell he had been drinking, so I left him sleeping and went out for breakfast.

We made it out to Corey's house later that day. He is one of the few blacks that lives in Sylvania Township. His house is a big two-story bi-level. The house has four bedrooms, three and a half bathrooms, a marble entry to the sunken living room, and a huge family room with a fireplace. The entertainment room includes a wet bar, two large flat screen televisions, gaming area, and a pool table.

Corey introduced Robert and I as family from Detroit. We had a good time and everybody was extremely nice. I spent most of my time with Corey's sisters, since Robert hung out with Corey and his boys. We left after Corey's big fireworks show ended.

When we made it back to the hotel, I ran a hot bubble bath and lit candles all around the bathroom. Robert found a jazz station on the hotel radio, got undressed, and slid into the bathtub.

I closed the lid on the toilet and sat down to slowly unbuckle and remove my sandals one at time as Robert sat in the bathtub and watched. I stood up and untied the bow on my wrap around skirt and let it slide down my legs to expose my white lace thong. I grabbed the bottom of my tank top and slowly removed it. I pulled it up unevenly to show one breast at a time. I stood there in my thong and twisted my hair into a ponytail. I slid off my thong, cut the lights off, and joined Robert in the bathtub. I sat between his legs with my back lying against the hair of his chest and his dick lightly touching the lower part of my back.

The aroma of lilac from the candles fills the air. The steam from the bath tub coated the mirrors. The warm illuminate glow of the flames dance on the ceiling and sensually outline our bodies on the walls. It's the perfect setting for a relaxing romantic bath.

"Baby moments like this I never want them to end," he admitted.

"It takes me back to the first time we made love. When you carried me to your bedroom and laid me across the bed than asked if I was sure. Saying yes was the best decision I ever made," I softly said.

"That turned out to be the best decision for both of us," he whispered in my ear.

"You are the only man for me. I dream of a long and happy future with you," I confided.

"Good because I don't plan on going nowhere," he assured.

"I hope you feel that way when I am old and wrinkled up," I teased.

"In my eyes you will never be old and wrinkled up," he cooed.

"You are the love of my life," I tenderly said.

"You are the love of my life as well," he replied.

Robert wrapped his arms around me and cupped my breasts. I slowly ran my hands up and down his thighs. He gave the back of my neck wet sucking kiss.

I softly nibbled on her shoulders as my hands move in a circular motion over her nipples. I could feel her nipples becoming hard to my touch. She grabbed my left hand and slid it down her tummy. She invited my fingers to enjoy her pussy. I ran my fingers along the inside of her virginal lips.

My insides are warming up from the anticipation of making love to my man. He used two fingers on his left hand to play with my clit. He moved his right hand off my breasts and down to my pussy. He slowly inserted a finger from his right hand inside my pussy. I grabbed hold of my breasts when he stuck his wet tongue inside my ear.

She moved her hips to the rhythm of my finger moving in and out her pussy. She moaned, held on to her breast, and slightly bit the bottom of her lip as her body enjoyed the stimulation.

I rotated the palm of my hands around my breasts with the rhythm of his fingers.

My dick began pulsating against her back as my hands continued to enjoy her hot pussy.

I arched my back out as my breathing became deeper when the sexual excitement was building in my body. I bit my bottom lip a little harder and twisted my nipples as I felt his throbbing dick swell to a full erection.

I removed my hands from her pussy and bent my knees up. She leaned forward, wrapped her arms around my thighs, and lifted her ass up so I could insert my hard dick into her pussy. Her body trembled as she slowly lowered herself engulfing my dick inside her pussy.

I rotated my hips as he pumped his dick up and down inside my pussy. The hair on Robert's legs lightly tingle my nipples as my breasts rubbed against his legs.

"Whose pussy is this?" he asked.

"It's yourrrrrs. Only yours," I moaned to him.

"Good this is the only pussy this dick wants," he said with his dick massaging me deeply.

"I love you," I moaned with pleasure.

"I love you too," he panted.

I turned around wrapped my legs behind Robert as my pussy descended back on his dick. I cupped my arms under his arm pit and held on to his shoulders. My nipples ran up and down his chest as my hips slowly rotated on the ride. We both moaned as our bodies sweated from the heat between us.

I grabbed her ass and pushed it towards me on her down strokes for deeper penetration. She gasped for air as her body exploded with excitement on each deep stroke of my dick.

"Oh, Oh, that's it baby make this pussy sing," I moaned with pleasure.

"I hear it singing my name," he moaned.

Holding onto his shoulder I leaned back so he could suck on my breasts while enjoying the ride. I rotated my hips as I continued to move up and down.

I continued to suck on her breasts until I felt my body preparing for an orgasm. The grasp I had on her butt became tighter as I pulled her in closer and held her tight while I busted a nut inside of her.

"Oh this pussy is good," he cried out in pure pleasure.

"Only for you," I moaned.

"I never want it to stop. Here I come," he warned pumping me faster.

"Oh, Oh, Oh, Oh, Ooooh, Oooooohhhhhhh!" we both cried out in ecstasy.

The thought of his dick cumming inside me made my body tremble with pleasure. We held each other tightly as are bodies trembled climaxing together. Our shadows on the bathroom walls enjoyed the sexual excitement as much as we did. We sat in the bathtub with sweat dripping down our faces sharing open mouth kisses as his hands ran down my back.

That next day we did not wake up until noon. We had just enough time to pack and get something to eat before hitting the road. I drove home, while Robert relaxed and enjoyed the drive.

Everything was going smoothly until a white Ohio State Troopers pulled up alongside the car. He drove besides us for ten minutes before slowing down and getting behind our car. My heart seemed to skip a beat when I saw the flashing lights of his police car in the rear mirror.

"Babe, wake up the police is pulling me over," I said.

"Treat this as a routine traffic stop. Do you want me to handle this?" Robert asked.

"Don't worry I can handle this," I answered.

"That's my baby. Remember, we were visiting family," he instructed.

The policeman walked over to the driver's side door and asked, "May I see your driver license, registration, and insurance?"

I handed the police officer my driver's license and the envelope with the rental car's information.

"Excuse me officer, what is the reason for you stopping me," I questioned.

"First you look too young to be driving and second you look to young to be across state lines with a male," the officer answered.

"He's nobody but my big brother," I replied.

"You don't look alike," the officer responded.

"That's because I got my good looks from my mother and he looks like his mother," I replied.

"So, he's your half brother?" the officer responded.

"Yes he is," I answered.

"That explains the difference in looks. What business did you have in Ohio?" the officer asked.

"We went to visit our grandmother in Cuyahoga, Ohio for the holiday," I responded.

"Take this as a warning. It would be wise for you to let your big brother drive to avoid from being pulled over again," the officer responded staring at Robert.

"Thank you very much officer," I replied.

He handed my information back and watched as we switch seats before he pulled off.

"I am proud of you. You handled that like a pro," Robert complimented.

"It was easier then calling my father from jail," I replied.

"Why would you be calling him from jail?" he asked.

"Baby, let's be real with each other. The trip down to Ohio was more for business then pleasure. I know that our luggage are not the only things going back home with us," I said.

"You did not have to come," he stated.

"Yes I did," I responded.

"What makes you say that?" he asked.

"If you didn't want me to come you would have never invited me," I answered.

"To tell you the truth I didn't want you to come, but it looks better for the cops to see me driving with you then by myself or with another nigga," he replied.

"I know you would never intentionally put me in harm's way. Besides, I was fully aware of your life style the moment I fell in love with you," I explained.

"I would never let you take the fall for my wrong doings," he assured.

"Lying to the police actually gave me an adrenaline

rush," I admitted.

"I have to confess, we do work well together," he commented.

"In two weeks Dean and I are flying out to North Carolina to visit my brother. I wish you were able to come. It would be nice for the two most important people in my life to meet face to face. I also would like you to see that he's not the monster the news made him out to be," he mentioned.

"It would be nice to finally meet the voice behind the phone calls," I said.

"One day you will get the chance to meet him," he said.

Chapter 24

I'm sitting at the dining room table eating a bowl of cereal when Robert bent over. I thought he was going to kiss me on the cheek. Instead, he started sucking me on my neck.

"Hey why did you do that?" I asked.

"I had to mark my territory to keep all the other niggas away while I'm gone," he advised.

"You're only going to be gone for one night. Besides, you don't trust me?" I questioned.

"It's not you that I'm worried about. Hell, why would any woman want to cheat on all this man?" he asked.

"There you go with that line again. Baby let me tell you the truth. I am only with you because I felt sorry for you," I teased.

"I know that you are going to miss me while I'm gone," he claimed.

"Yea right, if that's what you want to think," I responded.

"Remember if anything jumps off call Gator or Sean," he instructed.

"Don't worry I have no plans on getting into trouble," I mentioned.

"Sometimes trouble has a way of sneaking up and fucking up your plans," he warned.

"You be careful and have a nice visit with your brother," I said with a kiss on his lips.

Chapter 25

Robert and Dean flew into Raleigh-Durham international Airport in Morrisville, North Carolina. The airport is 19 miles outside of Butner. Even though the airport is on phase II of renovation, it still provides southern hospitality and high-tech amenities. They caught a quick shuttle from the airport terminal to a car rental. They drove directly to Butner Federal Correctional Institution Medium II Facility. When they arrived at the facility, they had plenty of time to visit with Thomas.

They walked up to the front entrance desk and handed the officer their driver's license. The officer gave them the Notification to Visitor form to read and sign before they were able to sign the Inmate Visitor's Daily Log. Dean waited in the lobby to give Robert some one-on-one time with his big brother. Robert was escorted to the inmate visitors area were the prison guard patted him down, checked his mouth, checked the bottom of his feet, and the inside of his shoes.

"Man it's good to see you," Thomas greeted.

"It's good to see you too," Robert replied giving him a hug.

"How is life on the outside?" Thomas asked.

"Business is doing very well. I decided to finally get my GED," he answered.

"I'm glad to hear that. I hope you are planning for your future, because you need to have a backup plan," Thomas said.

"I plan to open up a legitimate business," he responded.

"What kind of business are you thinking about?" Thomas questioned.

"I have a few ideas, but nothing concrete," he informed.

"Don't be a fool and jump in head first not knowing what you are doing," Thomas advised.

"I'm not. Come this January I am taking a couple of business classes at Wayne County Community College," he said.

"What about your startup cost?" Thomas asked.

"I am saving as much money as possible. My spending habits have been cut," he answered.

"Man I'm glad to hear that, but what's really going on in your life?" Thomas grilled.

"What do you mean by that?" he responded.

"It wasn't that long ago when you were acting like playboy of the year and now you have moved Selena in. She not even out of high school," Thomas answered.

"She has a key to my place but she has not moved in. Besides this is her senior year and there is only a two year age difference between us," he replied.

"She got plans after high school or does she plan on having you take care of her?" Thomas asked.

"Hell I have to force her to take money from me. She plans on going to college for accounting," he answered with a little extra bass in his voice.

"I did not mean to offend you. It's rare at your age in this game to find someone that's not with you for your money," Thomas suggested.

"I know. That's why I have to step up my game in order to keep her. I wish that you were able to meet her face to face then you could see she's special," he replied with a big smile.

"I am truly pleased to see you are happy but it's bizarre seeing you with a soft side," Thomas admitted.

"You sound just like Sherries," he replied.

"How is Sherries doing?" Thomas asked.

"She is doing well. She sends her love," he mentioned.

"How's Pops and the rest of his bastard kids," Thomas quizzed.

"He's fine. His other bastards have not changed. They still keep up all their drama," he stated.

"You know that you and Sherries are the only two siblings I claim," Thomas commented.

"I understand where you coming from," he agreed.

"Enough of that there are other important issues we need to discuss. Man I know Lamont was like a brother to you. What is your true take on the matter?" Thomas asked.

"He is a part of my past. No brother of mine would ever have jeopardized my life over money. I'm glad I didn't hear the whole story before delivering him," he answered.

"This hasn't made you question your loyalty to the family?" Thomas questioned.

"Lamont was my boy but my loyalty is to the family. You are the only person I would put over the family," he answered.

Beep! Beep! Beep! Beep! "All inmates report to the officers desk in an orderly fashion and remain standing for the count," one of the officers yelled.

The visit was interrupted by an official prisoner count. Thomas and all the inmates are required to report to the officers' desk. Thomas gave his prison number while one officer counted and another officer observed. He was identified by his inmate photo identification card and verification of name. The count was double because the officers reversed roles and inmates repeated their prison numbers. Thomas returns to the visit after the Control Center gave a good verbal count.

Dean entered the visitor's room after the official count was over. He walked in carrying a clear plastic bag with twenty dollars in coins from the front lobby change-dispensing machine. They ate a cheap meal from the vending machines while talking.

"How's Pilgrim coming along?" Thomas asked.

"We have the place up and running. Only a limited amount of people has access to it," Dean answered.

"It is very secure but easy to escape if needed. The cops that live on the block are on the payroll," Robert added.

"Remember nothing sold or bought there," Thomas reinforced.

"It is strictly used for separating the shipments and preparing packages for distribution. There is no late night activity at the house either," Dean replied.

"How are the other new business ventures doing?" Thomas asked.

"Both new locations are generating a very sizeable profit. Jason and Shannon have stepped up like men. Your brother taught them well. Jason is like a mini Robert and Shannon is like a mini Lamont before he strayed away," Dean answered.

"Talking about Lamont, did that cause any problems from his peeps?" Thomas asked.

"Lamont's hoe Cindy solved that problem for us. She made everybody aware that Lamont set-up shop in Pontiac from the money and drugs he stole from drug dealers he killed. She also ranted that he should not have been out wandering around Ohio with another tramp bitch knowing that he was a wanted man," Robert answered.

"Good that is about the same story I heard up here," Thomas replied in agreement.

"I did not have a problem with him branching out on his own. I had a problem with him wanting to take the family down to achieve that goal," Dean commented.

"It sounds like you two have everything covered. It feels like my input is not needed," Thomas added.

"This was something you and I started. If it weren't for you carrying the burden of the family in here there would have been nothing to build on," Dean expressed.

"We value your opinion. Man I love you," Robert added.

"I love you too little brother, but I need to talk with Dean," Thomas replied.

"I'll talk with you later," Robert said as he hugged Thomas and walked out the visiting room.

"Man thanks for giving me a little time alone with Robert," Thomas acknowledged.

"I knew you wanted some time with him," Dean replied.

"Tell me the truth, how is he really handling the Lamont ordeal?" Thomas asked.

"I know it bothered him that someone he considered a brother would stab him in the back like that, but he handled it like a pro," he stated.

"I am glad to see that the Lamont issue didn't mess up our connection," Thomas replied.

"You know I received positive feedback from Corey on Robert's trip to Ohio," he responded.

"I was a little concerned about him taking Selena to Ohio. How does he know that he can trust her?" Thomas asked.

"I know she is aware of his life style. When Lamont went missing, she helped Robert out at a few of the spots. Robert said when the Ohio State Troopers pulled them over she was able to talk them out of getting a ticket and having the car searched," he answered.

"Tell me what is really going on with that boy. He just doesn't seem the same," Thomas said.

"He's not the same. The man is in love," he informed.

"Is she worthy of him?" Thomas asked.

"She is fine as hell and it has calmed him down a lot. With all his talk about a future has made him more focused on the job," he answered.

"Ain't she a little too young for him?" Thomas asked.

"They are only two years apart. The biggest plus is that it keeps him out the streets. Hell, the other guys can barely get him to go out at night," he answered.

"That is a good thing. It's just that Robert threw me for a loop with that 360 degree overnight change," Thomas replied.

"We all found it funny that the same man that always talked shit about he was to good looking for one woman has finally settled down. I honestly believe he is going to be alright," he encouraged.

Chapter 26

"I'll be glad when you finally move in," Robert said picking me up from school.

"I told you after graduation. It would kill my father if I moved out now," I replied.

"Hell, you are at my house at least four nights out of the week," he commented.

"That's the advantage with having a lock on my bedroom door. They have no idea that my radio and TV have timers," I replied.

"Ok, slick ass I know this is your senior year and I hope you won't get mad at me, but I'm not attending any high school events with you," he responded.

"Why not?" I asked.

"I am a little old to be hanging out at high school events and I feel a little out of place," he answered.

"Do you feel out of place being seen with me, since I'm still in high school?" I questioned.

"It's not you or your friends. I'm talking about those underclass kids. I can't take another group of freshmen girls goggling over me," he explained.

"How many times do I have to remind you that nobody wants you but me," I replied.

"That's what you think," he said.

"No. That is what I know. So what about my prom, you plan on standing me up for that too?" I asked.

"I wouldn't do that to you," he answered.

"Oh that's good to know," I replied.

"I heard chicks turn into freaks after the prom and I wouldn't miss that," he responded smiling.

"How dare you think I will turn into a freak," I fussed.

"I know you can be a freak when you want to," he said grinning.

"It takes a freak to know a freak," I replied smiling.

"On a serious note, you need to stop hanging out at Ble Blobs," he ordered.

"Why is something going to happen up there?" I asked.

"Nothing but trouble hangs up there," he answered.

"Some days you act like my father," I replied.

"Just don't go up there anymore," he demanded.

Ble Blobs was a small corner store converted into an arcade on Woodward Avenue. I would periodically stop in to defend my title at Ms. Pac Man and Centipede. It was one of the few spots for local kids to hang out after school. The only down fall is that you are always guaranteed to see a fight.

To avoid an argument I agreed to stop going. It wasn't even two weeks later when the place was shot up because two local thugs were feuding over a girl that has slept with half the city. Every time their paths cross, they would start fighting. One of the thugs was standing out in front of Ble Blobs when a car pulled up and opens fire with a semi-automatic rifle. When the gunfire was over one person was dead and four others were injured. It never fails that the intended target never gets injured.

"Ok. Is there any other places you want me to stay away from?" I asked with a sarcastic tone in my voice.

"We don't need to argue about this. I do have something important to discuss with you," he answered.

"What is it?" I asked being puzzled.

"The last couple of weeks I have been thinking about our future. I know that the drug game is not going to last forever and I need to make plans for that day. I want a business of my own and I want it ran right. I'm getting my GED, so I can take a few business classes at Wayne County Community College," he answered.

"I am so happy to hear that," I replied with a big smile.

"I'm glad to hear that because we will have to cut down on our spending," he informed.

"Is there anything else that I can do to help out?" I asked.

"Yes, graduate from college. You can become my personal accountant," he encouraged.

I am so thrilled that this is my last year of high school, but I am more excited that Robert enrolled in evening classes at one of the Detroit Public School Adult Education programs in preparation for the GED test in October. Despite Robert's no high school event notice I am not going to miss any of my senior activities. I plan to party my ass off!

Since, all my class requirements for graduation are completed I enrolled in the school Co-op program. That means that I will only attend school half a day and work a part-time job while receiving credit as a full-time student. I was assigned to a job at a local bank in Highland Park as a part-time teller through the program.

My position at the bank gave me the perfect opportunity to hide the money required for Robert's retirement from the drug game. Robert and I took the time to start up several dummy businesses. We opened several personal and business bank accounts at different branch locations.

At night, I would count and rubber band his money and Robert would prepare the deposit slips. Since, I covered drive-thru during lunchtime Robert would bring in several large deposits through the drive-thru. This way no one in the bank saw me accepting deposits from him. I would re-verify the deposits amounts and wrap the cash in bank money straps before putting the money in my draw. Then I would process two or three of the large deposits slips while he was at the window. This way nothing suspicious about his transactions was caught on the surveillance cameras. The remaining deposit slips I processed between other customer transactions.

Spreading his deposits between customers insured they did not appear to come from the same customer. That way I'm able to avoid from filling out the Government Currency Transaction Report (also known as a CTR). CTR is a tool the government uses to catch money laundering of illegal money. The United States Government made it mandatory for all banks tellers to fill out a CTR on any customer that has a single transaction or several transactions totaling ten thousand dollars or more.

Homecoming fell on an Indian summer day. The weather is beautiful and we actually won our first homecoming game in years. The daytime temperature was in the mid-eighties and the evening temperature dropped to the mid-seventies. Baron is the Homecoming King and my date, since Robert refused to attend the homecoming dance.

"Just because you drove does not mean that we have to dance together," Baron said.

"Why would I want to ruin my reputation by dancing with you?" I asked.

"If nothing else being seen with the king will get you noticed," he answered.

"Nigga please! Because I'm your friend is the only reason why anybody voted for you," I replied.

"Nay, you got that wrong. My good looks got my votes. You practically begged me to run for king," he suggested.

"I felt sorry for your skinny ass!" I commented.

"That's ok. I know you want me and that you are just using Robert to make me jealous. Every girl in Highland Park wants me," he said being conceited.

"You are stupid and you will save a dance for me," I demanded.

"Just because Robert decided he's to grown for high school stuff you think I'm going to fill in for him?" he stated.

"No. You would not be able to fit in his shoes anyway," I answered.

"Now that is cold," he replied.

Not only did I have a good time at the dance, it was the first time a school event was not disrupted by a fight.

It seems like school just started and here it is the last weekend in October already. First thing Monday morning the principal asked all seniors to report to the auditorium. He announced that a classmate was murdered over the weekend.

He was not a popular kid in our senior class. He was a half- step from being a nerd. He was in the honor society, the student senate, the debate team, the science club, and the math club. He spoke to everyone even if they did not speak back. I had several math classes with him throughout high school and considered him a friend. He was stopped at a red light when his parent's car was carjacked. The carjackers stabbed him several times before leaving him lying in the alley amongst piles of trash to bled death.

For the next two months, there was a rave of death. Another male classmate was found shot in the chest at a crack house in Flint. A third male classmate shot in the head while ordering food in Popeye's Chicken drive-through in Detroit. A fourth male classmate discovered hung from a tree in his grandparents backyard in Hamtramck. A fifth male classmate shot multiple times by the East Point Police while in the commission of a crime. One female classmate died in a car accident on the Southfield Freeway. Two of Robert's friends were gunned down in a drive by shooting when they came out of a party store on Greenfield Avenue and Seven Mile Road.

It was sad to lose so many friends in such a short time, but with Christmas around the corner, Robert getting his GED, and he also enrolled in class at the local community college made it hard to stay sad.

The next few months were drama free. For Valentine's Day, we went over Robert's sister home for a dinner party. She stays Downtown Detroit, just a couple of blocks over from Robert in Orleans East Apartments.

"Robert. Selena. I didn't think you were coming," Sherries said surprisingly as she opened her door.

"You invited us," Robert replied.

"Yes but I thought you hated being around my friends," Sherries responded.

"Why would you think that?" Robert asked.

"You always calling them nerds," Sherries answered.

“Are we still invited?” he questioned.

“Come on in and enjoy yourselves,” Sherries answered swinging the door open.

There are about fifteen other guests. The atmosphere is filled with love. There is a lot of sexually arousing finger foods, dips, and champagne.

We made an attempt to mingle with the other guests. By my fourth glass of champagne all, that changed. This was the first time I drank champagne and I never imagined the effect it was having on me. I became extremely horny. All my attention was on Robert. It was as if he is the only person in the apartment.

I whispered to him that I’m horny and how much I want to fuck him. That turned him on. We did not want to embarrass his sister so we left early. As we were leaving, Robert grabbed a bottle of his sister’s champagne. Before we could completely pull out of her parking lot I could not help myself. I leaned over and started rubbing is dick.

“Sweetheart I’m not sure what’s going on but my body is hot for you. When we were in your sister’s place I wanted to rip your clothes off and fuck the shit out of you,” I said in a drunken slur.

“Baby it’s nothing wrong with you. That champagne made you more horny than normal,” he replied.

“Regardless to what made me horny my pussy is singing your name. Don’t you hear it?” I asked.

I lifted her skirt up, took my right hand, and placed it in her panties so I could feel how wet her pussy had gotten. “Damn, I can hear it singing for me! The minute we get home I’m going to plug it up with something good,” he said patting my pussy.

“I can’t wait,” I said grinding on his hand.

Her wet pussy excited me so much that I inserted my finger inside and proceeded to move it in and out. She moved her pelvis back and forth with the movement of my finger. She could see my dick throbbing with excitement.

Lucky, he only lives a couple of blocks from his sister's place because my insides are on fire. It took us under five minutes to make it to his apartment's garage. He pulled into his assigned parking spot and cut the car off. I noticed that his dick was budging out of his pants. There are no words spoken. I automatically climbed into the back seat and he followed.

I unzipped my pants and pulled my hard dick out. She lifted her legs up so I could slide her panties off her.

I wrapped my legs around him, put my arms above my head, and placed my hands on the backseat car door to get better leverage to push my pelvis as close as possible to him. His first deep stroke sent a wave of hot pleasure running through my veins. My body wanted him even more.

The scent of sex our bodies created filled the car. The heat from our bodies steamed up the dark tinted windows. The sounds from our bodies slapping together from each deep stroke and the moons of pleasure drowned out all background noise.

My mind and heart kept whispering out dirty thoughts filled with nothing but profound love for Robert. Pleasing his sexual needs was the only thing I wanted to do. I lifted my legs up and planted my feet on the ceiling so his dick could get deeper penetration.

"Take this pussy it's all yours," I ordered.

"This is all mines!" he stated.

"That's right it's all yours," I assured.

"Damn this pussy is hot and wet," he moaned with pleasure.

"Only for your dick," I whispered.

"Whose name is written all up inside this hot pussy?" he asked panting.

"Yours and only yours," I moaned to him.

"You want more?" he asked fucking me faster.

"Give me what you got," I begged.

I swung her legs over my shoulders and fucked her with quick deep strokes. I watched as she bit down on her bottom lip and screamed out in ecstasy.

I grabbed his ass when I felt my body coming to a full orgasm and he joined me with his last long deep stroke. I'm able to feel his dick inside me throbbing rapidly as we climaxed together.

We laid on the back seat for a couple of minutes engrossed in several deep kisses. The car windows were completely steamed up. I have no idea if any one heard us and I could care less if they did. We laid there in each other's arms for a while before heading to the elevator.

"Damn girl that was a fantastic," he complimented with a love tap on my butt.

"Only for you, baby," I said looking up at him.

I headed straight for the shower as soon as we made it in his apartment. He joined me a few minutes later. He lathered up the washrag and began to wash my back.

"I hope you enjoyed Valentine's Day?" he asked hugging me.

"I did. I love the beautiful cards, red roses, candy, outfit, and my handsome man," I said with a wet kiss.

"I was hoping not to disappoint you!" he said.

I gently looked into his beautiful eyes. "Baby you could

never disappoint me. The moment you gave me your heart is the only thing I ever wanted from you," I whispered. "Baby you stole my heart a long time ago. It was not hard falling in love with you," he said.

"I love you too," I said.

We both walked out the bathroom wrapped in our towels. I noticed that the bottle of champagne he grabbed from his sister's house was opened and sitting on the dresser next to a long jewelry box. I tried to act as if I didn't see the jewelry box.

"Are you going to open it?" he asked.

"I wasn't sure if it was for me," I commented.

"Tell me who else would I have a gift for in my bedroom? Open it!" he ordered.

I picked the box up and opened it. "This is gorgeous. I never saw a bracelet with a link like this. Thank you," I said hugging him.

"I had it made especially for you. It is my version of hugs and kisses," he said.

"I feel bad that I don't have another gift for you," I said.

"You loving me unconditionally is the only thing I want from you," he said putting the bracelet on my wrist.

"I can't imagine what life would be without you. Once upon a time I could not picture myself being this happy. You are my first thought in the morning and my last thought at night. I am still amazed about having you in my life. I cannot find the words to express how much I love you," he said positioning the bracelet on my wrist.

"I'm speechless," I said looking in his eyes, then at the bracelet on my wrist.

We embraced and shared a long passionate kiss. We drank a couple of glasses of champagne as we continued to share our feelings. I light the candles, cut off the lights, and opened all the bedroom blinds to allow the light illuminating from the moon to be our background.

Still wrapped in our bath towels she stood in front of me, while she continued to talk. I sat the bottle of champagne down as she unwrapped her towel to expose her perfectly shaped naked body. I leaned in and gently creased her breasts as if it was the first time that I laid my eyes on them. I gently started to suck on her nipples one at a time.

I ran my hands through his curly hair and down his back. His tender touches on my breasts sent a hot pleasurable rush through my entire body. My pussy became moist with a burning desire to please him developed into the only thought on my mind.

I unwrapped my towel to expose my fully erect dick. She climbed onto my lap. She placed one leg on each side of me as we sat facing each other. I continued to suck her breasts as she guided my dick into her hot wet pussy.

With both of us in an upright sitting position, I arched my legs up, wrapped my arms around him, and started to ride him. My pussy slowly stroked up and down his beautiful dick. I took my time to enjoy every inch of his dick with each stroke. The moans of pleasure could be heard from both of us as my nipples slide up and down his chest while I enjoyed the ride.

I wrapped my arms around her back and slightly grabbed her hair. I used the grip on her hair to control the movement of her head. I pulled her hair back and sucked on the middle of her neck. I pulled the right side of her hair to nibble on her left ear and suck on the left side of her neck. Then I repeated by pulling the left side of her hair to give her right side the same attention. I occasionally let loose of her hair and she would reciprocate by sucking on my neck.

The room felt thirty degrees hotter as the sweat began to build up between our chests. He wrapped his arms around me and slowly lowered his back to the bed as I rode him.

My hands ran down her back to her ass. I pushed her ass inward for deeper penetration as I rocked my pelvis upward on her down strokes. Her body trembled with pleasure as my dick took deeper plunges into her pussy.

My nipples began to throb with excitement as our moans grew louder on my down strokes. I allowed my throbbing nipples to rub up and down his sweaty chest as I continued to ride his dick.

She sat straight up and leaned herself back placing her hands on my knees for support. I touched her pussy lips and played with her clit. I enjoyed the hot juices flowing from her pussy as she rode my dick.

My body exploded with pleasure as his fingers slid along the sides of my pussy playing with my clit.

"Baby get on your knees it's time for me to take control of this ride," he whispered.

"Ok," I said.

I got on my hands and knees with my ass in the air as he held on to my waist and plunged his dick inside of my wet pussy. I moaned out as my body trembled from his deep slow strokes. The sweat from his body dripped on my back as he leaned in and fondled my breasts while we both enjoyed his ride.

I placed my hands on her back and motioned for her to lower her arms. This position allowed my dick deeper penetration into her pussy. My strokes became a little faster as my hands softly spank her across the ass.

I rested my elbows on the bed. I felt his balls slapping up against the lips of my pussy with each deep thrust of his dick. My legs and arms began to tremble as my body prepares to explode with excitement.

My strokes became even faster as her pussy vibrated during her orgasm. I took one last deep stroke inside her pussy. I enjoyed the throbbing feeling from my dick along the walls of her tight pussy as I came inside her.

We curled up in each other arms and shared several short sweet kisses. This was one of those moments when his kisses expressed nothing but love. He pulled the blanket up over our sweaty bodies and I dosed off with my head on his chest.

That next morning when I woke up, I noticed that his neck was covered with passion marks. I jumped up and looked in the mirror. There were passion marks covering my entire neck as well. The only thing that went through my mind was how the hell I will explain this to my father!

The skin on my neck is slightly sore from the bruises. I went to the kitchen and got some ice to wrap in a towel. I did not want to wake him so I stood in the bathroom mirror to see if the ice would make a difference. I was in there for about ten minutes before he woke up and came in the bathroom.

"What's with the towel on your neck?" he asked.

"It's filled with ice," I answered.

"What's the ice for?" he asked me.

I turned around and removed the towel. His eyes looked surprise. "Damn. I did that?" he asked laughing as he touched my neck.

"Yes. And it looks just like yours," I smiling.

"For real?" he asked looking in the mirror.

I started laughing as he turned to face the mirror. He touched his neck and said, "It was truly worth it."

"I can't walk into the house like this. My father is going

to kill me, besides that he would know that I lied about babysitting overnight. I need to stop at a store to pick up a couple of turtlenecks to keep my father from seeing the passion marks," I stated.

"So you need some turtlenecks to hide my love marks?" he asked.

"If I don't, my father and his bitch will raise hell!" I answered.

"Fuck them. You don't have to go home," he replied.

"You better watch what you are saying. One day I might take you up on that offer," I responded.

We stopped to grab breakfast at IHOP on Jefferson Avenue before heading out to Eastland Mall in Harper Woods. We ran into Macy's Department Store. I picked out several turtlenecks in different colors.

"Is that all you want?" Robert asked.

"Yes. I got exactly what I came for," I answered.

Before I could get my money out my wallet, he pulled out a large stack of money with a rubber band around it and paid for them.

"Thanks sweetheart. You did not have to pay for them," I replied.

"You're welcome. Do you want anything else before we leave the mall?" he questioned.

"No," I answered. "Are you sure?" he asked.

"I am sure," replied.

Chapter 27

The cold February morning started perfect. It is a Saturday night, the start of winter break at school, and my father believes that I'm spending the break over Lisa's house for my big eighteenth birthday. I have been looking forward for this day. Hell yea, I am legally an adult. It's only a couple of months left before graduation.

Robert is taking me to my first actual adult nightclub. His boy that owns the club is also going to let Leslie, Baron, Floyd, and Brandy in. After work, I'm getting my hair and nails done then heading over to Robert's. I'm going to wear the hot black sexy outfit he gave me last week.

I had just walked through Robert's front door when my cell phone started ringing. It was Baron's sister calling.

"Selena I have some bad news. My mother just got back from identifying Baron's body at the city morgue," she said.

"Can you tell your brother to stop playing and to call when he's on his way," I replied.

"This is not a joke," she responded.

"I do not have time for this. Tell Baron to call me when he is finished playing games. I will talk to you later," I said as I hung up the phone and called Leslie.

"Leslie, have you talked to Baron today?" I asked.

"I talked to him this morning. He was over his cousin's house. Is everything ok?" Leslie answered with a question.

"His sister called playing on the phone. She said he was dead," I answered.

"Are you serious?" Leslie responded.

"She sounded too damn calm for it to be true. I would have never stooped to this level to play a nasty joke like this," I answered.

"Let me call you back," Leslie replied.

The few minutes that it took Leslie to call back felt like hours had passed. "Hello," I said as I answered the telephone. All I heard on the other end was crying and at that moment, I knew it was true.

"His mother confirmed that he was dead. I'm on my way over to his house. Are you coming?" Leslie asked.

"Robert will be home shortly. I'm going to wait for him," I answered.

I hung up the phone and started yelling as I fell to my knees. "Why God? Why? Why God, why Baron?" I asked praying with tears.

I lost a lot of friends, but the hurt of losing one of my best friends was worst then I could ever imagine. It felt like a piece of my heart had been ripped out of my chest. I have just lost a person that I loved like a brother.

I blocked out the ringing from my cell phone and the house. I'm not in the mood to talk to anyone. I have been crying off and on for the last hour before Robert made it home.

"I'm home my Birthday girl," Robert called out.

Instead of answering him, I busted out crying. Robert walked over and sat on the couch.

"What's wrong?" he asked.

"Baron is dead," I answered.

"What are you talking about? I have not heard anything about that," he said.

"It happened over to his cousin's house in Detroit," I answered.

"Who told you?" he asked.

"His sister," I replied.

"Why didn't you call me?" he questioned.

"I don't know. I need to go over his mother's house," I answered.

We did not stay over the house much longer after hearing the senseless reason why Baron's died. By the time we made it back to Robert's place, my eyes were red, puffy, and burning. The pounding in my head was so bad that the only thing I wanted to do was take something for my headache and go to bed. I never imagined that I would be spending my eighteenth birthday crying. That shit fucked up my entire winter vacation school.

Earlier that afternoon Baron and two other boys were hanging over his cousin's house on the East side of Detroit. They were in the living room drinking beer and talking about the neighborhood girls. His cousin started talking shit about a girl that lived down the block.

"That stupid bitch would suck anybody dick," his cousin said laughing.

"I remember when you claimed to be in love with that hoe," one of the boys said jokingly.

"I only pretended so I could hit it," his cousin replied with a slight smile on his face.

"Man I wasn't going to say nothing! The hoe sucked my dick a couple of times before you started kicking it with her," Baron revealed.

“Why the fuck didn’t you tell me?” his cousin asked with bass added to his tone.

“Hell, when I found out you were messing around with that hoe you claimed to be in love. I did not want to hurt your feelings,” Baron answered with the look of surprise on his face.

“You’re supposed to be my motherfucking cousin. Your bitch ass is sitting up in my fucking house and smiling in my face knowing you fucked my bitch,” his cousin hotly shouted.

“What is your fucking problem? You knew she was a hoe. You can’t turn a hoe into a girlfriend,” Baron yelled back at his cousin.

“Ain’t that a bitch,” his cousin replied.

“You want to beef over a trick bitch?” Baron asked throwing his hands in the air.

“Who do you think you are calling my girl a trick bitch?” his cousin asked throwing his hands in the air.

“That trick ass hoe,” Baron yelled as he stared his cousin down.

His cousin stood up, picked a gun up off the table and BANG. Blood splattered all over the wall and ceiling as the bullet tore through the side of Baron’s head. Baron’s lifeless body slumped over and fell to the floor. The other boys started screaming at the sight of Baron’s body lying on the living room floor in a pool of blood. His cousin stood in shock with splatters of blood on him.

Chapter 28

I hated that my father worked afternoons, because that bitch Rita always start shit when he was gone. The last couple of months the tension at home has escalated between us. I cannot wait until graduation so I can move the fuck out this house.

I blew my top the day that bitch suggested that I should share my bedroom with her twelve-year-old daughter. Like a motherfucking fool, my father agreed. His bitch ass actually removed the lock off my bedroom door and moved her damn daughter's shit in my room. My father is letting that bitch run the house. Hell, I had a cure. I openly spent more time over to Robert's house.

"Selena can you go downstairs and talk on the phone so my daughter can fall asleep?" Rita tried ordering.

"This is my room!" I responded angrily.

"Damn. You always want to make things difficult," she replied.

"No. You should not have moved her ass into my bedroom in the first place," I responded rolling my eyes.

"It wasn't fair that she had to sleep in that extremely little room," she replied shaking her finger at me.

"Hell that was not my fault. It was unfair for you and your kids to move into my mother's house," I responded.

"I'll be glad when you get off that same old shit. You need to get over it. So find some way to you deal with it, because I'm not going anywhere," she replied.

“I don’t have to put up with this shit”, I responded.

“Where do you think you going on a school night?” she asked grabbing my arm.

“Don’t worry about where I’m going”, I answered pulling away.

“I know you’re not going over that thug’s house”, she replied.

“If I am what business is it of yours?” I responded with a cold look in my eyes.

“You better be back before your father gets home,” she instructed me.

“Fuck you!” I said as I walked out the front door.

The moment I walked out the door was the beginning to the end. I did not return home until the next day after school. It wasn’t surprising to see that my father stayed home from work.

“Selena what the hell is your problem?” my father asked with an attitude.

“You know what my problem is,” I answered rolling my head.

“That is still no excuse for your actions. Staying out all night! Not going to school! I asked you to stop driving around in that thug’s cars! You are not fucking grown!” my father yelled.

“For your information I did go to school. I hate being here with that bitch!” I responded.

“Watch your fucking language! This is my house!” my father said.

“Don’t worry, I won’t be here much longer,” I replied.

“What do you mean by that?” my father asked.

"I can't live like this. You got your new family so why are you concerned about me?" I asked.

"It's not like that. Rita has tried her best to get along with you, but you refuse to give her a chance," my father answered.

"You can believe that shit if you want. She moved in with us and want to completely change everything to her life style," I replied.

"You don't want to make this easy?" my father asked.

"Daddy, face it we will never be that big happy family that you see in the movies. I don't like Rita and I know that she doesn't like me," I replied.

"Where is all this anger coming from?" my father asked.

"I thought I could deal with this situation until after graduation. The day that you moved her daughter in my room was the last straw. I lost the only spot in the house that I could call my own. I give up on this shit!" I answered.

"So you plan on dropping out of school and hanging with that loser?" my father questioned.

"It's funny how it's ok for you call Robert names but it's not ok for me to say anything about your loser," I answered.

"This needs to stop!" my father replied.

"I feel the same way. I was going to wait until after graduation, but I think it would be the best for everyone if I make my move a lot sooner," I responded.

"You're move! I know you're not talking about moving in with Robert?" my father asked.

"I am eighteen. Legally I'm grown," I answered smacking my lips.

"Was this all his idea?" my father questioned.

"No. I've been contemplating this for some time. I

thought it would be best for me to wait until graduation, but I'm not happy here," I answered.

"Can we talk about this?" my father asked.

"There's not much to talk about. I should be completely out of here by the end of the month," I answered walking away.

By the end of the month, I officially moved out of my father's house. Our first official night as roommates Robert has a meeting with his boys. I'm staying home to rearrange his closets and drawers to make room for my remaining unpacked items. While I was cleaning out the closet in the master bedroom, I found several guns, two safes bolted to the floor, and his hidden stash of porno movies.

As I began to incorporate his porno movies with the movies on his dresser, I came up with the greatest idea for an additional birthday gift for him. This gift is going to be a surprise, in addition to the set of rims and tires he's expecting.

That next morning he noticed that his collection of porno movies is sitting on the dresser. He stood there puzzled not knowing if he should say something about them.

"I see you found my DVDs," Robert commented.

"I don't know why you had them on the closet floor," I replied.

"You're not mad?" he asked.

"Why would I be mad? I knew you were a freak when I met you," I said.

Robert realized it was best to leave well enough alone so he dropped the subject.

The morning of Robert's birthday, I let him sleep in. I was up getting ready for school when he woke up.

"Good morning Birthday Boy," I said giving him a kiss on his forehead.

"Good morning! Is that all you have for me?" he asked.

"Oh, here's your card," I answered tossing a card to him.

"Is that it? I thought you were getting back in the bed to give me my birthday gift," he replied.

"Catch up with me after school. By the way I need you to make a run for me around ten this morning," I responded.

"It can't wait until you get out of school?" he asked a little irritated.

"No. I have exams and it has to be done this morning," I answered.

"I have a full day. I have some business to take care of this morning with Gator," Robert replied.

"Just read your card," I said.

When he opened the card, a receipt fell out.

"You bought me tires and rims? How did you know I wanted them?" he asked.

"You were a little too obvious," I answered.

"What would make you say that?" he replied.

"I found all twelve copies of the quote you left around the house," I answered.

"When are you getting them put on?" he asked.

"I'm not. That is the ten o'clock appointment Gator is talking about," I answered kissing him on the forehead again.

"Thanks baby. You have a good day and I will see you later," he replied as I walked out the door.

I want to give him a birthday surprise he would never forget, so I went shopping after finishing my last final exam. I brought a movie camera for him and sexy lingerie set from Victoria's Secrets for me. While he was still out taking care of business, I was able to make the bedroom a romantic den. I placed the video camera on the dresser surrounded by bottles of perfume and cologne and scattered scented candles. Then I placed edible green apple flavored massage oil, a bowl of cut fruit, and a chilled bottle of champagne on the nightstand. I put in one of his freak movies in the DVD player.

I rubbed on one of my scented body lotions that he loves. I slipped into my new royal blue two-piece lingerie set and a pair of heels. When I heard him coming in the front door I turned on the video camera, started the DVD player, and stood in the bedroom doorway.

"Wow, that's my favorite color and you look damn good in it!" he said with a big smile on his face.

"Tonight it is all about the birthday boy. I plan to focus all my attention on fulfilling your sexually desires. Will you allow me to please you," I asked in a sexy tone.

"Now that's what I am talking about," he said kicking his shoes off getting comfortable.

We sipped on champagne while I fed him fruit. I let his hands explore my body as I slowly undressed myself with the freak movie in the background.

"There is nothing quite as stimulating and sensual as a silky full-body massage. I would love to give my Birthday boy full body massage," I told him.

"I give you permission to sexually take full advantage of me," he said with a smile.

I leisurely undressed him making sure that my hands caressed his well built body.

"Lie on your stomach and let me work my magic on you while you enjoy your movie," I instructed him.

I began by pouring oil in my hands to massage the back of his calves and legs. I climbed into the bed and poured oil on the back of his thighs and worked my way up to his perfectly shaped ass. I poured a line of massage oil up his spine of his back and slowly licked it off. I poured more oil up and down his back. I took my time and used my entire hands to make contact with his body. Using slow, steady, and smooth circular movements I worked my way up his back. I gave him short sucking kisses on his entire back, while enjoying the green apple edible massage oil.

He turned over on his back and I began to massage his feet. After working my way up both of his legs I intentionally skipped his entire private area. I poured oil in the crease of his six-pack. I started on his stomach. Once again, I took my time and used my hands to make contact with his body. Using slow, steady, and smooth circular movements I worked my way up his chest. My tongue licked its way up the creases of his six-pack. I sucked on and around his nipples as I massaged up and down his arms and hands.

While I lay on my back and she is straddled over me, giving me the opportunity to view her sexy naked body. She started talking dirty to me while she massaged oil on her breasts with one hand and played with her pussy with the other. "Damn this is a sight to see," he thought to himself.

"You make me so hot. I'd love to feel your dick inside of my pussy," I whispered.

"I love to have my dick up in your hot wet pussy," he whispered.

"My pussy is molded to your dick only," I cooed to him.

"That's right. Your pussy is mines and only mines," he agreed.

I stuck a finger into my wet pussy and then allowed him to suck my finger.

"My pussy is wet for you," I whispered.

I used the other hand to take his dick and rub it against my moist pussy lips and clit. I teased the head of his dick by sliding it back and forth across the opening of my pussy. I inserted just the tip of his dick inside my pussy then I took it out. I slid half of his dick gently and slowly inside my pussy then pulled it out again. I repeated that several times until I could not take it anymore.

"Please, let me fuck you?" I begged.

"Go ahead and fuck the hell out of me!" he urged me.

She lowered herself on me. Her pussy gladly accepted my dick. I had a full view of her sexy body. She grinded her pelvis around and around, back and forth with slow rhythm strokes. She gave me an extra treat by letting me watch her play with her nipples as she increased her speed and rode me like a horse. I moaned with excitement enjoying the race.

I leaned forward and rested my hands on the bed so Robert could suck on my breasts as I slowed my pace and continued to ride him. Up and down, around and around, side to side I moved my pelvis while he sucked on my breasts.

Without disconnecting, I rolled her into the missionary position. She squeezed and massaged my breasts as her hands moved in a circular motion. She raised her head up and sucked on my nipples when I slowed my strokes.

Robert's warm sweat dripping from his body aroused me more. To give him a deeper penetration I opened my legs wider, lifted them up, wrapping them around his waist. My hips and pelvis rotated in a circular motion complimenting his slow down strokes.

She got on her knees and I rode her doggy style. I know she's enjoying my balls slapping against her clit every time my dick thrust in her pussy. My thrusting became wilder when I grabbed and squeezed her sensitive hanging nipples.

"Mmmmmmm. That's it, fuck me like there is no tomorrow!" I yelled out.

"You love having this dick all up in your wet pussy?" he asked fucking me harder.

"Yes I do. I dream about your dick being up in my pussy. Mmmmmmmm," I moaned.

He turned me on my back and draped one of my legs over his shoulder while the other leg rested along his thigh.

"Whose pussy is this?" he asked.

"Baby, it's all yours," I assured.

"Damn your pussy is hot and wet!" he replied.

"It's always hot and wet for your dick," I commented.

I felt like a lusty conquering hero, spreading open the legs of my sweet maiden that simply love being taken by me. She thrust her hips to meet my every stroke. Her legs shook uncontrollably as her body came to a full climax when she felt my dick explode.

We enjoyed some lovely open-mouthed kisses. We paused for a while with our mouths still open and simply breathed each other's breath.

"This is a birthday I will never forget," he moaned with exhaust.

"You can watch that moment over and over again," I said.

"What do you mean by that?" he asked.

"Look," I said pointing.

I pointed to the video camera sitting on the dresser. He noticed that the red camera light was on.

"Where did that come from? When did you cut it on?" he asked.

"I cut it on just before you came through the front door. I wanted to give you something we both could enjoy," I told him.

"I would have never expected this from you," he said.

Chapter 29

In the blink of an eye, it's time for prom. I'm wearing a halter style backless ice blue form fitted short sequin dress with custom-made 4-inch ice blue sequin stilettos. Robert is wearing a white tuxedo, ice blue accessories, ice blue big block alligator shoes, and a white hat with ice blue trimming.

"Babe I know this is not traditional for proms but I wanted to give you something that you could look at anytime and remember this night," Robert explained. Instead of giving a corsage flower, I presented her with a piece of jewelry.

"They are beautiful. What kind of link is this?" I asked.

"I had matching custom made platinum bracelets with my own personal design of the infinity sign of love. My mother once told me that everybody has a soul mate and you are mine. This Infinity design is a symbol to express that my love for you will last beyond our life time," he recited.

Like a female, I cried happy tears. "That is the sweetest thing. I will love you in this life and my next life," I cried.

"I'm glad to hear that, but you need to stop that crying. I paid too much for you to have your make-up done professionally for you to mess it up," he teased.

"You always know how to blow a beautiful moment," I replied.

The prom is downtown Detroit in a banquet room inside of Cobo Hall. We stayed long enough to take pictures, get a few dances in, and to make sure everyone saw us. After leaving the prom, we stopped at Bouzouki Restaurant and

Lounge so Robert can meet with a few of his business acquaintances.

Once we entered through the big wooden doors off Lafayette Avenue the coat checkroom is the only thing that could be seen. On the other side of the wall is a bar and an elevated dance floor with tables and chairs around it. It felt strange when I realized that we had just walked into a strip club. The partially dressed women walking around and naked women on the stage was a dead giveaway.

Robert's friends are sitting at a table in front of the stage. Even though there are extra seats, he signaled for me to sit on his lap. This must be his way of letting the other men know that I'm his and off limits. Robert and his friends talked while I observed the full atmosphere of the club.

Men were there for pleasure as well as business. What amazed me was to see how many females are in the strip club as customers. Some are here for their own pleasure and then there are others like me, just hanging out with their man.

The dancers were rotating from dancing on the stage to entertaining customers on the floor. There seems to always be three to four women on the dance floor at all times. I noticed that the dancers and customers were disappearing into an area on the other side of the room. The partial wall and extremely high back from huge chairs concealed the view of that area. Robert informed me the area is for customers that pay extra for private lap dances.

"I can give you both a lap dance," a dancer said with a smile as she walked over to our table.

"Not tonight," Robert responded.

"Then I can give your lady a lap dance?" the dancer asked.

"Nope," I answered quickly.

"You have the prettiest legs I have ever seen," the dancer commented as she walked off.

"She was hitting on you," he said laughing.

"That's gross," I replied.

"You would be surprised at how many of them prefer women. That is why I had you sit on my lap," he stated.

"I thought you wanted me to sit on your lap as a sign to all the men that I was with you," I replied.

"No. It was a sign to all the lesbians that you are with me," he explained.

After leaving the strip club, we went to Captain's Bar and Grill. There was a long line of people waiting to get in. It was if we were celebrities. We walked straight up to head of the line. Robert gave the security guard a handshake. The guard opened the rope to let us in and the cashier greeted us as we walked through without paying.

His friends already had two bottles of champagne chilling at the table. The entire night we had endless bottles of champagne, rounds of drinks, and plates of food. I could only imagine what the bill came to. We partied like rock stars.

When we arrived at home, the champagne already has me feeling horny. I want to jump his bones the moment we walk through the door, but I would like it to be different this time. I will give him a show that he will never forget.

When we got home, I made him sit on the couch with a chilled bottle of champagne. I put in a romantic mixed CD, cut off the lights, and lit candles to give my body a soft glow.

"Baby, I'm going to give you a private striptease show. I might not be as good as the women at the strip club, but I will not leave you disappointed," I promised.

"I was hoping the prom freak would come out," he said smiling from ear to ear.

"Shhhhh. Don't talk just sit back and enjoy," I told him.

I moved to the beat of the music as I slowly and seductively slid my gown down my body. I briefly held the dress in front me before dropping it to the floor.

Damn she is a gorgeous sight! All my baby has on is a strapless bra, matching thong, 4-inch stilettos, earrings, and the infinity bracelet I gave her.

I slowly moved to the beat of the music while sensually caressing my breasts and ass. I stood in front of him and put one foot on his leg. He watched me move to the flow of the music as I rubbed the crotch of my thong. I slapped his hand, as it was moving towards my pussy.

"No. You are only allowed to watch," I told him.

"Come on baby let me get a little touch," he pleaded.

"I promise you will get your chance," I said.

I then proceeded to give him a lap dance. I straddle my legs over his legs and took I swig of the champagne then handed him the bottle. I stared in his beautiful eyes as I rotated my pelvis over his dick. I brushed my nipples against his chest with my body strokes as I rotated my pelvis.

She definitely is not like the strippers from the club, but I am enjoying her effort. My baby is trying her best for me. I appreciate her attempt at a lap dance.

I got off his lap and turned around with my back towards him. Then I slightly bent myself over and tooted my ass in the air. I gyrated my ass over his dick. I let him watch as I shook my ass and slid my thong down my legs. I turned to face him so he could observe me unsnapping my bra and slowly glide my hands over my nipples while removing my bra. After pulling a chair from the dining room table to use as a prop I sat on the end of the chair, leaned against the backrest, and arched my back.

I observed as she used one hand to masturbate and the other hand to fondle her breasts. Watching her pleasing herself is an ultimate turn on!

I could tell he was excited. He unzipped his pants and pulled his dick out. I continued to please myself as I watched one of his hands moved up and down the shaft of his dick. He was jacking off as he kept his eyes on me playing with myself. His dick was fully erect as my body writhed, shivered, and then finally exploded into an orgasm.

She walked over to the couch and helped me out of my pants and boxers. With her back to me she bent over placing the palms of her hands on the floor. I guided my dick into her pussy. I held on to her waist and pulled her body towards me on my upswings.

He had a tight grip on my waist as I swung my body to the rhythm of his stroked. I enjoyed the pleasure of his big dick in my pussy.

I sat back on the couch. She turned around and spread her legs around my thighs with her knees placed on the couch. I took a drink of champagne and drizzled a small amount of it down her breasts. I grabbed her breasts and took my time to lick and suck the champagne off her lovely breasts.

Damn his tender sucking on my breasts is making me hot. I want him now. I slowly descended my hot juicy pussy onto his waiting dick. I held on to his arms and proceeded to bump and grind as he sucked and nibbled on my breasts.

I wrapped my arms around her back and pressed her chest against mine while she continued to rotate her hips with her bump and grind. I enjoyed her nipples against my chest.

My nipples became highly sensitive with pleasure as they rubbed up against the soft hair on his chest. I engaged him in a passionate wet kiss as I continued to gyrate my pussy on his dick. He scooted us to the edge of the couch and laid me on the floor with our bodies connected.

I continued to fuck her in the missionary position. My dick's slow deep thrusting strokes felt wonderful inside of her hot wet pussy.

I thrust my pelvis up against him to allow his dick and balls to stimulate my entire vaginal area. I draped one leg over his shoulder and laid the other one flat on the floor. I held on to his arms as his strokes grew faster. We were both moaning from sexual pleasure.

I draped her other leg over my shoulder so my dick could gain a deeper penetration into her pussy. I slowed my strokes down to enjoy the deeper gratification.

"Whose pussy is this?" he asked.

"It's yours and only yours," I moaned.

"You want more of this dick?" he demanded to know.

"Yes, give it to me. Deeper. Harder," I begged.

"Dame this pussy is hot and extremely wet. I love feeling it dripping on my dick!" he moaned.

"That's because this pussy belongs to you and it love to feel your dick all up in it," I moaned.

"That's right, this is my pussy, and I love to be all up in it," he said panting.

"That's it baby," I urged him on.

We rolled over. With Robert on his back and me on my knees I further lowered myself so my pussy could completely devour his dick. Sitting straight up afforded his dick a deep penetration and gave him a full view of my body. I rotated my pussy around and around, back and forth. I concentrated on the muscles in my pussy. My muscles squeezed, pushed, pulled, and vibrated madly on his dick.

"Damn baby that feels good as hell!" he moaned out.

"It does feel good as hell," I cooed to him.

"I'm about to come," he warned.

"Fill me up with your juice," I told him.

My strokes became quicker as my dick grew thicker and stiffer. The muscles of her pussy tightened up around my dick as she exploded into an orgasm. I could no longer hold on. I erupted inside of her pussy.

My body exploded into an earth shattering orgasm as I felt the throbbing of his dick preparing to explode in my pussy. We laid there on the floor kissing. He snatched the blanket off the couch and we fell asleep on the floor wrapped up in each other's arms.

Chapter 30

If it wasn't for my little brothers, my father would never see my ass. His girlfriend Rita is the reason why I hate stopping by the house. Just the sight of that bitch makes my skin crawl. She's always starting shit then drags my father in the middle. I'm glad that my brothers are sitting on the porch. Maybe I can spend some time with them before that bitch knows I'm here.

"Selena!" They both yelled as I walked on the porch with four bags of summer clothing that I bought for them.

"Come show me some love," I said.

"I miss you," Milton said.

"I miss you more," Dwayne said.

"No he didn't," Milton said.

"Yes I did," Dwayne said.

"So you'll going to fight instead of talking to me?" I asked.

"No," they both said.

"What have y'all been up to?" I asked.

"Nothing we just play all the time," Dwayne explained.

"Were the other kids?" I inquired.

"They are over their fathers' house," Milton replied.

"Did you bring us anything?" Dwayne asked with excitement.

"You know I did. You want to see?" I asked teasingly.

"It looks like nothing but clothes," Milton pouted.

"It's not Christmas yet. Summer just started and you both need summer clothes and gym shoes," I told them.

"I don't ever want summer to end," Dwayne whimpered.

It was less than ten minutes when that bitch came out the front door. She opened her big ass mouth and started talking shit.

"You only have clothes for Milton and Dwayne?" Rita asked with an attitude.

"Yea, and what business is it too yours?" I commented.

"They are not the only kids living here," she said being snide.

"They are the only ones related to me," I replied.

"That is beside the point. It is not fair that my children have to see you buying all that expensive shit for Milton and Dwayne," she said being snooty.

"Hell they have a mother and a father that should buy their stuff," I responded with a sharp tone.

"I don't know who the fuck you think you talking to like that," she shouted.

"I'm talking to you. You're nothing but a blood sucking welfare bitch!" I responded.

"Jimmy, you need to come and talk to your smart mouth daughter. I am not going to tolerate her coming to our home talking to me any way she wants to," she called to my father.

"Your home? Bitch this is my mother's house. You will never be able to fit in her shoes!" I snapped.

"What is going on?" my father asked.

"You need to tell Rita that she doesn't even have to speak to me. I came by to drop off some stuff for the boys," I told him.

"Jimmy the problem is we are trying to build a family with the kids and by Selena only bringing things over for Dwayne and Milton it's causes problems for my kids," Rita explained.

"Daddy, she just said the key word her kids. Milton and Dwayne are my brothers," I replied.

"Sorry, Selena she is right about it's causing problems with the kids. She is here taking care of your brothers while you are running around with that good for nothing Robert," my father commented.

"It's not my fault that her broke ass baby daddies don't do anything for her kids," I stated.

"That's was not nice to say. You need to apologize," my father pleaded.

"She needs to worry about her own kids and stop worrying about what the fuck I'm doing," I replied.

I sat their clothes in the living room and got the hell out of there. Milton and Dwayne came running up to the car.

"Why are you leaving so soon?" Dwayne asked.

"I have someone to see," I responded.

"Can I have some money for the ice cream truck?" Milton begged.

"Here, don't spend it all on the first ice cream truck. Remember you have to share with Dwayne," I instructed.

"Thank you," they both said.

"I will see you in a couple of days," I said.

Stopping by my father's house put me in the mood to deal with one other person. That bitch Cathy has lost her motherfucking mind! She had the nerves to offer Robert a trick for a hit!

I am mad as hell at that bitch for propositioning him with some shit like that and pissed the fuck off at Robert for not telling me. With Highland Park being so fucking small, it was only a matter of time before word got back to me. It's common knowledge that crack heads will trade sex for drugs. Out of all the drug dealers in the city, she had to ask my Robert! I cannot believe that trifling hoe would stoop to that level and do some crack head shit like that! That bitch has to be checked!

I rode down on her as she was coming out of the party store on Grand. I bet she was not expecting me to confront her ass about this shit.

"That shit you tried on Robert will not be tolerated! I don't care what the fuck you are doing to yourself but you need to leave what's mine alone!" I snapped.

"What the hell are you talking about?" Cathy asked.

"That crack head shit! Thinking Robert would give you a hit for a trick," I said.

"That was not personal, it was just business," she casually stated.

"This is personal and Robert is my business!" I snarled.

"You are becoming as mean as that motherfucker you living with," she claimed.

"So fucking what if I am. Don't make me have your ass banded from all of his spots," I threatened.

"Like, he will turn down my money," she cracked.

"Bitch if you are out there offering your ass for drugs you don't have shit. Don't let us have this conversation again," I warned.

I made sure she saw that I'm packing a gun as I got back in the car. Now Robert got some explaining to do. I'll waited for him to come home before confronting him about not telling me about that crack head hoe.

"Robert we need to talk," I said angrily.

"What's wrong?" he asked.

"Why didn't you tell me that bitch Cathy tried to give you a trick for a hit?" I questioned.

"Because, it wasn't a big ass deal. What you don't trust me or something? You think I would sleep with a crack head bitch?" he asked being irritated.

"I trust you. I'm mad I had to hear about it in the street," I pouted.

"You want me to tell you every time a crack head bitch offers me a trick for a hit?" he complained.

"No. I would like to know about those fake ass ones that are smiling in my face," I said.

"I handled that situation and that is all that should matter," he said.

"You handling the situation is not the problem. If that bitch was bold enough to ask you for sex and then smile in my face, no telling what else she is capable of doing. It would help to know who I need to keep a closer eye on," I explained.

"Did you say something to her?" he asked.

"You know I did," I responded.

"What the hell did it accomplish?" he inquired.

"It made her aware that I know how foul she is and I am not the one she wants to fuck with," I replied.

Robert broke out laughing.

"What's so funny?" I asked.

"You, trying to act like a gangster," he laughed.

"Forget you. You better not let it happen again. This better be the last time we need to discuss some shit like this," I added rolling my eyes.

"Now that you are finished talking shit, I do have a surprise for you," he said.

"Ok, what is it?" I requested.

"Next week we're flying out to Miami," he said smiling.

"That sounds fun. Is anybody else going with us?" I asked.

"No, it's just the two of us. It was a hectic year and I thought it would be nice to get away," he said.

"You are truly a sweetheart," I said hugging him.

This past year was hectic and this trip to Miami is just what we need. Robert worked his ass off. He received his GED certificate and took an evening class at Wayne County Community College Downtown Campus during the winter semester. I lost Barron and several other classmates. I moved out my father's house. After graduation the branch manager was so impressed with my speed and accuracy that my senior co-op job turned into a permanent part-time position.

Our plan landed at the Miami International Airport south terminal just before noon. The towering windows with Florida themed artwork that ran along the escalators and stairs walls is a wonderful welcome sign to Miami. We grabbed our luggage, rented a car, and drove straight to the Trump International Beach Resort. The view of the Atlantic Ocean from our private balcony was breathtaking.

"It would be nice if this could be a cell phone free

vacation," I proposed.

"What do you mean by that?" he asked.

"Maybe we can cut our phones off. This way no one can disturb us," I suggested.

"I guess they can do without me for a couple of days," he agreed.

"You promise?" I begged.

"Yea, I can do that for you. You know what that means?" he insinuated.

"No. What?" I inquired.

"You are stuck entertaining me," he insisted.

"That won't be hard," I assured.

Ring! Ring! Ring! Ring! Ring! Damn his phone started ringing before he could turn it off.

"That's Gator calling," Robert mentioned.

"Don't answer," I pleaded.

Ring! Ring! Ring ! Ring! Ring! Damn there it goes again.

"That's Dean calling," he said.

"You promised," I pointed out.

Ring! Ring! Ring! Ring! Ring! What the fuck.

"That's Dean again," he repeated.

"Come on. Don't answer your phone," I requested.

"I have to. It must be important," he stated.

I started unpacking our clothes, while he talks to Dean. The change in his tone and the look on his face said it all. Shit it must be bad news.

"Babe, I know how much you were looking for this trip,

but we need to get home immediately," he informed.

"Is everything ok?" I asked.

"No, something jumped off at one of the spots. It is imperative for us to catch the first flight home. I have to make it up to you later," he promised.

"You don't have to make it up to me. You needed this trip more than me," I responded supportively.

I repacked the luggage as he called to reschedule our return flight back to Detroit. He then called Dean back to give him our expected arrival time. While he was talking, I stood in front of him and undressed myself.

I unbuttoned his shirt to caress his chest and suck on his nipples. Then I slid the shirt sensuously off his back with both of my hands. I massaged his dick through his pants in preparation of undoing the zipper. After unzipping his pants, I slipped one hand in his boxers and fondled his dick and balls before sliding his pants off. I continued to fondle him through his underpants until his dick grew into a soft erection.

Damn she was making it hard for me to concentrate on my telephone conversation. I hung up the phone and lay across the bed.

I removed his footwear before going for his pants. I glided his boxers slowly down his thighs. I smiled as his dick emerged. It was just like unwrapping a very special package.

She stroked my dick lovingly with her hands while talking sexy about it as I anticipated the coming attraction.

"Baby I crave this beautiful dick. I love the way it feels inside my pussy. I would love to taste it," I hinted

"That would be nice," he advised

"I love to lick it," I requested.

"That would be even better," he encouraged.

I started licking the head of his dick as if it was a chocolate ice cream cone. I ran my tongue along and across his ridge then down the underside of his dick. I sucked on the head of his dick as I flicked my tongue over the top.

She kissed and nibbled her way down my dick and back up to the head of my dick. While holding the tip of my dick with one hand she pointed her tongue and flicked it over the ridge of my dick between the head and the shaft. She stroked the rest of my dick with her free hand.

I opened my mouth, covering my teeth with my lips, and then slid his dick slowly inside. As his dick rested on my tongue, I moved my head up and down smoothly and continuously. With his dick in my mouth, I sucked firmly while shaking my head at the same time.

When she shook her head, it gave me a nice tingly feeling. I ran my fingers through her hair.

I climbed on top for him in the 69 position. I sat my wet pussy over his face. I returned to sucking his dick

I ate her pussy out. I grabbed her ass and slid my tongue in and out of her pussy.

I put my hand around the base of his dick and move it up and down in rhythm with the movement of my mouth.

I licked and sucked on both sides of her pussy lips and clit.

My tongue moved in circles around and around his dick while it slid merrily up and down.

Occasionally I would suck the hot juices flowing out her pussy while inserting my finger inside.

Using one hand I sucked his dick like a piece of hard candy and used the other hand to caress his inner thighs and balls.

I lightly licked the inside of her pussy while blowing on it.

"I'm so hot for that big beautiful dick," I moaned.

"Let me fuck you!" he said with excitement.

"Put that gorgeous dick in my pussy and fuck me. My pussy is wet for you," I told him.

After he aroused me into having several small orgasms, I lay on my back and pressed my knees to my chest.

She was inviting my big stiff dick into her hot wet pussy.

I draped my arms around my knees and let him put his dick in. His strokes were extremely slow but deep. I draped my legs over his shoulders as his hard dick continued to stroke in and out of my pussy.

I lifted her legs up and opened them wide for deeper penetration. She bit her bottom lips as she moaned with excitement from each of my dick's deep strokes.

I wrapped my legs and arms around him as we rolled on to our sides. We were on our side in a face-to-face position. He lovingly stroked his dick in and out my pussy as I gazed into his beautiful eyes.

This position allowed her pussy to stimulate parts of my dick and scrotum that I have never felt before. I had her to get on her knees so I could tear that pussy up doggy style. I slowed my strokes allowing me to enjoy it longer.

His slow deep strokes were extremely gratifying inside of my pussy. I contracted the muscles of my pussy on his down strokes. My pussy was thrilled from each stroke of his dick. I lost count of my small orgasms. We fucked in several positions like there was no tomorrow.

I held on to her hips and increased the speed of my strokes as I felt her body tremble into a major explosion. Her explosion set me off. I held my dick in her pussy and busted a nut from the excitement.

We had just enough time to get something to eat at the airport before boarding the plane. Robert was in deep thoughts so he did not talk the entire flight back. His occasional touch of affection let me know that he was still aware of my presence. We made it back to Detroit a little after eight that evening. The entire ride from the airport Robert spent it on the phone.

"Baby, something jumped off in Highland Park," he mentioned the last few minutes of our ride.

"Was anybody hurt?" I asked.

"No. Some punks ripped the front door off the house on Pasadena," he replied.

"Did they get anything?" I inquired.

"I won't know until I get there," he claimed.

"You can drop me and the luggage off at the front door," I suggested.

"You don't mind taking the up luggage by yourself?" he begged.

"It's no problem," I claimed.

"Oh, yea thanks," he replied.

"Thanks for what?" I questioned.

"Your performance back at the hotel," he said smiling.

"I wanted us to leave Miami with at least one memory," I explained.

"That was definitely a treat I was not expecting from you. Where did you learn that from?" he inquired.

"I learned from watching your other hidden collection of porno movies. You look surprised," I added.

"How did you know about them?" he quizzed.

"Why would you think hiding them in a shoe box was a good idea?" I asked.

"I know you were not snooping around," he implied.

"No. I found it strange for a pair of your big block alligator shoes to be out of the box. My only intention was to put them up for you," I described with a smile.

"Well did you?" he responded.

"No, I didn't want you to know that I found your collection. I thought it was cute that you felt the need to hide your deep throat collection from me," I teased.

"I did not know you like watching porno," he said.

"They are very educational," I informed.

"When you get upstairs, you can put my shoes back in their shoe box," he requested.

"I'll think about it. Be safe and I love you," I responded with a kiss.

"I love you too. I'm not sure what time I will be in, but I will call you later," he claimed.

Chapter 31

We own a two family-flat brick home on Pasadena. The front and back lawns are always neatly maintained. In the backyard, a cement slab floor is the only remains of a garage. We strictly use the house for storing and separating kilos of cocaine. There is absolutely no drug selling done at that location.

Both units are equipped with elaborate security measures. Steel security gates and doors are on the outside of the front, back, and basement entrances. The basement glass bricks windows are covered with steel security bars. Both back porches were completely removed to detour anyone from gaining unauthorized entrance.

The downstairs apartment has a steal security gate on the inside of the front door and stairway that leads to the basement. Steel security bars are installed on the outside and on the inside of each window. The dusty faded blinds remain closed at all times. The rooms' dull yellow walls with dingy white trimmed floorboards compliments the matted brown carpet. There is not one piece of furniture in the unit. From the absence of sunlight and fresh air the unit has an old stale smell.

The upstairs apartment has steel security bars on the outside of each window. Steel security gates on the outside of the front patio door and outside the door that leads to the none-existing back patio. We also installed steel security doors inside the upstairs unit front stairway door and the stairway door that leads to the basement.

The walls and floorboards are painted in the same dull yellow paint as the downstairs unit. Large piles of dusk balls lurk in the corners of the stained beige carpet. The kitchen is the only room with furniture in it.

There is an old white scratched up gas stove that sits in one corner and an old scratched up brown refrigerator with missing door handles that sits in another corner. Four mismatch chairs surround a round wooden table draped with a sheet. The light fixture is missing the glass cover exposing the single light bulb. More than half of the wooden cabinet doors are swollen shut. Several layers of dirt hide the white floor tile. The blinds remain closed throughout the unit, but the occasional smoking of cigarettes and cigars overpower the stale air smell.

The narrow basement stairways are dark and have one single hanging ceiling light at the bottom of the stairs. The stairways reeks a damp moldy smell from the basement. Several old molded bookshelves are the only items in the dark damp basement. A small sliver of light from the hanging stairway light exposes a large hole in the brick wall that separated the units' basements.

By the time, I made it to Pasadena the security door was being replaced and Dean had a lead on the punks that yanked the security door off. Having them run down the situation and coming up with a plan on the best possible way to handle this are the only things left to do.

"What up Robert!" Shannon and Sean both called when Robert emerged through the front door.

"I should be the one asking what up," Robert throws back at them.

"Me, Jason, and Sean were in the kitchen preparing the stash for the day when some punk motherfuckers tried to stick up the place. They snatched the fucking door right off the hinges. I thought it was the police at first. All I heard was a loud crash, a bunch of loud banging at the front door, then footsteps coming up the front steps," Shannon rambled off with excitement in his voice.

"It was funny hearing them trying to kick in the upstairs door. I wish we had a video camera. I can only imagine the expressions on their motherfucking faces when they finally got the upstairs door open," Jason added.

"Surprise motherfucking bitches, another fucking steel security gate," Sean cracked slapping his hands together.

"I bet that shit caught them off guard. They tried to catch y'all with your pants down," Gator commented.

"Were y'all still upstairs when they finally got that door open?" Robert asked.

"Hell naw! We had begun operation evacuation the moment we heard the crashing noise from the security door being snatched off. We put all the product on the sheet and grabbed it. Sean unlocked the basement security gate and door. Me and Jason hauled ass down the basement stairs as Sean made sure that the security gate and the dead bolt on the basement door were relocked. Our asses were through the hole in the wall and up the downstairs unit basement stairs before they got the stairway door open. Sean peaked out the front window and yelled it was a stick-up," Shannon explained on.

"We rushed out the fucking back door. You should have seen us jumping to the ground with our motherfucking guns drawn. Sean stayed behind with his shit out ready to blast anybody that came around the back," Sean rambled on.

"Three punks were jumping in a truck when we made it out front," Jason explained.

"It sounds like a few of the bitches were on the porch waiting for the other motherfucker to pull the security door off," Gator assumed.

"They jumped in a black Ford 150 pickup truck. They sped off like a bunch of hoe ass bitches as I let out off a round!" Jason detailed.

"Y'all motherfuckers were acting like Boys in the Hood," Robert laughed.

"Naw. My ass was like Old Dog from Menace to Society," Sean said.

"That's was some real gangster shit," Shannon ragged.

"So, did anybody pop a cap in at least one of them niggas asses?" Robert questioned.

"I'm not sure but I tried to stop that motherfucking truck. Those scary ass motherfuckers were ducking like bitches with a dick up their ass. We did shot out the back window and gave the truck frame a new look. I could not believe that the punks drove down the street with the fucking steel security door dragging behind it," Sean commented.

"That fucking door had to make a hell of a lot of noise," Robert inquired.

"You could hear the steel door rattling against the ground as they hauled ass out of Highland Park," Shannon said with a slight giggle.

"Those bitch niggas had to catch a lot of fucking attention," Robert assumed.

"The truck did receive a lot of attention. You know it didn't take long before several of the neighbors help piece together the license plate number," Gator said.

"I gave the shit to my cousin Stephen. He ran the license plate number and fingerprints lifted from the stairway through the police computer system," Dean informed.

Stephen Glass like most of the Highland Park Police force is family, friends, and neighbors of the local drug dealers. Stephen was the youngest detective on the police force. For a fair price, he warned them about all scheduled drug raids on their spots and shut down any rival drug dealers that tried to set up shop in Highland Park.

The stick-up punks were from the Harper/Gratiot area on the Eastside of Detroit. Robert drove Shannon and Jason by the addresses Stephen gave them to see if they recognized the truck and any of the punks. The first three houses turned out to be drug spots. The fourth house had kids playing on the porch and the black pickup parked in the backyard. Even though the security door was no longer attached, they were able to positively identify it from the shot out windows and bullet holes.

We need to send a message that this level of disrespect will not be tolerated. Everything was going as planned and everyone in place. Around 4 a.m. in the morning, cocktails simultaneously went flying through the front windows of the three drug houses. Like clockwork, the punk in the fourth house came running out the minute he heard the news about the other houses going up in flames. Wearing a long black leather coat to hide his shotguns he rushed to the truck. He leaped into the truck throwing his guns behind his seat.

"BOOM!" The truck explodes into flames the moment he turned the key in the ignition. The sound from the blast could be heard several blocks over. The impact from the explosion shook surrounding homes waking up his family as well as several neighbors.

It was just like something right out of the movies. The bitch jumped out of the truck engulfed in flames. His girlfriend and kids were screaming and crying from an upstairs window as they watched him frantically run to the front yard.

They ran outside and stood on the porch screaming for help. Several neighbors rushed out of their homes with blankets to help put out his flames. The crowd yelled for him to drop to the ground. He collapsed in a dirt pile at the end of his driveway.

The neighbors threw blankets and kicked dirt on him. One neighbor ran up with a fire extinguisher. When one of the neighbors' pulled the blanket from his head the flesh peeled right off his face. It was a terrifying sight to see. His girlfriend passed out and several people including the children vomited. The police, fire department, and paramedics pulled up after neighbors put his flames out.

His hands were so severely burnt that they were unrecognizable as human body parts. The heat fried his leather jacket and gym shoes to his skin. The paramedics attended to him while the firefighters hosed the truck's flames. The smell of burning flesh lingered in the air as the ambulance disappeared down into the darkness of the night.

The next morning I was sitting on the front porch with Dean and Gator. We were planning to conduct business as usual until Stephen stopped by.

"Hey. I'm glad to see the three of you here," Stephen said as he walked up the walkway.

"What's going on Stephen?" Dean asked.

"The Detroit Police opened an investigation on three house fires and a truck explosion. One of the bastards gave up several people that may have wanted revenge. He claims that it may be retaliation from a botched home invasion at a drug house in Highland Park as one of the possible leads. A Detroit Police detective on the case called the station this morning asking if any reports of a home invasion were reported yesterday," Stephen replied.

"Did he find any reports?" Robert asked.

"No and he's not going to. My sergeant assigned me to work closely with the detectives on this case. I will definitely see to it that they won't find what they are looking for," Stephen explained with a sly smile as they all started laughing.

"Is everything cool?" Gator asked.

"I hate to do this but you will need to shut this spot down for a while," Stephen requested.

"How long are you talking about?" Dean asked.

"It might be for a few days up to a couple of weeks. I expect the detectives will request a search warrant within the next day or two. Clear all evidence of drug activity, the installation of the new door, and clean up as many fingerprints as feasible. Also make it easy as possible for them to get in this place with a search warrant," Stephen ordered.

"Thanks for giving us heads up. We will take care of that immediately," Dean assured.

With rubber gloves and help from several family members, we washed the wall down in both units, and moved what little furniture to the basement. We covered the hole in the basement wall with the old bookshelves that are down there. To make it easy to enter the apartment we removed the cylinders from all the steel security doors and unlocked the deadbolts from the inside doors. Lastly we removed the meters from both electrical boxes to ensure the electricity to both units would be off.

Later that week Stephen accompanied the detective on a search warrant at the Pasadena house. He assisted with interviewing the surrounding neighbors that lived on the block and in the area. With no luck, they were unable to find witnesses that may have witnessed the truck fleeing Highland Park.

The Detroit Detective ruled out the Highland Park lead. They were unable to find any evidence or witnesses that could corroborate the allegations of a botched robbery attempt. The investigation is still ongoing, but the Detroit Detectives are looking into a possible drug territory feud.

Chapter 32

Since Robert was pulling another late night, I met up with my friends at a hole in the wall club. LaUmo's Night Club was just outside of Highland Park on East Seven Mile Road and John R Street. Like every Saturday night it's jammed packed.

When I got there, Leslie was holding a table while Floyd and Brandy were out on the dance floor. I'm sitting at the table and talking with Leslie when this ugly guy walked up. And I mean ugly.

"Excuse me pretty would you like to dance?" the guy asked.

"No thanks," I responded.

"Would you mind if I sit down, so we can talk?" he asked.

"Yes, I do mind. I have a man," I answered.

"Your man doesn't have to know," he replied.

"What part of I don't want to talk you don't understand?" I asked in a mean tone.

"Ohhhhh……. You're one of those stuck up bitches! It's your loss," he said in a grim voice.

"Go tell that to someone who cares," I said in a sarcastic tone.

Just then, Floyd walked up.

"What the fuck is going on? Is everything over here ok?" Floyd said staring him up and down.

"You're her motherfucking man?" the guy asked.

"No. If needed, I can beat the shit out of you like her man would," Floyd threaten.

"That bitch is not worth me fucking you up. You have no idea who you are talking too," the guy warned.

"Fuck him! He's not worth the trouble," I insisted.

The little punk waddled away as we laughed. He was all of four feet tall and three feet wide. His stomach was overlapping his two seasons' old blue jeans. His teeth perfectly matched his brown skin. His size five polished gym shoes look like Tic-Tacs on his feet. What would make him think I would be interested in his funny looking ass any way?

I always like to leave before the club closes to avoid the fights in the parking lot. Leslie and I were making our last bathroom run before leaving. When we came out the bathroom the short funny looking punk from earlier was standing against the wall.

"Ugly bitch!" he yelled out as I walked pass,

"Fuck you!" I replied putting up my middle finger.

The next thing I knew he slapped the shit out of me. My only reaction was to pull the knife from my purse and stabbed him in the side. Leslie grabbed me by the arm just as I swung to stab him for a second time. Floyd snatched me up and rushed us out the club.

I still had the bloody knife in my hand when we reached my car. Floyd took the knife out my hand and wrapped it in a paper bag that is lying on the ground. Brandy and Leslie pushed me in the front passenger seat. Floyd jumped in the driver's seat and everybody else jumped in the back seat of the car. Leslie called Robert while we were on route to Floyd's house.

"Hello," Robert said as he answered his phone.

"Hey, this is Leslie. I think you should meet us over to Floyd's house ASAP," she demanded in a shaky voice.

"Is Selena ok?" Robert asked.

"Some motherfucker at LaUmo's slapped her and we will explain everything when you get there," she responded.

"Do not let her leave. I will be there in a minute," Robert said and hung-up.

When Robert pulled up, Jason, Sean, and Shannon were with him. I could barely hear anything from the ringing in my head. The side of my face was extremely sore. The full hand imprint on the side of my face made Robert mad as hell.

"Baby what happened?" Robert asked.

"I guess this punk was still mad about me turning him down," I replied.

"Do you know who he is?" Robert questioned.

"No. That was the first time I ever seen him," I responded.

"Floyd, can I talk to you outside?" Robert requested.

"No problem," Floyd said.

"What really happened?" Robert requested.

"I walked up to the table and this punk called Selena a stuck-up bitch. I was like what the fuck is going on? Then he asked if I'm her motherfucking man. I checked his ass. Then he walked away. Everything was cool until we were getting ready to leave. Selena and Leslie were coming out the bathroom when that same punk bitch made a sissy move and slapped her. Man, it all happen so fast. I got over to her just as Leslie stopped her from stabbing him a second time," Floyd explained.

"What happen to the guy?" Robert wanted to know.

"I have no idea. My only thought was to get Selena away from LaUmo's before the police showed up," Floyd stated.

"Good thinking. Where's the knife?" Robert questioned.

"It is in a brown bag on the backseat floor," Floyd informed.

"I will take care of the knife. But I need you to make sure she gets home safe," Robert ordered.

Leslie followed Floyd Downtown in his parents' car as he drove me home in my car. Floyd pulled into the parking garage and walked me to my apartment door. I took a Tylenol for the headache and went to bed.

Robert, Gator, Shannon, and Jason went up to LaUmo's to see if they could get some information. The crowd had thinned out after all the excitement and the police wrapped up their investigation. Robert was able to get the punk's full name. Jason realized the punk lived down the street from his grandmother. It wasn't hard to figure out which hospital his friends took him too. They made a trip down to Detroit Receiving Hospital. It's a popular spot for gunshot and stabbing injuries, regardless if they have insurance or not. Gator knew one of the security guards. The guard let them into the back area were the punk was lying in a hospital bed.

"You have the wrong room," the punk commented.

"No. We have the right room the problem is that you slapped the wrong female tonight," Jason insisted.

"So who are you?" the punk questioned.

"I am her man and I don't appreciate anyone putting their hands on her," Robert explained as he leaned over to the bed.

"So what the fuck are you trying to say?" the punk asked trying to man up.

"It would be wise for you to forget how she looks. I don't want to make a visit on Kentucky Street to have a talk with your family," Robert threatens.

The punk's heart started to race as he bitched up. "Tell her I am sorry. Man you never have to worry about me," the punk said nervously. The fact that complete strangers knew where his family lived scared the shit out of him.

The next morning I could still hear ringing in my head. The side of my face was sore and a little red.

"Good morning beautiful," Robert said.

"Good morning to you?" I replied.

"Don't worry about last night. Nobody has the right to hit you," he stated.

"I'm surprised at my reaction last night," I commented.

"Hell, I'm impressed at your reaction. How do you feel?" he questioned.

"The side of my face hurt and I still hear ringing in my head?" I admitted.

"Are you staying in today?" he asked.

"I planned to stay in until the ringing goes away?" I replied.

"I have to get out of here, so I will see you later," he said.

"I love you," I replied.

"I love you too," he responded.

I stayed in the house for a couple of days until the ringing in my head stopped and the soreness went away.

"How's my sick and shut in?" Robert asked when he came in.

"Forget you. I'm glad to be going to work tomorrow, because I think I have had enough of this in-house rest," I mentioned.

"Shit, you have had company all weekend so it's not like you missed much," he laughed.

At a blink of an eye, summer was nearing an end. Leslie and I met up at Brandy's house. She came back from visiting her aunt in Louisiana early this morning.

"Summer went by fast," Leslie said.

"With Robert taking that evening class I did nothing but work," I replied.

"At least you and Robert were able to see the hottest concerts. Babysitting is all I did," Leslie commented.

"What about the trip to Miami?" Brandy asked.

"Hell the airport was about the only thing we got the chance to see," I responded.

"What about that train ride to Niagara Falls?" Leslie questioned.

"We spent a couple of days in Canada. It was beautiful," I explained.

"I bet you'll spent most of the time in your room fucking," Brandy joked.

"No. We left so I could shop," I threw back at her.

Leslie and Brandy both laughed at Me.

"Brandy, how was it in Louisiana?" Leslie asked.

"I was bored as hell! Try staying with an aunt that still thinks you are twelve years old!" Brandy complained.

"Did you get out and enjoy the city?" I questioned.

"Yea, with a bunch of old women," Brandy grumbled.

"It's sad knowing that everyone will be heading for college. Floyd will be at Florida A&M University, Brandy will be at Howard University, and you Leslie will be at Western University," I said.

"You're going to the University of Detroit Mercy," Brandy added.

"Yea, but I'm not leaving the state," I stated somberly.

"Girl, I'm not leaving Michigan. I'll only be in Kalamazoo," Leslie said.

"That's away from the city," I noted.

We sat on Brandy's porch for a couple of hours talking, eating, drinking, and laughing.

Robert and I did enjoy evening motorcycle rides, private picnics, concerts, a trip or two, and time with our families and friends. To close out the summer we went to the Michigan State Fair to see the "Old School Rappers" concert.

Robert talked with his boys, as I finished watching the concert with my girls. As the show was coming to a close, a guy ran up behind me and snatched my purse. Unfortunately, for the purse-snatcher he ran right into Robert's path.

Robert stepped forward and his fist caught the guy right in the eye. The next thing I know the guy hit the ground and they were beating the shit out of him. I ran over and kicked the guy before grabbing my purse back. We quickly walked off as security came rushing over.

"Are you ok?" Robert asked.

"Yes. I'm glad you were looking out," I answered.

"What was that kick for?" he laughed.

"I refuse to let you have all the fun," I said with a giggle.

"That was nice of you to make an attempt to help out even though we had it covered," he said.

"Make an attempt! You're lucky that I was around to help you out," I implied.

"Oh, so now you're protecting me," he joked.

"I thought that's why you keep me around," I teased.

"You're funny," he smiled.

"You laid that punk out," I complimented.

"Hopefully that will teach that bitch a lesson about snatching anything from a poor defenseless lady," Robert mocked.

"I know you are not talking about me, because I am not defenseless," I insisted.

"Ok, if you say so. I'm ready to go!" he mentioned.

"Me too, I have seen enough," I agreed.

Chapter 33

I finished my first year at the University of Detroit Mercy, Robert was two class left at Wayne County Community College entrepreneurship program, and all my friends were home from college for the summer. For the last two weeks, I partied my ass off! However, all good things come to an end. Starting Monday I will no longer be a part-time employee. I was promoted to a full-time employee. This weekend I'm going to spend it relaxing and catching up on some sleep. Friday night I got home early.

"Hey, I'm surprised to find you home early. I thought you were going to party until you drop," Robert surprisingly stated.

"I tried?" I responded.

"Well, I'm hanging with the fellas tonight," he said.

"You have a good time," I replied.

I made a light meal and curled in the bed with a Donald Goines book, "Black Girl Lost" while Robert got ready to go out with his boys. He gave me a long deep passionate kiss before he left. I sat in the bed and read until I fell asleep.

Chapter 34

I came home around 2:30 in the morning and Selena was dead sleep. Instead of waking her up, I sat on the bed and watched her sleep. This seems like the perfect time to get something off my chest.

"Baby, I know you are sleep and can't hear me but I need to tell you something. It was homecoming night your freshman year. You were standing outside of Brandy's house taking pictures when I saw you for the first time. At that moment, I knew you were the one for me. When I heard what Charles had done to you angered me and the only thing I wanted to do was kill his motherfucking ass.

I waited until the time was right. We were walking down the alley between Pasadena and Tyler. I wanted to hear from his lips how he attacked you, so I started a conversation about the hoes I had slept with. He started bragging about how he stole your virginity and how funny it was to see you trembling with fear, while you cried uncontrollably. I stopped in my tracks. My eyes saw nothing but red. A rage surfaced in me that I never experienced. The next thing I knew I shouted out. Hey, Charles," I disclosed.

When he turned around my gun was pointing in his motherfucking face.

"Robert, what the fuck is going on?" Charles asked.

"Every dog has their day and this is yours," I answered.

"What the hell did I do to you?" he nervously pleaded.

"This is for Selena," I angrily said.

“You’re going to shoot me over a bitch?” Charles asked.

“No. I am shooting you for being a bitch!” I said.

“I pulled the trigger and shot that motherfucking bitch in his face. It was the only punishment he deserved,” I concluded.

I leaned in close too softly kiss both of her eyelids before I climbed into the bed. I wrapped myself around here and kissed the back of her neck as I fell to sleep.

Chapter 35

That next morning I rolled over and was pleased to find Robert curled up next to me.

"Good morning baby," I said greeting him with a kiss.

"Good morning to you. Last night I wanted to wake you up when I came in," he mumbled out.

"You could have," I replied.

"You look so peaceful sleeping in my shirt. I couldn't bring myself to wake you up," he admitted.

"Well, I'm up now," I said in a cheerful tone.

Robert rolled over on top of me and we began kissing. I ran my fingers slowly up and down his back. Then he started nibbling on my ears while unfastening the buttons on the shirt.

I continued to unbutton the shirt as I kissed her neck and worked my way to her breasts. I cupped her right breast and put her left breast in my mouth.

Ring! Ring! Ring! Ring!

"Hello," Robert responded answering his cell phone.

"Hey, Robert it's me Gator. I am downstairs," Gator informed.

I'm gently massaging his dick while fondling his balls as he talked on the phone. I cupped his balls in my hands as I caressed the base of his dick with my fingertips.

"Man, can you run to the store and pick up the stuff? I will be ready when you get back," Robert requested with a little excitement in his voice.

"No problem," Gator replied.

"You can take your time," Robert suggested.

"Ok. Gone and get your morning freak on," Gator laughed.

When I hung up the phone Selena rolled me on my back. She lightly sucked on my bottom lip before licking down to my chin.

I slowly kissed down his neck. I licked, gently sucked, and kissed both of his nipples. I rubbed his nipples with my fingers as I proceeded to kiss down his tummy.

She reintroduced herself to my dick by lovingly stroking it with one hand and lightly messaging my balls with the other. She ran her tongue around the ridge of my dick and then sucked it like a delicious ice cream cone. She softly kissed and licked up and down my dick. Her tongue flicked over the ridge between the head and the shaft, while she strokes the rest of my dick with her free hand.

I opened my mouth and slowly invited his dick inside. I smoothly hummed as I moved my head up and down. I had one hand around the base of his dick moving up and down in rhythm with my head. The other hand cradled his balls as if they were precious jewelry. I finished up by sucking on the head of his dick as if it was a piece of hard candy and then blowing it dry.

I rolled her over on her back and engaged her in a deep kiss. She lifted her legs up to welcome my stiff hard dick into her soft wet pussy. Even though we did not have much time, we fucked like dogs in heat.

"Gator called while you were in the shower. I told him you will be down in a few minutes," I said.

“What time is your hair appointment?” Robert asked.

“It’s at 11 this morning?” I answered.

“I should be done around 8:30 this evening. You can pick me up then,” he instructed.

“I will be at Floyd’s house. Call me when you’re ready,” I replied.

After spending over three hours at the hairdresser I headed over to Floyd’s house. The gang is meeting over there since he’s leaving in the morning for a football clinic in Florida. I stopped and picked up a big order of fried shrimp and fries from Miley & Miley Shrimp Shack.

“It’s me,” I said entering the backyard.

“Hey did you bring enough food for everybody?” Floyd yelled out.

“I thought it would be rude for me to eat in front of you all. Besides I did not want to beat anybody down for trying to take my food,” I joked.

We sat out in the backyard talking, laughing, and eating for hours before Robert called.

“Excuse me, I need to take this call,” I said walking to quieter area.

Robert will be ready in fifteen minutes. I walked back out into the yard and gave out hugs as I prepare to leave.

“Sorry, I have to go. Bye, everybody,” I said.

“See you,” the gang responded.

I pulled up to the house on Pilgrim. I waited in the driver’s seat until I saw him surface from the house. I climbed over into the passenger’s seat.

“So you are going to make me drive?” Robert committed.

"I figured I would enjoy the ride?" I said.

"You don't mind if I make a little run?" he asked.

"Not at all?" I replied.

He pushed in Rich Boy's first CD and we hit the road. He drove over to Six Mile Road and jumped onto I-75 Freeway. We sailed up I-75 to the Big Beaver exit for Somerset Mall. We spent a couple of hours in the mall shopping. We hit most of our favorite stores; Guess, Gucci, Macy's, and Saks.

"Baby, I need to meet up with the boys tonight," Robert stated.

"Oh, so you took me shopping to make it easy for you to ditch me?" I sarcastically snarled.

"No. It's not like that. I thought you would like a few more outfits for the summer," he responded with a chuckle.

"Nice try," I replied.

"You want me to stop and pick you up something to eat before we make it home?" he asked.

"I ate over Floyd's house. You can stop and pick yourself up something to eat?" I responded.

"No thanks. We're going out to eat," he answered.

When he came home, I was laying in the bed watching re-runs of The Wire. He kicked his gym shoes off and got in bed. He laid his head on my chest and put one arm around me. I could smell he was drunk. I twirled my fingers in his silky black curls, while he dozed off to sleep.

"Wake up sleeping beauty. I have a surprise for you, but I will need your help," he said waking me up after getting out of the shower.

Seeing him with nothing on but a towel was a terrific way to wake up. As much as I wanted to pull him back in the bed, I went on and got up. I know whenever he asked for my help it always turn out to benefit me in one way or another.

"So what's my surprise?" I asked.

"If you help me get my packages together and count down the money, you get to have me to yourself for the rest of the day," he answered.

"What part of that is the surprise?" I jokingly questioned.

"I will be at your command for the entire day," he responded.

"Will I get to call all the shots this time?" I inquired.

"Yes, I will leave everything to you and will try not to interfere at all," he promised.

I jumped in the shower and got dressed for the day while he made calls. We were out the door by nine o'clock that morning.

The house on Pilgrim was our first stop. I sat at the kitchen table and helped Robert separate, weigh, and package up his stock.

He had me drive him to his drug spots. I counted and strapped up money while he took care of business. We completely finished his stops in record time.

"Ok, what do you have planned for me?" Robert asked.

"I want to spend the day cuddling with no interruptions. That means all phones off, especially your cell phones. We can pick up some movies and snacks before we make it home. Then the rest of the day you belong to me," I answered.

"Can we get something to eat first," he suggested.

"Outback sounds pretty good," I answered.

We went to the Outback Restaurant in Southfield on

Greenfield Road. The service was fast since the after church rush was over. We ordered two entirely different meals so we could eat from each other's plate.

I went into Target's and bought two movies while Robert sat in the car. We both ran into the party store to pick out snacks.

"What movies did you get?" Robert asked.

"You can see once we get home," I ordered.

When we got in the apartment, I made him go back down to the car and get our leftovers from Outback. That was my excuse to get him to leave the apartment so I can get my surprise ready. While he was gone, I rushed and switched the movie I knew he would hate.

"You bought American Gangster and Willy Wonka and the Chocolate Factory? I understand American Gangster but the other one," Robert said as he went through the bag.

"I thought it was my day," I complained.

"You're right," Robert admitted.

I changed into one of his tank top style undershirts that fit me like a mini dress. I cut the air conditioner on, grabbed a blanket out the closet, and a pillow from the bed. He placed the snacks on the end table, undressed down to his boxers, and laid on the couch. The temperature in the apartment dropped fast. I took my time getting the drinks ready and putting the movie in.

"I know it's your day, but is there any chance that we can watch American Gangster first?" he pleaded.

"No, so you can fall to sleep on my movie?" I stated.

When I bent over to put the movie in the DVD player, I made sure to bend over far enough for the tank top to ride up revealing I had no panties. My nipples got hard from the cold air.

When she turned around, I smiled at the sight of her hard nipples. I held up the blanket and invited her in. She positioned herself between my legs to lay on my chest. I was extremely shocked when the movie started. Instead of Willy Wonka, playing on the big screen it was one of the home made movies of us making love.

"I like this version of Willy Wonka. Is there a chance that I will get to play in your Chocolate Factory?" he asked.

"You definitely will get a chance to play all up in my Chocolate Factory," I replied granting him permission.

I put one hand down the front of her tank top to rub on her breasts and the other hand under the tank top to rub her pussy. When the video began showing one of my favorite positions, I thrust one of my fingers in and out of her pussy.

I enjoyed having my ass rubbing against his dick. I felt it getting hard. I slid my hands up and down his thighs as my body moved to the thrusting of his fingers in and out of my pussy. His thrust became swifter as his dick got harder.

When I could not take it any longer, I got up to take my boxers off. She lay back on the couch, lift her legs in the air, open them wide, and invited my dick inside her wet pussy. As I lowered myself down, my dick guided itself in her pussy.

I embraced him with my legs wrapped around his back. Thrusting my hips in the rhythm of his strokes ensured his dick to hit up against my G-spot. I could feel the muscles on his back flex as he enjoyed the ride.

"Uhhhhmmmmm. Baby, that's it. Your dick feels good inside," I cooed to him.

"You like this dick? Don't you baby?" he asked.

"Yes I do. I love every inch of it," I reinforced.

"Good. This dick loves to be all up in your pussy," he whispered.

I lay on my side in a semi-fetal position as he lies in the same position behind me for rear entry. We were like two spoons curled up together.

I wrapped my arms around her and played with her breasts and clits, while my dick performed its magic in her pussy.

I grinded my ass against Robert's pelvis as his dick plunge in and out of my pussy.

She raised her top leg over my legs. It„s gratifying for my dick to gain deeper access in her pussy.

The heat from his body made the room feel as if it was 100 degrees.

I flipped over on my back so she could take control.

With my back facing him, I straddled my legs over him. I leaned forward grabbing his ankles. I slowly lowered myself and engulfed his dick with my pussy.

I grabbed her ass and squeezed it on her down swings. I ran my hands up and down her lower back.

"Baby, turn around so I can see your breasts jiggle as you ride me," he requested.

"Anything for you," I said.

I turned to face him with my knees straddled on each side of him. I lowered my pussy on to his dick.

For deep penetration, I kept my knees raised to give her support as she leaned back.

I made sure that my breasts jiggled on my down strokes. He licked his lips as he enjoyed the sight.

I pulled her down to me so I could suck on her breasts. I enjoyed her breasts while my dick enjoyed her wet pussy.

I rotated my hips as I rode his dick. I enjoyed him sucking on my sensitive nipples.

I draped my arms around her back and pulled her in close. I wanted to feel her hard nipples sliding on my chest.

I laid my legs directly on top of his and the sole of my feet on his feet.

I held on to her waist and pushed her body down with my up stroke. On my final stroke, I held her ass and pushed it towards my pelvis.

My pussy tighten up around his dick as our bodies climaxed together. I lay on his chest with his dick still inside me until I caught my breath.

He got up to change the movie, I ran to cut down the air, and then we both got back under the blanket. I laid with my chest against his chest, he wrapped his arms around me, and I dosed off.

I woke up just as American Gangster was going off. We got up from the couch headed for the shower. Like normal, we talked and laughed as we washed each other. We both grabbed towels to dry off.

She was sitting on the bed putting lotion on her legs when I got the urge for a second round. I put Will Downing and Kem CDs in the CD player. I unwrapped her towel and laid her across the bed. I'm going to take my time and enjoy this.

I loved feeling his soft kisses all over my skin. He took his time too slowly skim his fingertips up and down every inch of my body. It was as if he was etching a permanent picture in his mind. I rolled over on my tummy when I noticed him going into the nightstand drawer. I waited with anticipation of the upcoming event.

I took time to kiss my favorite parts of her body. I opened the nightstand drawer and pulled out the strawberry flavored edible massage oil. I straddle myself over her legs as she lay on her stomach. I poured oil up and down her back. In a circular motion, I glided my hands up and down her back spreading the oil around. I poured more oil up the spine of her back. I bent over and licked her back up and down.

From the bottom of my spine, I felt the strokes of his tongue messaging the oil in. Then he nibbled on both sides of my spine before blowing the area dry. He took his time and traveled up my back repeating the tongue massage one small section at a time.

When I reached the top of her back, I sucked on the back of her neck. I lick down her spine and then back up with small sucking kisses. I nibbled across each of her shoulder blades then glided my hands down her back.

He did not speak a word. It was as if his hands were communicating with my body. His touch spoke from a deeper level of consciousness. It's no doubt in my mind that Robert loves me as much as I love him.

I pour oil on the back of her right calf, across her ass, and then down her left leg to the calf. With one hand on each of the cheeks of her ass, I massaged in slow circular motions but opposite directions. I continued the motion down the back of her thighs until I reached the calves. With both hands on the back of her right thigh, I glide my hands up then down. Then I switched and glided my hands up then down the back of her left thigh. Placing a hand on the back of each thigh, I glided up to her ass. I skimmed my fingertips in a circular motion over her ass.

From a light tap on my shoulder, he motioned for me to roll over on my back.

I poured oil on her breasts and stomach. In a slow opposite circular motion, I worked my way up and down her breasts and stomach several times. I poured oil on her right arm and nibbled on her right breast. I massaged her right arm as I sucked on her breast. When I finished with the right side, I repeated the action on the left side.

I held onto the sheets while biting my bottom lip. My insides were boiling with hot passion for this man. I wanted to pin him to the bed and have my way with him, but my heart knew that this was definitely different. Therefore, I continued to follow his lead.

I picked her left leg up and rested her foot on my shoulder. I poured oil on her leg and massaged the oil in. Then I poured several drops of oil on her knee and let it run down her leg. With my hands close together in opposite directions, I massaged up and down her thigh. I kissed down the inside of her thigh as I lowered her leg to the bed. I picked her right leg up and rested her foot on my shoulder. I poured oil on her leg and massaged it in. Then I poured several drops of oil on her knee that ran down her leg. With my hands close together in opposite directions, I circularly massaged up and down her thigh. I kissed down the inside of her thigh as I lowered her leg to the bed.

He spread my legs apart and carefully examined my wet pussy. His fingers explored the lips of my pussy before he inserted two of his fingers. I rotated my hips as his fingers moved in and out my pussy. His fingers were dripping wet when he pulled them out. I watched with excitement as he sucked his fingers clean. I ran my fingers through his hair as he lowered his head between my thighs.

I stroked my tongue upward against the shaft of her clit. I stimulated one side of her clit then the other side while occasionally inserting my tongue into her pussy.

The excitement of his mouth on my pussy was mind blowing. With a feather light twirling movement, his tongue moved in and out.

I ran my tongue up and down the inside lips of her pussy while I twisted the nipples of her breasts between my fingers. She was rotating and thrusting her hips to the motion of my tongue inside her pussy, as my mouth covered her pussy.

I grabbed hold to the end of my pillow as he gently sucked my pussy flicking his tongue back and forth. My legs began to shake as he rendered me totally helpless. It felt so good that I could not help myself from moaning aloud with pleasure.

When I felt her body coming to a climax, I pulled my tongue out and began to lightly blow on her pussy. I kissed my way up her stomach and stopping to suck both her breasts.

Our fingers interlocked as he held my arms straight out. He slowly kissed up my neck before engaging me in a deep wet kiss. I gasped for breath when his hard dick penetrated my wet pussy. I laid my legs flat on the bed and rotated my hips in the slow motion of his strokes. I moaned with pleasure from each deep dick stroke. I lifted my legs up and bent my knees close to my chest. I wanted to allow him deeper penetration into my pussy.

When she allowed me to plunge deeper into her wet pussy, it excited me so much I wanted more. I flung her knees over my shoulders and continued my slow deep strokes in her pussy. We both moaned with pleasure as we enjoyed the ride.

I climbed on top to straddle myself over him and inserted his hard dick into my hot wet pussy. With slow deep strokes, I moved back and forth. He grabbed my face and we engaged in another deep wet kiss while our bodies continued connecting with each stroke. The moans of pleasure were the only sounds between us.

She rolled over, got on her hands and knees so I could ride her doggy style. When my dick entered her pussy, my strokes were slower with deeper penetration this time. I cupped both her breasts and played with her nipples. I laid her flat on the bed without missing a stroke.

I felt his heat radiating from the sweat from his chest as it dripped on my back. I sucked on my bottom lip to lower my moans every time my body experienced a small explosion inside. I motioned for him to lie on his back. I mounted him in a squat with my legs planted firmly with him between them. I leaned back placing my hands on his thighs for support and rode him with the same slow strokes.

She turned around and continued to ride me with her back facing me. My hands rubbed her ass in a sensual circular motion. I would slap one of her ass cheeks when I felt her body releasing one of her small explosions.

I sat up and leaned my back towards his chest with one hand on the bed to keep my balance and the other to fondle his balls as I continued the ride.

I'm able to fondle her nipples. Occasionally I softly wiped sweat off her back with my hands.

I felt my body preparing for a major orgasm. I leaned forward and grabbed his ankles to allow the deepest penetration during this moment.

I responded by pushing my dick further up her pussy. That orgasm tired out every muscle in my body.

Lying in his arms with my head on his chest listening to his heartbeat is my favorite spot.

"I want you to always remember that I love you more than I ever loved anyone. You are my heart and soul. You are my soul mate in this lifetime and my next lifetime," he whispered in my ear. "What's wrong?" he asked as I began to cry.

"Nothing. It was as if you were reading the thoughts of my heart. You will never know how many times I wake up out my sleep to make sure this is not a dream. I am thankful that you are in my life and I never want to envision life without you. I truly love you with every breath that I take," I told him through my tears as he held me tighter.

Chapter 36

Glad to see Monday come to an end. It is always seems to be the hardest day of the week? Robert is meeting up with his boys and will not be in until late. Guess I go to bed early.

The next morning I noticed he never came to bed, so I walked to the living to check if he fell asleep on the couch. I even checked the spare bedroom to see if he has passed out in there as he has done once before.

This is not like Robert! It's not like him at all! He has never stayed away from home without letting me know. If something happened in the streets, he calls to inform me of his where about no matter what time it is. This is totally out of his character. I'm truly concerned.

All morning I tried calling his cell phone but it keep going straight to voice mail. Around noon I checked his voice mail and after hearing the messages from his boys, I realized that I was not the only person looking for him. I was unable to concentrate that entire day at work. Robert is the only thought on my mind.

I pray he is ok. I hope it's a very simple reason why he has not contacted me. Maybe he got locked up or something. As the day went and not hearing from him my fear turned into sheer panic. My knees got weak, as a cold chill of fear ran through my body. My stomach knotted up, sweat ran down my forehead, and my hands became clammy. I never felt this lost before.

I call Dean, Gator, and a few of his other friends.

Hopeful at least one of them heard from him. Once I got off work I drove over to each one of his drug houses, but there is no sighting of him.

Ring! Ring! Ring! I expect it's some news concerning Robert. "Have you heard from him yet?" Gator asked.

"No. I've been checking his voicemail all day. From the messages it sounds like nobody has heard from him," I answered.

"When was the last time you saw him?" Gator questioned.

"Yesterday afternoon. He came up to the bank and took me to lunch. I went to bed early last night, since I knew he was meeting up with you. It wasn't until this morning I noticed he hasn't come home," I answered in a distressful tone.

"We all left Dean's house shortly after midnight," Gator replied.

"I am truly worried. This is not like Robert!" I responded with panic in my voice.

"Have you talked to his sister or mother?" Gator asked.

"I talked with Sherries but not his mother. She hasn't heard from him either. I'm pulling up to his mother's house right now and Sherries. car is in the driveway," I responded.

"Talk with Sherries only. I do not want his mother to know anything until it is absolutely necessary. Meet me over to his father's house in about an hour," Gator ordered.

I talked with Sherries on the porch so his mother couldn't overhear us. It's hard as hell holding back the tears, but I knew I had to keep it together until I hear from him. After I told her that I'm meeting Gator over to their father's house, she decided to ride with me. The ride is silent we both were unable to stop thinking the worst.

"Yesterday when we sat in the parking lot sharing our last good-by kiss and hug there was a feeling that came over me that did not want to let him go. I held him tight and kissed him one last. He told me that he loved me before I got out his car," I reminisce to myself.

When we got there, Gator and his father had started calling all the local hospitals, police departments, and morgues they could think of. So far, there is no one admitted to the hospital, arrested, or found dead under his name or description. That could be a good or bad sign.

Dean came by with some news from his cousin Stephen. "Stephen ran Robert's license plate through the computer system and got a hit. His Benz was impounded this morning. They found it abandoned in the middle of the street at Linwood and Six Mile. Stephen is treating it as a missing person case. Highland Park Police are in the process of picking up his car from the Detroit Police impound," Dean said.

I began shaking and crying uncontrollably after hearing Dean's news.

"Selena, I hate to do this but was everything ok at home?" Dean questioned.

"Yes. Why you ask?" I answered.

"I have to rule out all possibilities," Dean replied.

"Our relationship is solid if that's what you're hinting at. Just this past weekend was magical," I responded.

"Did he mention having problems with anyone?" Dean grilled.

"No, I assumed everything was ok. He seemed like himself," I responded.

Dean's cousin called an hour later with an update. "Stephen said they had possession of Robert's car and found traces of blood in the truck. They need one of his parents to come down to the station to give a DNA sample to determine if it Robert's blood," Dean said.

"Sherries I need to get home just in case he is there hurt," I mentioned.

"I'm going to ride to the police department with my father," Sherries replied.

"Selena call when you get home to let me know if he is there," Dean requested.

All night his boys, his father, and Sherries keep calling to see if I heard from him. I flinched every time the phone rang. I could not stop thinking the worst. I put on one of his shirts that still have his scent on it. I sniffed and hugged on his pillow as I cried myself to sleep. Every time I dozed off, I dreamt of hearing his voice telling me he loves me and we will meet again. I would wake up in a cold sweat and I lie there with my eyes wide open and motionless. Every muscle in my body was completely stiff, while fear ran throughout my veins as my heart raced.

The next afternoon the lab department report released the DNA results. They determined that it's Robert's blood in the trunk of his car and speculated it had been there for eighteen to twenty hours. The police already considered him dead and that its drug related. Sadly, that notion entered my mind, but the hope of finding him alive overpowered all my bad thoughts. Unfortunately, his mother needed to be informed.

While Robert remained missing, I came straight home from work. I lay in the bed, held on to his bed pillows and remembered the last time we were together. There were moments when I closed my eyes to imagine hearing his voice, feeling his touch, and smelling the scent of his body. Every time anybody walked down the hallway, I would run to the door hoping to see Robert on the other side. I called my voicemail repeatedly to replay all the old messages Robert left for me. It helps to hear him saying, "I love you."

Friday, the five o'clock news reported the Detroit Police found the remains of an unidentified black male in an abandoned building around noon. My heart instantly dropped. I knew it was Robert, but did not want to believe it. I immediately went over to his mother's house. I pulled up a minute or two before Stephen did.

Stephen delivered the news confirming the remains belong to Robert. It felt as if someone ripped my heart out of my chest and stomped all the life out of it. That's when reality hit that I will never see my man again and all my dreams of a future with him crumbled away.

It was a hot summer day and almost a week after Robert went missing, his remains were found in an abandoned building in Detroit off Livernois and the Lodge Freeway. The building has sat abandoned for over ten years. Time has taken a terrible toll on its structure. Between the weather, thieves, crack heads, and the local gangs the building's appearance resembled a movie set from a horror picture. It's so nasty inside even a homeless person would have refused to stay there. Stray animals, rats, mice, roaches, and the occasional junkie that needed a place to shoot up at were the only creatures that ventured in there. It's hot, smelly, and dark inside. Filth covered the floors and mold coated the walls. All of the lower floors windows are boarded up and the doors left ajar.

The smothering heat in the building accelerated the decomposing of Robert's body and filled the air with a foul odor from his decaying remains. Some crack heads stumbled into the building to get high. The smell did not detour them from their mission, but the sight of a portion of his head in the doorway sent them running. They ran out the building yelling, "A dead body is in there!" One of the neighbors overheard and called the police.

Police found several remains of Robert's bones fragments scattered around the building's basement stairway. In the darkest corner of the basement majority of Robert's torso remains were still attached to a chair laying in a pool of slime from his decomposing body fluids. His partial clothed torso is missing the head, both arms, and both legs. Rotten flesh and uneaten organs are the only things left. The remains are infestation with maggots, flies, and insects. His skin is covered with bit marks from the rats and mice that nibbled on his flesh and stray dogs that ripped the flesh and bones from his lifeless body.

Shattered fragments of his skull are found throughout the basement. His legs and arms bones are mulled clean. They found the palm of one hand and only six of his ten fingers. Both feet were missing all their toes. Between the years weather damage, insects, stray dogs, rodents, and trespassers the entire crime scene is too contaminated for any possible leads. The police are left with very little evidence to go on.

Chapter 37

After leaving the fellas I head straight home. I pulled into my assigned spot in the parking garage for the night. I got out of my car and started walking towards the elevator. The parking garage is completely full but not a person insight. The nighttime insects mating are the only noise to be heard in the still night air.

Robert stood waiting for the elevator. He watched the floor numbers decreased as it got closer and closer. As he placed the car keys in his pocket, he received a blow to the back of his head. He felt the tense pain only for a second. The blow knocked him unconscious causing him to fall to the ground. He was totally unaware that someone laid waiting for him with a bat.

The peaceful spring night is shattered at the sound of four men rushing from behind a parked van. They ran over to help their partner. One of the men rambled through Robert's pockets taking his car keys. Then rushed to open Robert's car trunk as the other men carried his limp heavy body and throwing him in the trunk. The slamming sound of the car trunk echoed through the parking structure.

When I regained consciousness, I found myself tied to a chair in the basement of an abandoned building. The area is dark, damp, and reeked of mold. The glare from the flash lights exposed the mice running along the back wall.

They have my chest tied to the chair's back and each leg to a chair leg with rope. My hands are handcuffed together behind the chair. I have a splitting headache with streaks of dried blood on his face. My gym shoes and all my jewelry is missing.

"What the fuck is going on?" I asked in a very mean tone.

"Bitch this is pay back for my nephew. It may have taken some time to catch up with your punk motherfucking ass," one of the men answered.

"Fuck you motherfucking bitches!" I replied in a meaner tone just before they taped my mouth shut. The next thing I felt were blows to my face and head. By the time the blows stopped, my eyes are swollen shut, my jaw shattered, and ringing from my busted right eardrum.

I could faintly hear a purring sound in the background. The sound got louder, louder, louder, and louder. The closer it got I realized it was the roaring of a chainsaw. My insides exploded as I felt the most excruciating pain in the world the moment the blade of the saw made contact with my shoulder. Blood began squirting out as the blade tore clean through my flesh and bones as it sawed my right arm off at the shoulder. With my mouth-taped shut and jaw broken, I'm unable to release the screams of anguish that's yelling inside my head.

After my right arm fell to the side of my body it swung on the ground still attached to the handcuff. My right shoulder was throbbing with pain as blood ran down the side of my shirt. Even though it left my other arm free, he is unable to successfully use it. The weight from my dangling right arm, the pain in my shoulder, and the fact he is not able to open my eyes left him at a disadvantage.

The yelling inside my head is so loud it's completely blocking out the cowards cussing about my blood hitting their cloths and the laughter about torturing me. This is the end for me. I'm going to cover up the screams in my head with memories of what makes me happy. I let my mind escape to the conversation with Selena on the Bob-Lo Boat.

The men bitched and argued over who would get to use the chainsaw next. Without warning, I felt the same excruciating pain as they started to saw my left arm from the shoulder. When the chainsaw separated the last piece of skin and flesh from my left arm, both arms hit the floor. The sides of my shirt, pants, and beautiful black curly hair are drenched from blood splattering.

I had the wind knocked out of me as someone kicked me in the chest. The blow to my chest caused the chair to fall backwards to the floor. My head hit the cement floor so hard it bounced up.

The next person decided to saw off a leg at the knee. He held the chainsaw up in the air and then swung downwards in a counter clock movement. His swing was so swift that he sawed both Robert's legs off below the knee with the chair legs still attached to them. Robert's body shocked and shivered as it immediately went into shock.

I no longer felt any pain. My cold and numb body lay on the floor bleeding while they attempted to clean evidence out of the basement. As I lay bleeding to death, I'm still able to keep my reality blocked by revisiting my life with Selena. The moment I began to visualize running my hands up and down Selena's body a shotgun was placed under my chin.

They pulled trigger blowing his head into pieces. They wanted to make sure his family would not be able to have an open casket funeral.

Chapter 38

Between Robert's father, Dean, Gator, and myself we made sure Robert was sent off like a king. Mr. Harris arranged for Thomas to attend the funeral. As much as Robert wanted the two of us to meet face-to-face I hated that it's under these circumstances. Five armed federal agents escorted Thomas to the funeral in his orange prison jumpsuit and shackles.

The closed casket service was standing room only. I had no idea he knew this many people. All of his brothers and sisters and their children and grandchildren as well as other family members from his father's side came. His mother had family from Mexico and New York came in town to support her. Corey and other members of their crew drove in from Ohio. Classmates and two of his professors from Wayne County Community College came. There is a large turn out from the old neighborhood. Even a few of his loyal customers. lurked in the back. It did not surprise me to see several of his old hoes in attendance, especially Wanda. I'm surprised to see my father and Rita. It was heartwarming when I noticed that his parents mentioned that I was the love of their son's life in his obituary.

At the cemetery his mother fainted as they lowered his body in the ground. The burial is so final. It hurt so bad knowing I would never see Robert again. Having his plot in the same cemetery as Baron's plot is the only comfort. In a morbid way, I'm glad to see that he is not there alone.

The days following the funeral, I did not have the desire to get out of bed. All I did is hold on to his pillow and cry until I could cry no more. I miss him so much. I am not sure if I will ever stop hurting.

Damn those phones wouldn't stop ringing. I unplugged the house phone, silenced my cell phone, turned Robert's cell phones off, and cut the volume on the door intercom system down. I just wanted to be alone.

A couple of days passed without anyone being able to contact me. That's why I was shocked to hear someone knocking at my front door. Out of the peephole, I saw Leslie and Brandy. They were able to talk the security guard into allowing them to come up and check on me.

"We know you are in there," Leslie said.

"We are not leaving until you open this door," Brandy demanded.

After they knocked on the door for ten minutes, I decided to let them in.

"We came to see how you were doing, since no one has spoken to you in days," Leslie mentioned.

"I just don't feel like being bothered," I replied.

"We know you're mourning but there are a lot of people concerned. I cannot say that I know how you feel but you need to know that we care about you," Leslie explained.

"Brandy what are you doing in my kitchen?" I asked.

"Cleaning up! When was the last time you did a good house cleaning?" Brandy questioned.

"A few days before Robert went missing," I replied.

"It's not like you to leave stuff just sitting around," Leslie commented.

I yelled out as Leslie bent over to pick up Robert's gym shoes that he left beside the couch. "Leave Robert's stuff alone! I will pick them up later," I announced.

"Sorry, I didn't mean to upset you," Leslie said.

"I know that wasn't your intention, but I need to mourn at my own pace. I just need some time to myself," I clarified.

"We're not going to stay long. We just needed to check up on you," Brandy ensured.

"Thanks for coming by. I really mean that," I claimed.

Chapter 39

"Gator, this is a major hit for the family," Dean said.

"They did not have to butcher Robert like that," Gator replied.

"You're right about that! We need to find out who did this," Dean responded.

"And we need to find out as soon as possible," Gator agreed.

"Let's not jump to fast. I do not want to go after the wrong person or crew. How do we know if it's was intended to be an act of revenge against just Robert or if they have vengeances for the entire family?" Dean asked with concern.

"That may take a minute and we do not have time like that," Gator answered.

"We need to cover all our bases," Dean replied.

"You're right," Gator responded.

"I am flying out tomorrow to North Carolina to talk with Thomas. There are just some things we cannot discuss over the phone," Dean replied.

"Send him my condolences. I know Robert's murder is killing him. It has to be a devastation feeling that he is not able to hunt down his brother's killer," Gator replied.

Dean flew into North Carolina, rented a car, and drove straight to Butner Federal Correctional Institution Medium II Facility. Thomas was expecting his visit.

"Hey man. I am glad to see that you were able to make it up here so quick," Thomas acknowledged.

"This is a matter that must be addressed with urgency. There's no way I can go forward without your input," Dean replied.

"I loved the hell out of my little brother," Thomas admitted.

"We all loved Robert," Dean agreed.

"It's anguishing not being able to do anything. I wish I were out there to hunt the motherfuckers down that did this to my brother. Knowing how monstrous they killed him is ripping me to shreds on the inside. I have gone over a list of suspects in my head that I would like to ask about," Thomas stated.

"Go ahead," Dean replied.

"Who was dealing directly with Corey?" Thomas questioned.

"It was just Gator, Robert, and myself," Dean answered.

"By chance were any of Corey's boys looking for additional payback from Lamont's fiasco?" Thomas questioned.

"Luckily that stupid motherfucker unknowingly left a witness alive that were able to confirm that he was working alone. Everything is cool on that end," Dean answered.

"Would Lamont's whore Cindy have a way to make a payback like that?" Thomas questioned.

"She is a cracked out whore working the streets of Pontiac. She doesn't have the mental capacity or means to pull off something like that. Besides she's screaming whoever killed Lamont probably killed Robert, and they are after all of us," Dean answered.

"What about Lamont's family?" Thomas questioned.

"Even though Cindy told them about Lamont sticking-up drug houses and killing people is the reason for his disappearance we have not ruled out that possibility," Dean answered.

"Is there anyone in our family that wanted to branch off like Lamont?" Thomas questioned.

"They all seem happy about their positions in the family. Besides that, I have avoided bringing in anybody that does not have blood ties into the family. But it's still a path worth keeping under investigation," Dean answered.

"Any new competitors in town?" Thomas questioned.

"No, Stephen keeps us posted on any new activity," Dean claimed.

"What about the independent spots in the neighborhood?" Thomas questioned.

"Most seem contented dealing enough to make ends meet. The others spots are not in our market. We are also checking into that possibility," Dean explained.

"What do you know about the stick-up guy that tried to rob Shannon and them?" Thomas questioned.

"He was a punk that was known for robbing dealers. There were several open contracts on his life from dealers all over. So it was only a matter of time before he was going to meet his maker, but Gator is looking at his family ties," Dean replied.

"How about any of Robert's ex-whores, did any of them what him dead?" Thomas questioned further.

"Most of them seem satisfied cussing him out whenever they saw him. Besides, Selena has had him on lock down for the past four years so most had moved on," Dean informed.

"Robert giving up his player card shocked the shit out of me," Thomas stated.

"That shocked the shit out of a lot of people," Dean responded.

"Was Selena cheating?" Thomas questioned.

"That is funny she loved the ground he walked on," Dean answered.

"Was Robert cheating?" Thomas questioned.

"Believe it or not that's just as funny. That girl had his nose open so wide that you could have drove a semi-truck up it," Dean answered.

"What about that bitch Selena stabbed in the night club?" Thomas questioned.

"That fat fucker works at McDonalds, lives with his grandmother, and catches the bus. He does not have any street connections," Dean encouraged.

"Is Sherries dating anyone that Robert had to check?" Thomas questioned.

"She's still dating the same stiff ass college boy from Memphis," Dean answered.

"The bitch in the truck explosion," Thomas said.

"That's another one we are looking into," Dean responded.

"I have not ruled out the possibility that someone want to pay me back by taking my brother out," Thomas replied.

"I have also tossed that question in my head wondering if it's part of our past coming back to haunt us," Dean responded.

"Make sure you investigate all leads. Check to see if there is any family link we need to be worried about and make sure their entire family is destroyed," Thomas ordered.

Chapter 40

The last couple of months I spent most of my time locked up in the apartment. Going to the cemetery, work, or the grocery store are the main reasons for me leaving out the house. From time to time I would pull myself together to visit my little brothers and Robert's mother.

The mornings I would wake up from dreaming of Robert my insides would scream for my loss as I reached out and he wasn't there. Those would always be the hardest days at work. All I want to do is go home, crawl into bed, and cry myself to sleep.

After all this time I still refuse to pick up any of the items Robert left out of place before he went missing. He left a shirt on the back of a dining room chair, a pair of gym shoes next to the couch, and a baseball hat on the entertainment center. The items help me to cling on to the hope that this nightmare is only a hoax and Robert is coming back to me.

On this beautiful Sunday in August, I sat at Robert's grave right next to his marble head stone and ran my fingers over the embedded picture of him. It's been three months since Robert's death and today my heart aches just as bad as it did the day his body was found. This was not just my daily visit to the cemetery, but our anniversary.

"How come life has to be so unfair? We should be on a little island wrapped in each other's arms. The spot where my heart resides feels so empty and lonely without you. I don't want to accept that you are never coming back to me. This is not how it was supposed to end," I cried at his grave.

I was still talking with Robert when Dean walked up. He bent over and gave me a hug.

"How are you Dean?" I asked.

"I am fine, but the question is how you are? Everyone is worried about you. No one has seen or heard from you since the funeral," Dean asked with concern.

"I'm surviving. Some days are better than others days," I answered.

"Every time I stop in the bank you're never there," Dean replied.

"I transferred to another branch. It was too hard for me to concentrate on my job. Whenever the door swung open I anticipated seeing Robert walking through it," I responded with sadness.

"Nobody expects for you to get over his death quickly. I loved Robert like a brother and I somewhat understand your grief. I want you to know that there are many people that love you and are truly concerned," Dean replied.

"I know but I need some time to myself to deal with this at my own pace," I said sniffling.

"I know how much he loved you and he would hate to see you hurting like this. You need to focus on all that you both gave to each other while he was alive. I know for a fact that you gave him something to look forward to each day," Dean ensured.

"He is still my first thought in the morning, my last thought at night, and every thought in between. We had such big plans for our future together. I was to start my second year at the University of Detroit Mercy while he finished his last business classes at Wayne County Community College," I explained trying to hold back tears.

"Fulfilling the dreams that you shared with him would be the best way for you to honor his memory. He wanted nothing but the best for you. You can't let him down now," Dean insisted.

"Thank you, I needed to hear that," I admitted.

"Remember Fran and I are always here for you no matter what time it is," he added.

Dean was right, Robert would be very disappointed at me for giving up on life. I still had time to register for fall classes. At first I threw myself only into school and work. As time went on, most weekends I found myself either driving up to Western University and staying on campus with Leslie flying up to Howard University and staying on campus with Brandy, or flying down to Florida A&M to catch Floyd's home games. I even began spending more time at my father's house and with Robert's mother.

However, the days surrounding holidays are still truly unbearable. Sweetest Day, Thanksgiving, Christmas, and New Years Eve I find myself back in the same emotional wreck as the day of Robert's funeral. I'm barely able to drag myself out of bed. I would hide behind my fake face to spend a few hours visiting Robert's and my family as well as friends. The moment I got home I remove the fake face, put on one of Robert's shirts, and spend the rest of the evening crawled up in a blanket on the couch. I cry and laugh as I watch our homemade movies and looked at pictures.

Chapter 41

Several months later Dean is in the visitors. room at Butner Federal Correctional Institution waiting to see Thomas. He wanted to be the one to deliver the update about revenge on Robert's killer.

"Hey, there Dean. I am surprised to see you. What brought you down here on this May morning?" Thomas asked.

"I wanted to update you face to face," Dean answered.

"I hope it's good news?" Thomas replied.

"It is. The person responsible for Robert's death has been identified," Dean informed with a smile on his face.

"That is damn good news. How were you able to figure out that connection?" Thomas questioned.

"Unbelievably, with help from Selena and your brother," Dean announced.

"You need to explain this," Thomas requested.

"Let me take you back to the last week in February," Dean explained.

Chapter 42

I'm not sure what made me accepted the opportunity to work the next six Saturdays at my old branch. The commercial teller went on maternity leave so I am filling in for her. Luckily, the branch is only open for half a day. That leaves me plenty of time to visit Robert's grave.

"Damn it's my birthday. I wish I could stay in the bed and sadly sing happy birthday to myself. The only gift I want for my birthday is for the people responsible for Robert's death to pay," I thought aloud as I stared at the calendar.

When I got to the bank it was cold as hell inside the building. I'm glad I brought a sweater to wear. So far, everything is going well and my last customer is walking up to the window. "Who is this very well dress, six foot tall, out of shape male with a raspy voice stepping up to my counter," I wondered as a strange feeling came over me.

His dark complexion makes his small pouty pink lips and gold teeth stand out. Too bad, he is not able to hide the fact that his hairline is receding. The turtleneck sweater he's wearing is slightly hiding the large cheloids on his neck. His thick bushy eyebrows brought unnecessary attention to his large scary eyes. His swagger shouts he's a drug dealer.

Fuck, his transactions are going to take some time and I want to get off on time. He has a very large deposit that is spread between six different business accounts. Guess Robert and I were not the only ones using dummy companies to hide our money in the bank. I am glad his deposits total is ten dollars short from me filling out the government's CTR report.

While, working on the last deposit he pulled up his sleeve to look at his watch. My heart stopped and my throat felt like it was swelling shut. "What is he doing wearing Robert's Infinity link bracelet? Robert had them bracelets made especially for us! What the fuck is Robert's bracelet doing on this man? Does this motherfucker have any connection to Robert's death?" Why can't I stop those questions from playing over and over in my head? Let me take a few deep breathes. I need to collect my thoughts. It's no way I'm going to let this man leave my counter without getting some information.

"That's a nice bracelet. What kind of link is that?" I questioned.

"I have no idea," the customer answered.

"I like unique looking jewelry," I replied. I pulled up the left sleeve of my sweater and showed him a few of my one of kind bracelets.

"Those are unique links," the customer responded.

"I'm having the hardest time finding a jewelry store that specializes in one of kind pieces. I hope asking where you purchased your bracelet at is not too bold of a question?" I asked.

"It's not a bold question but unfortunately, an acquaintance gave it to me before he passed away," the customer responded with a smirk.

"I hate to hear that. Sorry for your loss," I replied.

As bad as I want to ask this motherfucker more questions I could not help from quickly finishing his transaction. I can feel myself becoming extremely angry.

"You enjoy the rest of your weekend," I said.

"Thank you and you do the same," the customer replied.

The moment he exited the bank, I locked up my area and ran to the bathroom. I needed to calm my nerves down. There was no doubt in my mind that was definitely Robert's bracelet.

I went back to my area and balanced out my drawer. I took a minute and copied down the stranger's bank accounts numbers before turning in my paperwork. Shit I cannot seem to get out of the bank fast enough. I have to call Gator about this.

"Hi Selena, I was going to call you later and wish you a happy birthday," Gator said.

"Gator can you meet me at the cemetery?" I requested.

"When do you want to meet?" he asked.

"I am on my way and it is very, very important," I demanded.

"Yea, I will be up there in fifteen minutes," he replied.

I'm standing over Robert's grave nervous as hell when Gator showed up.

"What's wrong, you're shaking like a leaf," Gator said giving me a hug.

"I saw someone with one of Robert's bracelets on," I responded.

"How do you know if it's his?" he asked.

"He was wearing the one that matches this bracelet," I answered pulling up my right sleeve to show him my Infinity bracelet.

"I was at the jeweler's with Robert when he designed that. Where did you see this person at?" he questioned.

"A customer walked up to my window wearing it," I said.

"Are you sure?" he drilled.

"Yes, I struck up a conversation about the link. He had no idea what kind of link it was but said an acquaintance gave it to him before passing away," I explained.

"Are you sure that Robert had it on the last time you saw him?" he grilled.

"He had it on when we meet up for lunch that afternoon. He never took that bracelet off," I answered.

"Did you get a name?" he questioned.

"No. All his deposits were for business accounts but I wrote down all his account numbers. When I go to work on Monday I will look up his information," I promised.

"Did you get a good look at him?" he asked.

"Yes I did," I answered giving Gator a very detailed description of the mystery man.

"If you think of anything else give me a call," he responded.

"I will. Thanks for coming," I replied.

I stayed and talked with Robert for a little while longer before heading over my father's house. I promised my father that I would stop over for an early birthday dinner.

Gator caught up with Dean to discuss the conversation he had earlier with Selena.

"Man, I talked with Selena at the cemetery. She said a guy came into the bank with one of Robert's bracelets on," Gator said.

"How does she know that it was one of Robert's bracelets?" Dean questioned.

"Remember when he had those Infinity bracelets custom designed?" Gator asked.

"Yes," Dean replied.

"She said this guy came into the bank wearing Robert's. He told her an acquaintance gave it to him that passed away," Gator explained.

"Do you think it could have fallen off Robert's arm?" Dean asked.

"There is no way that could have happened. He had special claps put on the bracelets to ensure they wouldn't fall off," Gator ensured.

Dean sat silent before responding.

"Do you think he knows Selena's and Robert's connection?" Dean asked.

"I'm not sure but I have hired two of our best guys to watch her just in case," Gator informed.

"Did you tell her that she's going to be watched?" Dean asked.

"No, I thought it would be best not to scare her," Gator said.

"Did she get a name or any information on him?" Dean questioned.

"She plans to pull his records Monday at work," Gator answered.

"This is the best lead we have. When she gives you the information we need to jump on this immediately," Dean suggested.

Wanting to find the relationship between this man and Robert's death has given me motivation that I have not had since the day before Robert went missing. Monday morning at my original branch, I dedicated every free moment gathering all the information I could on the mystery man's account numbers.

Not one business account has the same address, but that's not strange. Every account had multiple authorized names on them. Isaac Brown is the only name that appears on each one. I wrote down all the information. I made a copy for Gator and a copy for myself. After work, I stopped by the drug house on Puritan and gave Gator his copy.

This week went by extremely slow because I couldn't wait until Saturday. I'm hoping the mystery man would come in. Hot damn, he came in around the same time as last week and that bastard is still wearing Robert's bracelet. Regardless how much it hurts, I am going to strike up a conversation with this bitch. Maybe that motherfucker will slip and reveal more information that Gator and Dean could use to track his ass down.

"Good morning sir," I greeted cheerfully.

"Good morning to you," said the customer.

"How is your day going?" I asked politely.

Ring! Ring! Ring! "Hello," he said answering his cell phone.

"Damn, a fucking phone call. The bastard has the nerves to back away from my window. Move closer motherfucker so I can hear your conversation. Let me hurry and finish his fucking transactions," I thought to myself.

"Sir I am finished with your transactions," I said.

He nodded and walked out the bank. If he was going to do that shit and talk on the phone the entire time, he did not have to stand in my line.

Selena is completely unaware that Dean and Gator are staking out the bank parking lot. They're trying to catch a glimpse of this mystery man. Two men fitting the description came through the bank.

"Gator I can't believe there are two ugly motherfuckers that fit Selena's description," Dean observed.

"Later this evening I am going to stop downtown and talk with Selena. I need to set up something so she can make a positive ID on this guy. We do not need to waste time following the wrong one," Gator said.

"I'm going to have my cousin Stephen run both their license plates for now. We definitely need a positive ID," Dean said.

"If either one of them had anything to do with Robert's death I will personally make him pay for it!" Nobody hurts my family and get away with it," Gator promised.

Buzzzzzzzzz! Buzzzzzzzz!

"Who could that be downstairs in the main lobby? I'm not expecting anybody nor do I feel like being bothered! I should have let security know that I'm not to be disturbed," I thought aloud.

Buzzzzzzzzzz! Buzzzzzzzzzzz! Buzzzzzzzzzzzzz!

"Who is it?" I asked.

"There is a gentleman by the name of Gator," said the front desk security guard.

"You can let him up," I replied. Maybe Gator has some good news. I could use some right about now.

"Sorry for stopping by without calling," Gator said coming in.

"No problem. I hope you got some good news for me?" I asked.

"Somewhat. Dean and I were sitting in the bank parking lot this morning. Two guys came out of the bank fitting your description. Next Saturday I will need you to make a positive I.D. on this bastard," he said.

"No problem," I replied.

"What time does he show up at the bank," he asked.

"Around twelve o'clock. He is always one of my last customers?" I disclosed.

"I will certainly be up there Saturday. I need you to point him out to me," he said.

"What kind of signal do you want me give you?" I asked.

"Let me think for a second. Touching your hair or ears is too obvious. Is there anything in your window that you can move?" he asked.

"There is. I can move my name plate to the other side of the window when he gets in my line," I told him.

"That's a good idea. Promise me you won't go acting like a superwoman. I want you to leave this to grown men," he demanded.

"I promise?" I said with my hands behind my back and fingers crossed.

"See you Saturday," he said leaving.

Saturday could not get here fast enough. I'm so glad to see Gator walking through the bank doors. He got here twenty minutes before eleven o'clock. Since, the bank is extremely packed, nobody even noticed Gator sitting in a lobby chair pretending to be reading the newspaper. He has a perfect view of all customers in my line.

Like clockwork, the mystery man steps in my line a minute or two before twelve o'clock. I moved my name sign as Gator peeked from behind the newspaper. The moment he walked up to my window, I had a feeling of confidence that his days are coming to an end very soon.

"You are a very beautiful young lady. Your smile can light up a room," the customer said.

"Thank you," I said cordially smiling knowing his motherfucking murderous ass days are numbered.

"Do you have a man?" the customer asked.

"Yes I do," I said with a smile.

"Let him know that he is a lucky man," the customer complimented.

"We are both lucky," I responded.

"Just in case he forgets how lucky he is," the customer replied handing me a piece of paper with his name and cell phone number.

His name is Isaac. Isaac puck bitch Brown. This proves he's the Isaac Brown that is on all those business accounts. Stupid motherfucker, little do you know you need to be concerned about your own luck! You have no idea your luck is running out!

"You have a good day sir," I replied hurrying to get him out of my window.

The moment Gator followed the bitch out of the bank I sent him a text message with Isaac's name and cell phone number. Gator has to solve this soon! I am not sure how much more I can take seeing that bastard wearing my man's bracelet! Every dog has their day and his is coming soon.

Gator went straight over to Dean's house after following Isaac.

"I followed that punk Isaac Brown to a home in an exclusive subdivision in Farmington Hills," Gator reported.

"Have you ever seen or heard of this guy before?" Dean asked.

"No. That what's concerns me," Gator replied.

"I understand. We need to find out more information about him. Like who he is associated with, where is he from, and how is he connection to Robert's murder," Dean explained.

"Your right," Gator agreed.

"If this motherfucker had anything to do with Robert's death he will pay for it," Dean promised.

"Hell everybody in his family will pay for it," Gator added.

"We will sit back, observe, and collect as much information as we can. I'll have Stephen pull up information on the Farmington Hills address. When the time is right we will hit our mark with a fool proof game plan," Dean added.

It's getting down to the wire, this is my fifth Saturday, which leaves me with only two more opportunities to find the connection this black ugly ass bitch has to Robert's murder.

"Baby, I'm hoping that you can hear me. I need your help. I know Dean and Gator ask me to let them handle it, but knowing that your killers are still out there haunts me. The desire for revenge consumes every fiber of my body. I will not rest until those that violently ripped you out of my life pay for it. Please send me a sign to let me know if my feeling is right about this Isaac Brown," I request as I talked to Robert at his grave.

I made it to work with the anticipation of Isaac Brown coming in. I felt like a kid waiting for Christmas hoping that Robert would send me a sign. A half hour before closing the commercial window I become frustrated. That punk Isaac has not come in yet. Just as I put up my close sign, the bastard walked in.

"Excuse me for being late. Is there any chance that you can take me? I would hate to stand in the other line?" Isaac asked.

"It's no problem. I can take you," I said wearing a fake smile.

He really doesn't know how much I was wishing he would show up. During our conversation I had became very disappointed, because there was no concrete evidence or information to confirm my suspicions.

"I know this is a commercial window only, but is it possible of me making a couple of personal deposits?" Isaac asked.

"I can take them since you are my last customer," I politely answered.

"Thank you," he said.

My heart hit the floor when he opened up his mink coat to get his deposit slips out of the inside pocket. He was wearing a platinum byzantine chain and medallion. It wasn't just any medallion but the sign I have been waiting for. It confirmed my suspicions about this punk motherfucker.

That medallion definitely belonged to Robert. It's a circle outlined in diamonds with a diamond traced symbol in the middle. Most people have no idea that the diamond symbols are small case letter "r" and "s" overlapping each other. Robert said the letter "r" represents him and the letter "s" represents me and they symbolized the unity of out two souls.

My insides began to scream "killer!" on the inside. A very cold chill ran down my back when his hand slightly touched mines as he handed me the deposit slips. I have to get him out of my window. I'm not sure how long I can hold back my hands from shaking with anger and hatred. Wait until Gator hears about this shit!

I'm determined to collect as much information before getting the hell out of here today. I quickly balanced out my drawer which leaves me plenty of time to collect as much information before getting off. I pulled up information on every personal account number he gave me, and his name is on every account. The mailing addresses are for out of state residences. I wrote down everyone's information including names, driver license numbers, social security numbers, and both in state and out of state mailing addresses.

The moment I walked out of the bank I called Gator. When the voice on the other end of his phone said, "Please leave a message," my mind went into a state of desperation. "Damn Gator, where the hell are you? Why are you not answering your phone? Fuck it I'm going to stop over on Pasadena," I said on his voice mail.

A slight sigh of relief overcame me when I noticed Dean's car parked out front. When Dean opened the front door, he could tell something is wrong.

"Girl it look like you seen a ghost," Dean commented.

"I did. That bastard came to the bank with Robert's chain on. He is wearing Robert's platinum chain and diamond medallion with our initials united. I know this punk knows what happened to Robert!" I explained.

"Did you get any more information about the motherfucker?" Dean asked in a calming voice.

"He has several personal accounts with out of state addresses. Here, I copied everything down," I said as I handed him a piece of paper with all of Isaac's personal banking information.

"You don't know how badly it hurts seeing this bastard standing at my window with Robert's jewelry on," I fussed.

"I could only imagine. Don't worry when the time is right Robert's killer or killers will pay for what they have done. You need to go home and relax," Dean advised.

"I will after I stop by Robert mother's house. I am supposed to be going out to lunch with her and Sherries," I mentioned.

"I'm glad to see that you still keeping in touch with Mrs. Harris," Dean commented.

"It helps being around people that misses Robert as much as I do?" I responded.

After Gator wrapped up his meeting with the crew, he met up with Dean.

"Good afternoon Fran, is Dean at home?" Gator asked when she opens the door.

"Hello Gator. You can have a seat in the living room. Dean will be down in a minute?" Fran said.

"Hey Dean, what's going on?" Gator greeted him.

"That motherfucker showed up at the bank wearing Robert's medallion!" Dean informed.

"Did she do anything stupid?" Gator asked.

"No, but she hit the jackpot. She was able to obtain personal information. Here take a look?" Dean said handing him the information.

"Gator as you can see she was able to get us names, driver license numbers, social security numbers, and addresses," Dean mentioned.

“Man this will help us to locate and eliminate his connections that would have a reason to retaliate,” Gator replied.

“I hate that there is no immediate remedy to this. Selena could become a problem,” Dean said.

“You think she will try going after this man?” Gator asked.

“I don’t think she will jeopardize her safety, but seeing Robert’s medallion truly freaked her out. I am not sure how she will react if sees him at work next Saturday,” Dean indicated.

“As much as I care for Selena, we cannot go after this Isaac Brown without having all our ducks in a row,” Gator explained.

“Have your boys keep a closer eye on her. Have one of them inside the bank next Saturday. The moment that motherfucker walks in make sure they stop her from doing anything stupid,” Dean recommended.

“I understand,” Gator said.

Chapter 43

"Robert was that corny?" Thomas asked with a chuckle.

"No he was not corny, that boy was in love. Your brother had several pieces of custom made jewelry that expressed his love for that girl," Dean expressed.

"I did not know his nose was open that wide for her," Thomas replied.

"Yea. That was a side of your brother that shocked the shit out of me too," Dean explained.

"Obviously Isaac has out of state connections," Thomas added.

"Taking down everybody involved is the only way to ensure that there would be nobody left to come back for retaliation," Dean made clear.

"How do you plan to stop his family members from retaliating?" Thomas asked.

"Selena took care of that," Dean said.

"How the hell does she fit in this picture again?" Thomas questioned.

Chapter 44

I am so glad that this is my last Saturday at this branch. I'm more surprised to see that punk Isaac walking up to get at the end of my line. I Gator and Dean would have taken care of the situation by now.

The thought of him standing in my window wearing Robert's jewelry made me sick to my stomach. The closer he got to my window the worst I felt. Just as I finished up with the customer ahead of him, all hell broke loose inside of me. Justice for Robert consumed my thoughts. My blood boiled with hatred and revenge throughout my body. I wanted to run to my car, get my gun, and shoot this bastard in his motherfucking face. My hands started shaking, sweat started rolling down my face, and my stomach erupted. I began to vomit uncontrollably as the punk walked up to my window. The head teller immediately closed my window and had one of the other tellers process his transactions.

I went to the employee's lounge to get myself together. I balanced out my window, sold all my cash back to the vault, and left for the day. I'm glad to see my time at this branch come to an end.

I went to the cemetery with the anticipation of finding the strength to stop me from gunning down that bastard Isaac. When I pulled up at Robert's grave, the ground is covered with a fresh layer of snow. The surroundings are so calm and serene, yet my mind is consumed with nothing but hate and revenge. I so badly want to kill that bastard myself for ripping my live apart. I stood at his grave wondering how I mentally got to this place.

I dropped to my knees on the fresh layer of snow that covered his grave. "Where do I go from here?" I shouted out loud as I held onto his headstone and cried my eyes out. I cried like the first night I had to accept he was never coming home to me. The cries of my sorrow from a broken heart pierced the silence looming in the air. My tears dripped onto his headstone leaving thin streaks of frozen icicles down the front. I wished my mother were alive.

I know Gator and Dean asked me to leave it to them. On my way home, I could not help from driving by and taking pictures of each one of the addresses of on Isaac's business accounts. Every damn address I rode by is either burnt out, tore down, or boarded up.

Later that day at home I ran a hot bath, lit candles, cut on the smooth jazz station, and opened a bottle of White Zinfandel. Maybe a relaxing bath will take my mind off today's events, but my mind kept racing with ways to get that motherfucker back. Killing him wouldn't do much good since there are probably others tied to Robert's murder. The idea of hitting him and his family in the pocket popped in my mind.

Coming up with a revenge on Isaac Brown sparked a fire inside me. Half way through my bottle of wine I got out of the tub. I went to FedEx Office with all the information and pictures I collected on Isaac Brown. I wore gloves to avoid my fingerprints from being on anything. I made copies of everything and placed them in an overnight envelope. I used Isaac's name and Farmington Hills address as the sender's information. Yes, I decided to send banking accounts information, driver licenses, social security numbers, and the pictures of the vacant, abandoned, and nonexistent business addresses contacted to Isaac Brown's to the FBI's Michigan office. I drove out to Farmington Hills to dropped the package in a drop box to avoid from being caught on a surveillance camera.

The FBI found the package to contain enough information to launch an investigation into a possible money laundering case. They connected the money trial to drug activity in four other states. The Michigan investigation on Isaac Brown revealed him as being a key suspect in another large drug investigations in Illinois that spanned to drug ties activities in several other states. The FBI had more than enough information for the Grand Jury to hand down indictments on individuals in four different states.

In a matter of weeks, it was on every news channel the arrest of over one hundred seventy-five people spanning four states. The FBI gave credit to a local Michigan bank that complied with the Government Currency Transaction Reporting System that helped crack the case. The news flashed the face of Isaac Brown, two bank employees, and twenty-three other people indicted in Michigan for money laundering and drug trafficking. It's not the revenge for Robert's death that I was looking for but it was better than nothing.

"Gator, do you know if Selena turned information over to the Feds?" Dean asked as he met with Gator for lunch.

"No I don't know. I told her to leave it alone," Gator replied.

"It's nothing we can about that bastard now. That man is too hot," Dean said.

"If we sit back and wait for the perfect opportunity, I think there might be a way we can still hit our mark," Gator reasoned.

Chapter 45

About a month later, Isaac is pulling into his garage for the night. He got out of his car and waved goodnight to the FBI agents parked in front of his house. The second the garage door closed, Gator stepped from behind a freezer with a ski mask on and his gun drawn.

"Bitch hand over your coat!" Gator demanded in a low mean voice.

"So you want to stick me up?" Isaac asked as he handed over his coat.

Gator tossed his coat to the floor.

"Shut the fuck up and take all your jewelry off. Place all of it on the hood of your car!" Gator ordered.

Isaac continued to talk shit while he was taking off the jewelry. "Take this shit! You must be one stupid motherfucker. One day we will meet again!" Isaac warned.

"Not in this lifetime," Gator promised

"If you are looking for money I can get you a lot more. Just spare my life. I have thousands in a safe inside the house," Isaac pleaded.

"You really think I'm a stupid motherfucker! Bitch this has nothing to do with money!" Gator snapped.

Gator picked all the jewelry that belonged to Robert, put it in his pocket, and threw the other jewelry in Isaac's face.

"This is for the owner of the other jewelry!" Gator replied. Then he placed the barrel of the gun to Isaac's forehead as Gator continued talking shit to Isaac.

"Stupidity must run in your fucking family. First, your dumb ass nephew tried to play stick-up man, but that literally blew up in his fucking face. Then you had to flash my man's jewelry in his girlfriend's face at the bank. Yea, motherfucker she is the one that turned your ass over to the feds. But you will never be able to tell anyone!" Gator threatened.

Isaac squint his big scary eyes and thought about how his nephew had suffered from the car bomb. He received 3rd degree burns over 75% of his body. The doctors had to cut his charred jacket, clothing, and gym shoes from his scorched skin. All his skin nerve endings were destroyed which caused extreme pain to the exposed burn areas. One of his ears and both lips were completely burnt off. He lost sight in both eyes and what appeared to be skin had a glossy leathery look. He died a week later from infections and complications from the burns. Gator pulled the trigger and fled out the garage side door that led to the backyard as Isaac's body fell to the ground.

The agents watching Isaac's house heard gunfire and noticed someone running from the side door of the garage. They gave chase through the woods behind Isaac's house. Gator reached the getaway car and drove off just as the agents surfaced from the woods.

Chapter 46

"She turned over all his banking information to the FBI. Not only did they link Isaac to money laundering, murder, and drug ties they were able to identify him as the head of his family. The investigation led to a multi-state drug bust a couple of weeks ago," Dean answered.

"Are you talking about the big drug bust that spans several states?" Thomas inquired.

"That's the one," Dean replied.

"I caught that one on the news. They arrested almost two hundred family members across four states," Thomas said.

"Thanks to Selena's interference Gator was able to take the bastard out last night without any problems. The Feds think someone in his family wanted to silence him. There was a rumor claiming he made a deal and was about to roll over on his connections," Dean explained.

"She took a big ass risk going to the FBI with that information. She really loved my brother," Thomas had to admit.

"She still loves him. She has taken his death very hard," Dean informed.

"I feel bad for her but I am glad that my brother was able to find true love in his short life. It's very rare to find true love in our life style. I wish there was something I can do for her," Thomas expressed.

"You do not have to worry about that. Gator took care of that this morning. She should be receiving the package right about now," Dean explained.

Chapter 47

I hate when I wake up early. It looks like another cold crispy morning. I have a couple hours before my first class. Guess I will cook a real breakfast this morning. Bacon, eggs, grits, toast, and a glass of orange juice sounds good. Maybe I can still catch the morning news.

I sat at the dining room table to eat breakfast. The moment I turned the news on they announced breaking news story updates right after commercial break. That's funny if the story was that juicy why go to a commercial break? Let me see what this breaking news story is. That looks like that black motherfucker Isaac. I cut the TV up and listened carefully to the newscaster.

"Isaac Brown, the key suspect in one of the largest multistate drug investigations was gunned down in his garage around four o'clock this morning. Apparently, it was not a robbery attempt since all of his valuables and money was left behind. It is rumored that he was in negotiation of a plea bargain with the FBI. The Feds are looking into all Mr. Brown's acquaintances that would want to keep him from testifying. Federal Agents conducting the surveillance on Mr. Brown was only able to identify the shooter as a male dressed in all black clothing and a skullcap. They were able to get a description of the car and the license plate number. The car was reported stolen a week earlier from an elderly white woman out of Port Huron who has no connection to the case. The Southfield police found the car several hours later ten miles from the shooting behind a commercial building engulfed in flames. It appears the flames may have destroyed any chances of the police retrieving evidence from the car. The Feds are asking if anyone has information on this case to please contact them or their local police department," the newscaster reported.

That is the best fucking news I could have ever heard. I wonder if Dean and Gator heard the news yet.

Ring! Ring! Ring! Ring! "You have reached the voicemail of Dean please leave a message at the beep." Ring! Ring! Ring! Ring! "This is Gator leave a message." "Damn is anybody answering their phones", I said.

Ring! Ring! Ring! "Hello," Fran answered.

"Hey Fran this is Selena," I replied.

"How are you doing?" Fran asked.

"This is the best I have felt in months," I answered.

"What's going on?" she asked.

"I was trying to get in touch with Dean and Gator," I replied.

"Dean is in North Carolina and I have not heard from Gator this morning. Is everything ok", she inquired.

"Did you hear the breaking news", I asked her.

"No. What happened?" Fran asked.

"The bastard that I saw wearing Robert's jewelry was murdered. The newscaster reported that it happen early this morning right under FBI surveillance," I explained.

"Did they say anything about the shooter?" Fran asked with a little concern.

"They think somebody connected to the case wanted to keep him from testifying. I wasn't sure if Dean had heard the news," I told her.

"I don't think so," she answered.

Knock! Knock! Knock!

"Hold on a minute Fran there is someone at my door," I said.

"Who is it?" I asked calling out to the door.

"It's the security guard from the front desk. I have a package for you," the person on the other side of the door answered.

"Fran I have to go," I said.

"Call if you need to talk," she requested.

I opened the front door and noticed the security guard holding a box.

"I'm sorry to bother you but this package came and I need you to sign for it," the security guard stated.

"Who is the package from?" I asked.

"A private carrier delivered the package without a sender's name attached. You can call the carrier service for that information," the security guard advised.

"Thank you," I replied as I signed for the package.

After all, that I have been through the last couple of months I'm a little uneasy about opening the box. Let me check the internet to see if the carrier is even listed. There they go. Why would anybody send me a package by a carrier service in Detroit?

"Hi, I just received a package without a sender's name. Is there any way that I am able to find out who sent it?" I asked.

"Yes you can. All I will need is the twelve digit tracking number listed in the bottom left corner of the attached shipping label," the person from the carrier service requested.

"It is 4-5-K-1-2-3-N-8-1-1-7-6," I replied.

"The signature obtained from the gentleman say Mr. Robert Harris," the person from the carrier service answered.

I ripped open the package and to my surprise, it's all of Robert's missing jewelry! Tears rolled out my eyes as I pulled each piece of Robert's jewelry carefully out the box. This time the tears were more of a joyful reason. Isn't this a bitch, that bastard Isaac Brown death was definitely revenge for Robert's murder. I put his jewelry back in the box. This will be the first trip to the cemetery I will be happy to make.

Ring! Ring! Ring! Ring! "This is Gator leave a message." It went straight to voice mail. "Gator I don't want to know who sent me the package, but I want the person to know that I am truly grateful for getting a part of my Robert back," I said with tears spilling into my message.

I sat on the ground hugging Robert's headstone. "Baby I will never know if I played a role in taking Isaac Brown down nor do I need to know who actually killed him. I believe that he is not the only person involved in your murder. However, I am satisfied to see that his entire drug family is paying for it. This is the first time that I have been able to see a little light in my dark gloomy days and nights without you. When I received that package with your jewelry, it felt like I received a piece of you back. Even though that punk ass bitch ripped you out of my life, he was not able to erase my memories of you. You are and always will be permanently etched in my heart and soul forever. No matter what path I walk down there will never be another man in my lifetime that could ever compare to you. You are my soul mate and I know that we will meet again. I will always love you," I said getting up.

Angela Hairston grew up in the City of Highland Park, Michigan and graduated from the University of Detroit Mercy with duel degrees. She is presently residing in the metropolitan area of Atlanta, Georgia with her family where she is working on establishing a career as an author. Currently she is working on several other titles to follow "Permanently Etched In My Heart", which is her first installment under Highland Park Publishing. In 2009 she made her publishing debuted as one of the premier authors in "Cosmos Anthology 2010", published by 3-Queens Publications, which introduced an excerpt from her second installment of books, "Karma Is A Bitch".

To write author:

Highland Park Publishing

Attn: Angela Hairston

P.O. Box 724651

Atlanta, GA 31139

To email author

hairston@highlandparkpublishing.com

hairstonbooks@yahoo.com

Follow on Facebook and Twitter

hairston@highlandparkpublishing.com

To contact the model/actress

Asia Mills

hairston@highlandparkpublishing.com

To contact the photographer/graphic designer

Anthony Thomas

Ecmanthony@gmail.com

www.anthonythomasphotography.com

Highland Park Publishing

Introduces titles written by

Angela Hairston

Permanently Etched In My Heart

Karma Is A Bitch

Karma Is A Bitch 2

Yana's Tale

Ho Know Your Place

Richard Doe

Also a premier author in "Cosmos Anthology 2010" published by 3-Queens Publications

(Excerpt from)

Karma Is A Bitch

I would love to have a small traditional wedding. I can picture myself in a white wedding gown standing at the altar and looking into his eyes and seeing the beautiful live we will share together. We will have at least two kids, a dog, and a lovely three story home with a two-car garage. I even imaged us as senior citizens sitting in the backyard watching our grandchildren playing on the swing set that once belonged to their parents.

The past few years it seem as if God has given me a chance at real happiness. This is the first time in my life that I'm actually in love. I found a man that completes me mentally, emotional, and definitely physically. He is a kind, loving, gentle, patience, full of life, compassionate, understanding, strong, educated, and still has an edge of a bad boy side. The fact that he has a banging body is an extra bonus.

His parents and sisters treats me as if I have always been part of the family. Being around them is the closet to a normal family I have ever been a part of. His mother reminds me of my mother during her good days. His sisters and I share what I didn't have with my siblings.

I have not given up the search for my siblings. I hope that it's not too late for us to build a relationship. I would love for them to finally accept me for the woman I have become and not as a reminder of my father. It's been over twenty-five years since I have seen or heard from either one of them. I wonder if they have gotten married, how they look, and if they have kids. I don't even know if I'm an auntie or not. It would be nice to get back in touch with them and possible build a relationship with them. All I want is to love them and have them love me back.

I never expected any shit like this. Out of all the people, whose paths I crossed I would have never imagined that anyone would bestow such destruction to my life. I knew that several of them hated the ground I walked on, but I never image any of them despising me this much. This motherfucking bitch totally caught me off guard. I had no idea someone could hate me this much!

I cannot get this hoe's last words out of my head. The bitch let me know that this was for every person that I have misused in my past. What the fuck made this motherfucker think that I treated them any different. Shit, it was only part of the game. Hell, I got mine at any means possible and there was nothing stopping them from getting theirs.

I don't remember ever giving any of them a hint that I really cared. Come to think of it, I treated a bunch of people like shit. This is going to shock the hell out of those that love me. Shit, I am still astonished that this motherfucking bitch put me in a situation like this.

Was I that self-centered that I fuck over people

that bad without even knowing? Was I that blind? How could I have missed all the warning signs?

I can faintly feel the bastard breathing next to me. Here this bitch is lying next to me holding my hand like this makes the shit ok. I'm delighted to feel this bastard's heartbeats are slowing down to an occasional thumb. I'm fucking glad to hearing their voice decrease to a low mumble as they continue struggling to talk bullshit. Isn't this a bitch, the motherfucker still has the bloody knife in their hand. It's only a matter of time before this hoe dies on me.

This is not how I am supposed to spend the last day of my vacation. Why does it seem the moment that everything in my live is going right, the mistakes from my past fucks it up? I hate to see all that is good in my life coming to an end so soon.

At this time my outcome looks very bleak. It would be nice to survive this. I suspect that all my dreams are nothing but dreams. Here I am lying next to the person that is attempting to shatter my dreams. As much as I intensely dislike this person at this moment, I wonder why they waited until now to do this to me. Hell, the motherfucker did a lot of talking but none it made any sense for their actions. The bitch gave me a weak explanation for their actions as they kept plunged the knife into me, but that still doesn't justify their actions.

It's funny I would have never expected my life to end like this. I am stuck lying in this pool of blood. My body is too injured and tired to move from this spot. I could feel myself bleeding from every stab wound. It is amazing how my body is becoming cold as it slowly shutting down. I hope somebody comes looking for me before it is too late. If not I hope, I ended up in heaven with my mother and not hell with my father. It would be nice for my eternal life to be drama free.

If this bitch is right, I shocked how I let it get to this point. If I knew this was the outcome I would have taken responsibility for my actions which lead me down that path. I never once claimed to be perfect but I can't believe my actions were bad enough for someone to take my life this violently.

Am I to pay the price for every woman that choose financially gain over love? Am I to pay the price for every woman that feels they can use their looks to get over on people? Was I that shallow? If this is true, then Karma is a Bitch.

Highland Park Publishing

Order Form

Name:____

Address:____

City:____

State:____________________ Zip:___________________

Telephone:_________________________________

Email:____

Quantity	Title		Subtotal
________	Permanently Etched In My Heart	$14.95	________
________	Karma Is A Bitch	$14.95	________
________	Ho Know Your Place	$14.95	________
________	Richard Doe	$14.95	________
		Subtotal	________
	Add 6% sales taxes for purchases shipped to Georgia address		________
	Add $4.99 for Shipping charge		________
		Grand total	________

Mail Orders by check or money orders made out to Highland Park Publishing:

Highland Park Publishing
P.O. Box 724651
Atlanta, GA 31139
404-707-7670

Web orders over the web at www.HighlandParkPublishing.com